GREAT ILLUSTRATED CLASSICS

THE ADVENTURES OF TOM SAWYER

Mark Twain

adapted by
Deidre S. Laiken

Illustrations by
Pablo Marcos Studio

ABDO
Publishing Company

GREAT ILLUSTRATED CLASSICS

edited by
Malvina G. Vogel

visit us at
www.abdopub.com

Library edition published in 2002 by ABDO Publishing Company, 4940 Viking Drive, Suite 622, Edina, Minnesota 55435. Published by agreement with Playmore Incorporated Publishers and Waldman Publishing Corporation.

Printed in the United States.

Library of Congress Cataloging-in-Publication Data

Twain, Mark, 1835-1910.
    The adventures of Tom Sawyer / Mark Twain ; adapted by Deidre S. Laiken ; illustrated by Pablo Marcos Studio.
        p. cm – (Great illustrated classics)
    Reprint. Originally published: New York: Playmore: Waldman Pub., 1989.
    Summary: The adventures of a mischievous young boy and his friends growing up in a Mississippi River town in the nineteenth century.
    ISBN 1-57765-679-2
    [1. Mississippi River--Fiction. 2. Missouri--History--19th century--Fiction.] I. Laiken, Deidre S. II. Pablo Marcos Studio. III. Title. IV. Series.

PZ7.C584 Ad 2002
[Fic]--dc21

                                                          2001055386

Contents

CHAPTER   PAGE

1. The Great Whitewash 7
2. Tom Meets Becky 19
3. Heartbreak for Tom 33
4. Tragedy in the Graveyard 43
5. Tom and His Guilty Conscience 61
6. The Cat and the Pain-Killer 69
7. The Pirates Set Sail 77
8. Tom's Visit Home 93
9. The Pirates Return 99
10. Back Home Again 11
11. Aunt Polly Learns the Truth 12
12. The Salvation of Muff Potter 13
13. Digging for Buried Treasure 14
14. Trembling on the Trail 15
15. Huck Saves the Widow 16
16. Lost in the Cave 17
17. Escape! 19
18. Buried Treasure 20
19. A Home for Huck 22
20. Respectable Huck Joins the Gang ...23

Mark Twain

About the Author

Mark Twain was born Samuel Langhorne Clemens in a small Missouri town in 1835. After piloting river steamers along the Mississippi for four years, he began writing humorous short stories for newspapers.

The Adventures of Tom Sawyer was Twain's first full-length novel. Many of thee adventures of Tom and Huck Finn actually happened to Twain in his boyhood.

Even though Twain wrote this book mainly to entertain boys and girls, he hoped that adults would read and enjoy it, and recall their own childhood.

Mark Twain died in 1910. But he left the world a true picture of American life and the American spirit in his novels, short stories and other writings.

Sid Tells About Tom's Mischief.

CHAPTER 1
The Great Whitewash

Tom Sawyer was always getting into trou ble. He was the kind of boy who just coulc not resist adventure.

Tom lived with his Aunt Polly, his cousir Mary and his half-brother Sid. Everyone wa; used to Tom's mischief, but Sid never missec a chance to tell Aunt Polly when he though Tom was up to no good. That's how she founc out that Tom was playing hooky from schoo and going swimming.

Now, as a punishment for his behavior Tom found himself faced with the chore o whitewashing 30 yards of fence on a sunny Saturday afternoon. And what was worse—it was one of those warm summer days when everyone else was out playing ball or swimming. And there was Tom, all alone on the sidewalk with a long-handled brush and a bucket of whitewash.

He looked at the fence. It seemed enormous, and he knew it would take all day to give it only one coat. Tom began to think of all the fun he had planned for this day, and his sorrows multiplied. Soon his friends would come down the street, and he shuddered to think of how they would laugh to see him whitewashing a fence on such a beautiful day. There must be a way out of this situation.

Tom emptied his pockets and looked at his worldly wealth—bits of toys, marbles, and trash. He might be able to bribe someone else to help him for a while, but there wasn't

A Fence to Be Whitewashed

early enough to buy a whole day of freedom. Tom thought for a while . . . then an inspiration burst upon him!

He picked up the brush and began to spread the whitewash slowly and peacefully over the fence. In only a few minutes, Ben Rogers came walking by, eating a big, juicy red apple. Tom's mouth watered at the sight of such a treat, but he kept on painting and pretended not to see or hear Ben at all.

"Hey there, Tom, what's up with you?" called Ben. "It's too bad you have to work on a day like this. I'm just on my way to the river for a swim. Too bad you can't come along!"

Tom looked at Ben for a moment, then said, "What do you call work?"

"Why, ain't that work?" asked Ben, pointing to the fence.

"Well maybe it is, and maybe it ain't," answered Tom. "All I know is that it suits me

Ben Wants Tom to Go Swimming.

ust fine."

"Come on now, don't tell me you actually *ike* it!"

"*Like* it? Well, I don't see why I shouldn't ike it. It isn't every day that a boy gets to whitewash a fence."

That puts things in a new light for Ben. He stopped eating his apple and began watching Tom work. Maybe there was something to his whitewashing after all, he thought.

"Hey, Tom, let me try it for a while," Ben asked.

"No, no!" protested Tom. "Aunt Polly encrusted this fence to me, and I can't just let anyone take over such a big job."

But Ben continued to beg Tom to let him have the privilege of whitewashing for just a little while. Tom kept refusing until Ben offered him the rest of his juicy red apple. That had been what Tom was waiting for.

Tom sat in the shade and munched the ap-

An Even Exchange

le while Ben swished the brush back and forth, sweating at his work. It was a wonderful idea, and as other boys came by, Tom kept trading with them too.

By mid-afternoon, the fence was completely whitewashed, and Tom was the proud owner of all sorts of treasures. His inspiration had certainly worked. All he had to do was make his chores seem to be fun, and the other boys were eager to do them for him.

When the fence was completed, Tom went into the house. "Can I go out and play now, Aunt Polly?" he asked.

"What! Already? How much have you done?"

"It's all finished, Aunt Polly."

"Tom, don't lie to me. I can't bear it," she warned.

"Look for yourself," answered Tom as he led his aunt to the window.

"Well, I never!" exclaimed Aunt Polly.

14

"Look for Yourself."

You really *can* work when you put your mind to it."

She was so pleased with Tom's work that she presented him with a large juicy apple and told him he could go out, but to be home in time for dinner. Tom smiled, and when she turned her back, he slipped a sugar-coated doughnut into his left pocket.

Within minutes, Tom was out on the street as free as a bird. As he passed the house where Jeff Thatcher lived, he saw a girl in the garden—a new girl he had never seen before. She was lovely. Her blonde hair fell in two long braids almost to her waist. Tom fell in love instantly!

He tried to attract her attention by standing on his head and showing off in all sorts of silly ways, but she ignored him. Tom vowed that before the week was up he would win her love. He skipped down the street, his head full of romantic plans and adventures.

The Girl Ignores Tom.

A Loose Tooth

CHAPTER 2
Tom Meets Becky

It was Monday morning and Tom Sawye was miserable. He was always miserable o Monday mornings because it meant he ha to go to school. Tom began to scheme. Ther had to be a way, some way, to avoid going t school. He could be sick and stay home. Bu as much as he tried, Tom could not find th least little thing wrong with himself.

He thought for a little while longer an then realized that one of his upper front teetl was loose. This was really a lucky break. Jus as he was about to begin groaning an writhing in pain, he remembered Aunt Polly's way of pulling loose teeth, and Tom was in no hurry to suffer *that* particular pain again.

So he went back to thinking. He remembered hearing the doctor describe an illness that had laid up a patient for two weeks and threatened to make him lose a finger. Tom had a sore toe—something he hadn't looked at or thought about in days. Now he wondered if he could possibly fool Aunt Polly. Since he didn't know the details about the illness, he figured a few loud cries of pain might do the trick. So Tom began to groan and moan with considerable spirit.

Sid, who lay sleeping in the next bed, did not even stir. Tom increased the volume and frequency of his cries, but his half brother snored on. Finally, Tom shook Sid until his sleepy eyes opened in surprise. Tom began to groan again.

"Tom! What's going on?" shouted Sid.

Tom Moans and Groans.

"Oh, don't jump around so," moaned Tom.

Despite Tom's protestations, Sid ran down-tairs to tell Aunt Polly about Tom's appar-nt agony.

"I . . . I think he's dying," stammered Sid.

"Rubbish! I don't believe it," snapped Aunt ᵖolly. But she ran up the stairs as fast as she ould. By the time she reached Tom's bedside, ᵊer face was white with fear.

"What's the matter with you, Tom?"

"Oh, Aunt Polly, it's my sore toe. It feels ᵼs if it's about to fall off."

Aunt Polly sank into a chair with relief. ᵊhe laughed a little, then cried a little, and ᵊhen did both together. This made her feel so ᵑuch better that she snapped at Tom, "Stop his nonsense, get out of bed, and get off to ᵊchool immediately!"

All this made Tom feel quite foolish, and ᵊe stopped his awful groaning immediately.

"Oh, Aunt Polly," he said, "it just hurt so

"I . . . I Think He's Dying."

much I never minded my tooth at all."

No sooner were the words out of his mouth than Aunt Polly was carefully examining the loose tooth. In minutes, she had tied a loop of silk thread to the tooth and the other end of the thread to the bedpost. Tom pleaded with Aunt Polly not to pull it this way, but it was no use. She left the room, only to return moments later with a hot log from the kitchen stove. She thrust the log dangerously close to Tom's face. He jumped back and gazed in horror at the tooth dangling by a thread from the bedpost.

On the way to school, the obvious gap in Tom's front row of teeth attracted the attention and envy of all the other boys. Maybe the pain was worth it after all, thought Tom.

As he neared the school, he came upon Huckleberry Finn. Huck was the son of the town drunkard and was free to come and go as he pleased. He was always dressed in cast

Pulling Tom's Tooth

ff clothes and incredible rags. He slept in oorways or empty barns and never had to o to school or church. In short, Huck was the nvy of every boy in town, but he was treated s an outcast by their mothers.

Tom waved to Huck, and the two boys got nvolved in a serious conversation about the est way to cure warts. Then Huck showed 'om a tiny tick that he had managed to cap-ure. Tom's eyes lit up at the sight of the little reature, and he made a quick trade—his ooth for the tick.

This little transaction made Tom late for chool, and when he entered the classroom, Ir. Dobins, the teacher, demanded an expla-ation.

Tom was about to concoct a wonderful lie hen he noticed the lovely girl with the long londe braids. Tom also noticed that the only mpty desk in the room was on the girls' side, ext to this mysterious beauty.

Huck Finn Shows Tom His Tick.

Without a moment's hestitation, Tom answered, "I was with Huckleberry Finn."

Everyone in the class gasped! Even the teacher was astonished. No one would ever actually admit being with the town renegade. In an instant, the teacher brought out the switch of hickory twigs and whipped Tom as a punishment. Then he ordered Tom to sit with the girls. This, of course, was exactly what Tom wanted. He quickly slid into the empty seat next to the new girl.

Tom tried desperately to attract her attention. He offered her a lovely ripe peach, but she only tossed her head and looked away. Next, Tom began to draw something on his slate. He covered his work with his hand and appeared to be very involved in this activity.

Soon, the girl's curiosity got the best of her, and she made an attempt to see the drawing. But Tom kept on working and pretended to be totally unaware of her attentions. At last,

A Switch of Hickory Twigs

she gave in and hesitatingly whispered, "Let me see it!"

Tom partly uncovered a drawing of a house with a brick chimney and smoke curling into a blue sky. The girl's interest grew. Soon she asked Tom to draw in people.

"It's such a nice drawing," she said. "I wish I could draw."

"It's easy," whispered Tom. "I'll teach you."

The girl told him that her name was Becky Thatcher. Tom and Becky agreed to spend the lunch recess together, with Tom teaching her how to draw.

Tom went back to his drawing, but this time he hid the slate from Becky. She begged to see it, but he refused. Finally, he gave in and showed Becky the slate. The words "I love you" were printed in Tom's own steady handwriting. Becky blushed, but anyone could see she was pleased.

"It's Such a Nice Drawing."

Tom Watches the Tick.

CHAPTER 3
Heartbreak for Tom

Tom thought that the lunch recess would never come. The air in the classroom was utterly dead. Not a breath was stirring. It was the sleepiest of sleepy days. It took all of Tom's strength just to stay awake. His hand wandered into his pocket, and he pulled out the tiny matchbox which held the tick he had traded his tooth for. Tom released the creature and watched it crawl along the long flat desk.

Joe Harper, Tom's best friend, sat next to him. Joe, too, was grateful for the diversion of a tick on such a dull Monday. Tom poked at the tick with a pin, and the creature changed his direction at every poke. Joe took a pin out of his lapel and joined in the sport.

In a few minutes, Tom complained that they were interfering with each other, and neither was getting the fullest benefit of the tick. So he put Joe's slate on the desk and drew a line down the middle. One side was to be Tom's territory and the other side, Joe's.

The poor tick scurried from one tormentor to the other, and the two boys bent their heads over the slate, giving all their attention to the game. It didn't take long before they began to argue, and Tom reached over into Joe's territory and poked the tick with his pin.

"Tom, you let him alone!" shouted Joe.

"Look here, Joe Harper, just whose tick is it anyway?" answered Tom.

The boys were so involved in their game

A Fine Game

that they didn't notice the hush that had come over the class. They didn't realize that Mr. Dobins had tiptoed towards them and was now standing and watching their game. Before they knew it, they felt the harsh smacks of hickory twigs on their shoulders. The punishment ended their game.

When school was let out for lunch, Becky was waiting for Tom. The two walked off together to a secret place in the yard behind the school.

For a while, Tom drew on his slate as Becky, obviously impressed, watched him in silence. After some time, Tom looked up and asked, "Were you ever engaged, Becky?"

"I don't know," she answered. "What's it like to be engaged?"

"Well, you just tell a boy that you won't love anyone but him, ever, and then you kiss. Anyone can do it."

At first, Becky hesitated, but Tom ex-

36

A Punishment at Hand

plained over and over again the importance of the kiss and the pledge of undying love.

When Becky agreed, Tom kissed her. Then he relaxed and told her of the rest of the agreement.

"We'll always walk to school together, and at parties you choose me and I choose you. We'll always be together, when nobody is looking, that is."

"It's so nice. I never heard of being engaged before," whispered Becky with a sigh.

"Oh, it's a lot of fun! Why me and Amy Lawrence . . ."

Becky's wide eyes filled with tears, and Tom realized he had made a terrible mistake. He tried to comfort Becky and explain that he had no feelings for Amy anymore. But Becky would hear none of it. She turned her face to the wall and went on crying.

Tom got up and walked around the schoolyard for a while. Then he returned to Becky's

An Engagement Kiss

side and once again told her that she was his only love. But Becky kept on crying.

Tom reached into his pocket for his most important treasure—a brass doorknob. He passed it to Becky and said, "Please, Becky, won't you take it?"

Becky threw the doorknob on the ground.

Tom got up and stomped out of the school-yard. He headed for the hills outside of town and didn't return to school at all that after-noon.

Becky soon regretted her actions and began looking for Tom everywhere. She called his name over and over, but there was no answer. She had no companions but silence and lone-liness, so she sat down to cry again.

As the rest of the students filed back into the school, Becky looked hopefully for some sign of Tom, but it was too late. Her heart was broken, and she was sure she had lost him forever.

Tom Offers His Treasure to Becky.

Life Is Pain and Trouble.

CHAPTER 4
Tragedy in the Graveyard

Tom ran through the back roads until he was far away from the dreaded schoolyard. He sat for a long time by the side of the road with his elbows on his knees and his chin in his hands. It seemed to him that life was nothing but pain and trouble. He had only meant the best for Becky Thatcher. What had he done that was so terrible? Nothing!

She had treated him like a dog. Oh, she would be sorry some day—maybe when it was too late!

Tom's mind wandered to thoughts of death.

He could almost see it all now. They would carry his poor body into the church, and Becky and Aunt Polly would cry and cry. They would say all sorts of kind things about what a brave, wonderful boy he had been all along.

Tom was awakened from his fantasy by his old friend, Huckleberry Finn. The boys were overjoyed to see each other and began to play a lively game of Robin Hood.

When Tom realized that it was close to dinner time, he said good-bye to Huck. But they made arrangements to sneak out that night and meet in the graveyard, where they planned some more adventures.

At half past nine that night, Tom and Sid went to bed as usual. Tom waited for what seemed like eternity for Huck's signal that the coast was clear. Finally, Tom heard the "meow" that meant Huck was waiting down by the woodshed.

Overjoyed to See Each Other

Tom opened the window, slipped out, and joined his friend. Huck was waiting with his dead cat, for they planned to swing it over a grave to see if this method would cure warts.

The boys walked about a mile and a half out of the village until they reached an old graveyard on a hill. Grass and weeds grew over the grounds, and many of the older graves were so sunken in that the grave stones could not be seen at all.

"Huck, do you believe that these dead people would like us being here?" whispered Tom.

"I wish I knew. It's awful solemn, isn't it?" answered Huck.

Just then, Tom thought he heard something. He grabbed Huck's arm and the two boys froze.

"Did you hear it?" asked Tom. "There's something coming this way, no doubt about it!"

Tom Slips Out to Meet Huck.

Some shadowy figures approached through the gloom. One was swinging an old-fashioned tin lantern. Huck shuddered and whispered, "It's the devils, sure enough. Three of them. We're goners now, Tom, can you pray?"

Just as Tom was about to begin praying he recognized one of the figures. "They're humans!" he whispered. "One of them, anyway. It's old Muff Potter. I know his voice."

The boys sat very still watching the three figures standing over a grave. The lantern light revealed their faces. It was young Dr Robinson, Muff Potter, and fearsome Injun Joe, a murderer.

Potter and Injun Joe were unloading some rope and shovels from a wheelbarrow. Dr Robinson stood beside them, urging them to hurry and dig open the grave before the moon came out.

After a while, their shovels struck something with a dull, woody sound. They hoisted

48

Shadowy Figures in the Graveyard

a coffin out of the ground with their ropes, pried off the lid, and removed a body. The corpse was placed in the wheelbarrow and covered with a blanket.

"Now it's done," said Injun Joe with a grunt. "Five more dollars or here it sits."

The doctor protested, "But I paid you both in advance."

But Injun Joe had been carrying an old grudge against the doctor's father ever since the old man had him jailed for threatening his life. Now, he raised his fist to the doctor's face.

Dr. Robinson struck out suddenly and knocked Injun Joe to the ground. Muff Potter jumped on the doctor, and the two men began to fight. In an instant, Injun Joe was on his feet. Wild fire was in his eyes. He snatched up Potter's knife and crept around the fighters, seeking his chance to use it.

At the moment the doctor freed himself

The Fight!

from Potter's strong grasp, Injun Joe picked up a heavy tombstone and knocked out Potter with it. Then he drove his knife into the doctor's chest. The doctor reeled and fell on top of Potter. His blood was everywhere.

Injun Joe stood looking down at his two victims. The doctor groaned, gave a last gasp, and then was still. Injun Joe knelt down and went through the doctor's pockets for money and other valuables. Then he placed the fatal knife in Potter's open right hand.

In a few minutes, Potter came to. His hand closed upon the knife. He raised it, glanced at it, and dropped it with a shudder.

"Lord, how did this all happen?" he cried.

Injun Joe then told Muff Potter that he had seen the whole thing. "Potter," he explained, "you were so drunk that you got into a fight with the doctor and wound up stabbing the poor man to death."

At first, Potter refused to believe what In-

Injun Joe Frames Potter.

jun Joe had told him. But Injun Joe was so convincing, that Potter eventually accepted the story as true and begged his partner to keep it a secret. When this was agreed upon, the two men slipped silently away into the night. The murdered doctor, the blanketed corpse, the lidless coffin, and the open grave were all that remained of the night's terror.

The two boys fled back towards the village, fearful of every shadow and speechless with horror.

"Huck, what do you think will happen?" Tom whispered breathlessly.

"If Dr. Robinson dies, I guess there will be a hanging," answered Huck in between gasps for air.

Then both boys realized that they had been the only witnesses to the crime. Muff Potter had been out cold. Only Huck and Tom could point an accusing finger at the real killer. It was then that they understood the great dan-

Tom and Huck Flee.

ger they were in. Injun Joe was not likely to let them go on living if he suspected that they had seen the murder and might give him away.

Once the boys were safely back in the village, they stopped to talk inside an old ruined building.

"Hucky, do you think you can keep mum about all this?" asked Tom.

"We *got* to keep mum, Tom. That Injun Joe would wipe us out in a minute if we were to squeal. Now listen, Tom, we've got to swear to keep quiet about all this."

The boys agreed. In the darkness of night, they wrote out an oath on a piece of bark. It read: HUCK FINN AND TOM SAWYER SWEARS THEY WILL KEEP MUM ABOUT THIS AND THEY WISH THEY MAY DROP DOWN DEAD IN THEIR TRACKS AND ROT IF THEY EVER TELL.

Then they pricked their fingers and signed

Writing the Oath

heir initials in blood. They buried the bark
ind whispered all sorts of magical words dur-
ng the ceremony.

Now it was done. The oath had been sealed
n blood. Tom and Huck would never tell anyone what they had witnessed that awful
night. Their lips were sealed forever!

Sealing the Oath in Blood

Tom Sneaks In—Unnoticed?

CHAPTER 5
Tom and His Guilty Conscience

After the boys said good-bye, Tom returned to his house and crept silently in his bedroom window. He undressed with great care and fell asleep congratulating himself that no one knew of his adventure. He was not aware that the gently snoring Sid was awake and had been so for almost an hour.

When Tom awoke the next morning, Sid was dressed and gone. Something was wrong. No one had bothered to wake him. Within five minutes he was dressed and downstairs feeling sore and drowsy.

After breakfast, Aunt Polly took Tom aside and wept. He had broken her old heart.

"Go on and ruin yourself," she cried. "It's no use for me to try and raise you like a good boy. I know you sneaked out last night."

Tom pleaded for forgiveness and promised to reform. He was so miserable he didn't even think of ways of getting even with Sid for telling on him. He moped to school, feeling sad and gloomy.

With hardly a sound, he slipped into his seat. His elbow pressed against something hard and cold. He held it up and unwrapped it. A long lingering sigh followed and his heart broke. It was his brass doorknob. Becky had returned it!

Tom hardly had time to wallow in his sorrow. By noontime, the whole village was alive with news of Dr. Robinson's murder. Everyone in town was drifting towards the graveyard. Tom's heartbreak over Becky flew

Tom's Gift Is Returned.

way, and he joined the procession. As soon as he reached the scene of the bloody crime, he felt a slight pinch on his arm. It was Huckeberry Finn. They looked into each other's faces and felt tense and uncomfortable because of the secret they shared.

Within a few minutes, Injun Joe and Muff Potter appeared. Without a moment's hesitation, Injun Joe told the sheriff a grisly tale, calmly explaining that Muff Potter had stabbed the doctor during a drunken rage.

Huck and Tom stood frozen in their tracks as the stony-hearted liar reeled off his story. The boys were astonished. An innocent man was going to hang, and only they could save him.

Tom's fearful secret and gnawing conscience disturbed his sleep that night and every night that followed. After several nights of Tom's moaning and tossing, Sid complained to Aunt Polly. She questioned Tom, but all

A Stony-Hearted Liar!

he said was, "It's nothing, nothing at all."

But Sid, who seemed just a bit too concerned, had to say, "But you talk so much, Tom. Last night in your sleep, you kept screaming something about blood and telling somebody something."

This made Aunt Polly think that Tom was only having nightmares about the murder, just like other people in the town were. Although Tom nodded his head in agreement, Sid suspected that something much more dramatic was bothering Tom.

Every day or two during this time, Tom went to the little jail window and smuggled small gifts to Muff Potter. Cigars and bits of fruit and food were silently passed to the prisoner. Muff thanked Tom and figured it was the boy's way of thanking him for the few times they had gone fishing together. But to Tom, these offerings were the only way he had of easing his guilty conscience.

Tom Eases His Guilty Conscience.

Tom Watches Becky's Window.

CHAPTER 6
The Cat and the Pain-Killer

This was a bad time for Tom Sawyer. Aside from his sleepless nights, he had another problem. Becky Thatcher had stopped coming to school. Tom began finding himself hanging around her house, watching her window, and feeling miserable. He'd heard she was ill. What if she should die!

There was no joy in life for poor Tom. He put away his bat and his ball and dragged himself through each day.

Aunt Polly became alarmed. She had never seen Tom this way. She tried all sorts of

69

homemade remedies on the boy, but nothing seemed to work. Instead of getting better, Tom just seemed to grow paler and more dejected. What bothered Aunt Polly more than anything was Tom's total indifference to all her usual remedies. Ordinarily, he would put up an incredible fuss when he had to swallow medicines, take hot oatmeal baths, or suffer under hot compresses.

Then Aunt Polly heard of "Pain-Killer"—a medicine she saw advertised in a magazine. When it arrived, she tested it. It was horrible! But, at least if Tom complained, he would show some spark of his old self again.

She gave him a teaspoonful and watched for the result. Her fears were instantly put to rest, for Tom showed an unusual interest in the medicine.

What Aunt Polly did not know was that Tom was becoming bored with his unhappy existence. He was also tired of all her at-

An Advertisement for "Pain-Killer"

empts to nurse him back to health. So he thought of various plans for getting out of his situation. It finally hit him that the best thing to do was to pretend to actually enjoy the "Pain-Killer." He began to ask for it so often that he became a nuisance, and Aunt Polly wound up telling him to simply help himself. Little did she suspect that Tom was pouring the liquid into a crack in the parlor floor when nobody was looking.

One day, when Tom was getting rid of the medicine this way, his aunt's cat, Peter, came into the parlor. Peter eyed the spoon in Tom's hand and seemed to beg for a taste.

"Don't ask for it unless you want it, Peter," said Tom.

But Peter meowed that he *did* want it.

"You better make sure."

Peter was sure.

Tom pried open the cat's mouth and poured down the "Pain-Killer." Peter sprang a cou-

Giving Peter the "Pain-Killer"

le of yards into the air and let out a loud
var whoop. Then he set off around the room,
anging against furniture, upsetting flow-
rpots, and making a mess of the house.

Aunt Polly entered the room and stared in
mazement as Peter did a few double som-
rsaults and sailed through the open window,
arrying with him the rest of the flowerpots.

Tom lay on the floor laughing so hard he
vas crying. But he finally did manage to tell
is aunt what had made the cat act so crazy.
'he old woman's face broke into a smile. She
ad to admit that it was a cruel thing for the
oy to have done, but at least it was a sign
hat Tom had his old lively spirit back.

Peter Acts Crazy.

Becky Won't Look at Tom.

CHAPTER 7
The Pirates Set Sail

Just when Tom's life seemed to be worth living again, misery set in. Becky Thatcher finally returned to school. Tom was overjoyed when he saw her familiar blonde hair and glowing face in the schoolyard. He tried to get her attention by jumping over the fence, yelling, laughing, doing handsprings, standing on his head, and throwing secret glances in her direction. But nothing worked. Becky never even looked at him.

Tom's cheeks burned in shame. He had made a fool of himself. He couldn't stay at school and be miserable, so he gathered his things together and sneaked off.

He walked and walked until the school was only a tiny black speck in the distance. He was gloomy and desperate. Nothing mattered now. He was a friendless, forsaken boy, and nobody cared whether he lived or died.

He was so deep in his misery that he didn't see his old friend Joe Harper heading towards him. Joe looked worse than Tom. He explained that his mother had just punished him for drinking some cream which he had never even tasted. He swore he was completely innocent.

The two boys walked along, spilling out their misery to each other. They made a pact to stand by one another as brothers and never separate till death.

They began to plan some way of escaping from their lives of misery and pain. Joe wanted to be a hermit and live on crusts of

Deep in Misery

bread and water, but Tom had a much more exciting idea. He suggested that they become pirates.

Tom knew of the perfect pirate hideout—a small, uninhabited island out in the Mississippi River called Jackson's Island. He and Joe sought out Huck Finn and invited him to join them on this wild adventure. When Huck agreed, they made plans to meet at a lonely spot on the river bank two miles above the village at midnight. Each would bring fishing hooks and lines and as much food and other provisions as he could steal.

It was a starry and very still night as Tom made his way out of the village. The mighty river lay like an ocean at rest. When Tom reached the bank, he heard nothing, so he gave a low, distinct whistle. It was answered. Both Huck and Joe appeared from behind a bluff. Joe carried a side of bacon, and Huck carried a skillet, a bag of tobacco, and corn-

A Midnight Meeting

cobs from which to make pipes. Tom showed them the boiled ham cakes he had brought.

The boys loaded their provisions onto a small raft tied up on the bank, and they pushed silently away from shore.

About two o'clock in the morning, the raft grounded on Jackson's Island. The boys jumped off, tied the raft to a nearby tree, and set out to gather wood for a fire.

They built their fire against the side of a great log and cooked some bacon for dinner. The climbing fire lit up their faces and threw its ruddy glare on the trees, foliage, and twisting vines.

When dinner was over, the boys stretched out on the grass and fell into a deep, contented sleep.

Tom awoke the next morning wondering where he was. It took a few minutes for him to realize that he had actually run away from home. Joe and Huck were fast asleep. Tom

Reaching Jackson's Island

woke them, and they all began talking ex-
citedly. In a minute or two, they had stripped
off their clothes and were chasing each other
and tumbling about in the shallow water.

They returned to camp wonderfully refreshed, happy, and very hungry. Soon, Huck
had the campfire blazing again. They had a
delicious breakfast of coffee, bacon, and fried
catfish which Huck had caught.

After filling themselves until they could
eat no more, the boys explored the island a
bit. They discovered that it was about three
miles long and a quarter of a mile wide. The
shore that lay closest to the mainland was
separated from the island by a narrow chan-
nel hardly two hundred yards wide.

The boys took a swim every hour, so it
wasn't until mid-afternoon that they finally
returned to camp. After feasting on cold ham,
they threw themselves down in the shade to
talk. But the talk soon began to drag . . . and

A Life of Swimming and Eating

hen died. The stillness and the sense of lo-
neliness began to affect the boys.

Soon they all realized that they were truly
homesick. Even poor homeless Huck Finn
was dreaming of doorways and life back in
town. But the boys were all ashamed of their
feelings, and none of them was brave enough
to utter a word.

Suddenly, the boys became aware of a peculiar sound in the distance. It was a strange,
muffled boom.

"Let's go see what it is!" shouted Tom.

They sprang to their feet and hurried to
the shore. They parted the bushes on the
bank and peered out over the water. A little
ferryboat was steaming up the river about a
mile below the village, its deck crowded with
people. Suddenly, a great puff of white smoke
burst from the ferryboat's side, followed by
that same dull, booming sound they had
heard earlier.

A Great Puff of White Smoke

"I know now!" exclaimed Tom. "Somebody's drowned!"

"That's it!" cried Huck. "They did that last summer when Bill Turner drowned. Now I remember. Folks say that the boom will make a drowned body rise to the surface."

"I sure wish I was over there now," said Joe. "I wonder who it is that drowned."

The boys stood still as they listened and watched. Presently, a thought flashed through Tom's mind, and he shouted, "I know who's drowned—it's *us*!"

They had become heroes in an instant. They were missed. They were mourned. Hearts were breaking because of their running away. The whole town was talking about them. Here was their triumph at last! Being pirates was worthwhile after all.

As twilight drew on, the boat went back to the dock in town, and the pirates made their way back to camp, excited over their discov-

"I Know Who's Drowned—It's *Us*!"

ery.

They caught a fish, fried it over the open fire, and talked all during dinner. Their conversation centered on what people might be saying about them and who was missing them.

But when the shadows of night closed in, they stopped talking and sat gazing into the fire. The excitement was gone now, and Tom and Joe could not help thinking about the people back home who were not enjoying this little adventure at all. They began to have misgivings, and soon they drifted into sad, troubled moods.

Joe was the first to timidly mention these feelings. He asked Tom and Huck how they might feel about returning to civilization. But the two boys only laughed and denied any homesickness at all.

When the fire had died, the boys all turned in for the night—all, that is, except Tom.

Fresh Fish for Dinner

Tom Looks in the Window.

CHAPTER 8
Tom's Visit Home

Tom waited to make sure Huck and Joe were fast asleep. When he was absolutely sure, he tiptoed cautiously among the trees until he was out of hearing. Then he ran straight for the raft on shore.

By ten o'clock, he was back in town. He flew along the streets and alleys and shortly found himself at his aunt's back fence. He climbed over it and looked in through the sitting-room window where a light still burned. Seeing no one inside, Tom went to the door and softly lifted the latch. When the opening was just big enough for him to fit through, he slipped into the sitting room and quickly hid under the bed. From his hiding place, Tom could see two people enter the room, and he could hear Aunt Polly talking.

"But, as I was saying," she cried, "he wasn't bad—only mischevious. He never meant any harm, and he was the best-hearted boy who ever was." She sank down onto the bed and cried.

"It was just like that with my Joe," sobbed the other voice, which Tom recognized as Mrs. Harper's. "He was always full of the devil and up to every kind of mischief, but he was just as unselfish and kind as he could be."

Tom went on listening and realized that everyone assumed the boys had drowned while taking a swim. Then, when the raft was discovered missing, there was hope that they had gone down the river to the next

Talking About the Drowned Boys

town. But when that hope vanished too, the boys were believed to have drowned somewhere in the middle of the river. If the bodies were not found by Saturday, the boys' funeral would be held at noon on Sunday.

Tom shuddered when he heard the news. He watched as Aunt Polly knelt down and prayed for him. The tears fell as she whispered words of love and endearment for him.

After Mrs. Harper had left and Aunt Polly was asleep, Tom crept out from under the bed and stood looking at the old woman by the light of the candle. His heart was full of pity for her. He thought he should write her a note and tell her that he was really alive.

So Tom took a piece of sycamore bark out of his pocket, put it on the table, and began to write. But then he got an interesting idea and quickly put the bark away.

As he started out the door, Tom bent over his aunt and kissed her. He would return another time.

A Kiss for Aunt Polly

Hunting for Turtle Eggs

CHAPTER 9
The Pirates Return

It was morning when Tom finally returned to camp. Huck and Joe were already up and glad to see him. They had begun to worry where he had gone. During a sumptuous breakfast of bacon and fish, Tom recounted his adventure back in the village. When he finished, he hid himself away in a shady nook and slept until noon.

The day passed slowly, with the boys hunting for turtle eggs, fishing from the shore, and swimming until they were tired and ready to rest. A sadness came upon each of the boys, and they fell to gazing across the wide river to the town. Tom found himself writing "Becky" in the sand with his big toe.

Finally, Joe broke the silence. "Oh, let's give it up," he said. "I want to go home. It's so lonesome here."

"Oh no, Joe, you'll feel better soon," said Tom. "Just think of the great fishing that's here."

"I don't care for fishing. I want to go home."

Tom tried again. "But Joe, there isn't another swimming place like this anywhere."

It was no use. Soon, even Huck was convinced that it was time to give up and go home. Tom, however, remained firm; he refused to leave the island.

By this time it was beginning to get dark, so Huck and Joe began gathering their things. They didn't want to leave without Tom, but he absolutely refused to consider giving up and going home.

"BECKY"

"Tom, I wish you'd come too," said Huck. "Now you think it over. We'll wait for you down by the shore."

Tom stood watching as Joe and Huck walked slowly away. Suddenly, an idea hit him and he ran after his friends yelling, "Wait! Wait! I want to tell you something."

Joe and Huck stopped and turned around. When Tom reached them, he began explaining his secret plan. The boys listened quietly until they saw the point he was driving at.

Yes, they agreed, Tom had a wonderful plan, even though it meant they would have to stay on the island four more days until Saturday.

Somehow, knowing that they would be going home soon helped Tom, Huck, and Joe pass those days quickly. They fished, swam, played games, and made plans for their return.

When Sunday finally came, the town was

Tom Has a Wonderful Plan.

mournful and silent. The Harpers and Aunt Polly's family were full of grief. The villagers hardly talked, and there was a strange feeling of sadness in the air.

Becky Thatcher found herself moping around the deserted schoolyard, feeling miserable and talking to herself.

"Oh, if only I had that brass doorknob again!" she murmured. "But I haven't anything now to remember him by." And she choked back a little sob. Becky regretted what she had done to Tom. Now she was sure she would never see him again. Just the thought of this touched her so deeply that tears began to roll down her cheeks.

Nearby, a group of boys talked in low voices about Tom and Joe. They retold stories of their two lost friends and shook their heads in disbelief at the thought that they were really gone forever.

At noon, the church bell began to toll. The

Becky Mourns Tom.

villagers gathered in the church, and only the sound of whispering was heard. No one could remember when the little church had been so crowded. A hush came over the villagers when Aunt Polly entered, followed by Sid and the whole Harper family. As the silent, black-clad procession made their way slowly down the aisle, the whole congregation stood in respect.

The funeral service began with the minister describing the boys in glowing terms. He related many incidents in their young lives, and as he talked, the congregation became more and more moved. Soon, there was hardly a dry eye in the church.

A slight rustling sound in the gallery went unnoticed, but a moment later, the creaking of the church door interrupted the service. The minister raised his weeping eyes and stood transfixed! First one, then another pair of eyes followed the minister's gaze. Then,

The Funeral Service Begins.

almost at the very same instant, the congregation rose and stared at the three "dead" boys marching up the aisle. They had hidden in the gallery and listened to their own funeral sermon!

Aunt Polly and the Harpers threw themselves upon the boys and smothered them with hugs and kisses.

Suddenly the minister shouted at the top of his voice, "Praise God! Sing! And put your hearts into it!"

And the whole congregation did. The sound of their voices shook the rafters, while Tom Sawyer, the Pirate, looked around the church at his friends and confessed in his heart that this was the proudest moment of his life.

Three "Dead" Boys Return!

Tom Tells Sid of His Adventures.

CHAPTER 10
Back Home Again

That was Tom's great secret—the plan to return home with his brother pirates and attend their own funeral. They had paddled over to the town on Saturday and slept in the woods at the edge of the village. At daybreak on Sunday, they crept into the church and finished their sleep in the gallery.

At breakfast on Monday morning, Aunt Polly was very loving to Tom, but he was busy chattering away with Sid about the events of the day before. After a while, Aunt Polly broke in.

"Tom, I don't say it wasn't a fine joke—to keep everybody suffering almost a week so you boys could have a good time. But it was a pity you were so hard-hearted as to let me suffer so. If you could come over to go to your own funeral, you could have come over and given me a hint some way that you weren't dead. I suppose if you really loved me, you would have wanted to do that."

This made Tom feel guilty. He *had* actually come to tell Aunt Polly that he was all right. He had even written her a note telling her just that. But instead of owning up to the truth, Tom made up a story of a dream he had on Jackson's Island.

"I dreamed I was right here in this very room, Aunt Polly. Mrs. Harper was here too. The two of you were crying and saying how much you missed us. I think you were saying how even though we got into trouble, we were always kind-hearted boys."

"You Were So Hard-Hearted."

Tom gave such a perfectly detailed description of that unhappy night that Aunt Polly was truly amazed. This dream seemed to convince her that Tom had a special gift. She was so pleased that she took a big red apple from the cupboard and gave it to him to eat on the way to school.

What a hero Tom had become! He did not go skipping and prancing, but moved with a dignified swagger as became a pirate who felt that the public eye was on him. And indeed it was. Tom tried to ignore the looks and remarks as he passed people, but they were food and drink to him—he was enjoying every moment.

Smaller boys flocked at his heels, and older boys were consumed with envy. They would have given anything to have his swarthy, sun-tanned skin and his sudden fame.

At school, the children made such a fuss over Tom and Joe and gazed at them with

Tom Is a Hero!

such admiration, that the two heroes quickly became "stuck up." They told and retold their adventures to eager listeners who wanted to hear the whole story over and over again.

Tom decided that he could be independent of Becky Thatcher now. His fame and glory were enough. He would live for that alone. Now that he was so distinguished, maybe she would want to make up. Well, let her, he decided. She could try all she wanted.

When Becky arrived at school, Tom pretended not to see her. He moved away and joined a group of boys and girls and began to talk. Soon he noticed that Becky was tripping gaily back and forth, her face flushed and her eyes dancing. She pretended to be busy chasing schoolmates and screaming with laughter.

When Tom pretended not to see her at all, Becky came closer and once or twice glanced wistfully toward him. Soon she noticed that

Tom Is Independent of Becky Now.

Tom was talking more to Amy Lawrence than to anyone else. She felt a sharp pang and grew disturbed and uneasy. In a moment of anger and jealousy, Becky announced that she was planning a party during the vacation. Soon everyone was begging for invitations. Everyone, that is, except Tom and Amy. Tom just turned coldly away and took Amy with him.

Becky's lips trembled and tears came to her eyes. She hid these signs and went on talking gaily. As soon as she could, she sneaked away by herself and burst into tears. She'd think of some way to get even with Tom.

At recess, Tom continued his flirtation with Amy, but only after he'd checked to see if Becky was still watching. When he looked across the schoolyard, he saw something that made his blood boil. Becky was sitting cozily on a little bench looking at a picture book with Alfred Temple. They were so absorbed

Becky Sits with Alfred Temple.

hat their heads were almost touching. Jealousy ran red-hot through Tom's veins. He began to hate himself for throwing away the chance Becky had offered for making up. By noon Tom couldn't take it any longer, and he left school and ran home.

Once Becky saw that Tom was no longer around, she lost all interest in Alfred and the picture book. She burst into tears, got up, and walked away.

Alfred ran after her, trying to comfort her, but she snapped, "Go away and leave me alone, can't you! I hate you!"

The boy stopped in amazement and wondered what he could have done. He was humiliated and angry once he figured out the truth. Becky had simply used him to make Tom jealous, but he would get back at Tom. The question was *how*.

Then he thought of the perfect way to do it. He went inside the classroom and found

"Go Away and Leave Me Alone!"

om's spelling book on his desk. He opened
the lesson for the afternoon and poured ink
ll over the page.

At that moment, Becky was glancing in
hrough a window behind him. She saw the
hole thing, but she moved on and said noth-
ng. So Becky started on her way home, in-
ending to find Tom and tell him what Alfred
ad done. She hoped that Tom would be so
hankful, that all their troubles would be
ver.

But before she was halfway home, she
hanged her mind. She thought back to the
ay Tom had treated her, and she was filled
ith anger. Let Tom get punished because of
he damaged spelling book, she decided. And
he also decided to hate him forever.

Alfred's Revenge!

"I've a Notion to Skin You Alive!"

CHAPTER 11
Aunt Polly Learns the Truth

Tom arrived home in a dreary mood, an his aunt's first words showed him that he ha brought his misery to the wrong place.

"Tom, I've a notion to skin you alive!" crie Aunt Polly.

"What have I done?" asked Tom in sur prise.

"Done? You've done enough! Here I go ove to Mrs. Harper's house like an old softy, ex pecting to make her believe all that stuf about your dream, and then she tells me tha Joe told her the whole truth. You really *wer* ere and heard the talk we had that night. Tom, I don't know what's to become of a boy who acts like that. It makes me feel so bad to think you could let me go to Mrs. Harper and make such a fool of myself and never say a word."

Tom hung his head for a moment. He had no answer to give his aunt. He could only try to explain that he didn't think it would turn out this way. But his explanation only made Aunt Polly angrier. Finally, Tom gave in and told his aunt that the real reason he had returned that night was to tell her that he really hadn't drowned and to ease her mind.

Aunt Polly looked up sternly and said, "Tom, I would be the thankfulest soul in this world if I could believe that you ever had such a good thought, but you know you never did. And I know it too!"

Tom pleaded and tried to convince his aunt that he really was telling the truth. "When

Tom Explains His Visit.

ou and Mrs. Harper got to talking about the
uneral," he said, "I just got all full of the
dea of our coming and hiding in the church.
t seemed like such a terrific plan, I couldn't
ear to spoil it. So I just put the bark back
n my pocket and kept mum."

"What bark?" Aunt Polly asked.

"The bark I wrote on to tell you we'd gone
pirating. I wish now you'd woken up when I
kissed you. I do, honest."

The hard lines in his aunt's face relaxed,
and a sudden tenderness dawned in her eyes.
She couldn't believe that Tom had really
kissed her. But she could tell that the boy
was speaking the truth. Still, she had to be
sure.

When Tom had gone off to school, Aunt
Polly ran to the closet and took out the jacket
he had worn on the pirating trip. She hesi-
ated before putting her hand in the pocket.
If Tom was lying this time, she couldn't bear

Aunt Polly Checks Tom's Jacket Pocket.

t. Twice she put her hand in the pocket and twice she pulled it away. But she could not resist. On the third try, she withdrew Tom's piece of bark and read the note through flowing tears.

"I could forgive the boy now," she cried, 'even if he'd committed a million sins!"

Aunt Polly Forgives Tom.

The Measles!

CHAPTER 12
The Salvation of Muff Potter

Summer brought with it the usual adven
tures, hopes, and disappointments. It was
Tom's unfortunate luck to catch the measles
and he had to stay in bed for almost three
weeks. Those weeks seemed like an eternity
and when at last he was out again, the whole
town was buzzing with excitement.

Muff Potter's murder trial was finally
starting. It was the topic of every conversa
tion. Tom could not escape it. Every mention
of the murder sent a shudder through him
and kept him in a cold sweat all the time.

When he couldn't stand it any longer, Tom looked for Huck. He had to have a talk with him. It would be some relief to unseal his tongue for a little while. In addition, he wanted to assure himself that Huck had kept the morbid secret.

"Huck, have you ever told anybody about . . . *that*?" whispered Tom.

"About what?" asked Huck.

"You know what."

"Oh! Of course I haven't."

"Never a word?"

"Never a solitary word. So help me!"

Tom felt more comfortable, but he insisted that they swear again to keep mum about what they had seen that fateful night.

After Huck and Tom sealed their pact with another oath of blood, they discussed the fate of poor Muff Potter.

"I've heard talk that the people plan to lynch him if the court frees him," said Tom.

Swearing Again to Keep Mum

The boys took a long walk and had a long talk, but it brought them little comfort. As twilight drew on, they found themselves hanging around the neighborhood of the jailhouse. They somehow hoped that something would happen to clear away their problems. But nothing did.

The boys did as they had often done before. They went to the cell grating on the ground floor and gave Potter some tobacco and matches. Luckily, there were no guards around. Muff was always so thankful for their little gifts, that it only made their consciences ache more.

After the visit, Tom went home miserable. That night, his dreams were full of horrors.

Each day during the trial, Tom hung around the courtroom, drawn by an almost irresistible impulse to go in. But he forced himself to stay out. Huck was having the same experiences.

Tom's Nightmare

Finally, the great day came—the day that the jury was to make its decision. The villagers filed into the courtroom and sat waiting for the news. The judge and jury entered and took their places.

Shortly afterward, Potter was brought in. He looked pale and haggard, timid and hopeless. All eyes were on him. Injun Joe sat in the gallery, looking fierce and angry.

Instead of waiting for the jury to reveal its decision, Potter's attorney rose to make an announcement. He had an important new witness and wanted to change Potter's plea to "not guilty."

In a firm clear voice, he said, "Call Thomas Sawyer to the stand."

Looks of puzzled amazement appeared on every face in the courtroom, Muff Potter's included. Every eye fastened itself on Tom with interest as he rose and took his place on the stand. He was scared, but he took the oath

"Call Thomas Sawyer to the Stand!"

without hesitation.

Then the defense attorney asked the fateful question. "Thomas Sawyer, where were you on the seventeenth of June, about the hour of midnight?"

Tom glanced at Injun Joe's iron face, and his tongue froze. The audience waited breathlessly for Tom's reply, but his words refused to come.

After a few moments and a few deep breaths, Tom relaxed enough so that his words began to flow. He told the whole story. He explained why he and Huck had been in the cemetery that night and described every detail of the ghastly murder.

On hearing Tom's story, Injun Joe sprang from his seat, tore his way through the crowd, and leaped through the window.

As a result of Tom's testimony, Muff Potter was set free. But Injun Joe was still alive and out there somewhere, waiting . . .

Injun Joe Escapes!

The Hero!

CHAPTER 13
Digging for Buried Treasure

So once again Tom was a hero and his name even appeared in the village newspaper. Tom's days were filled with happiness and praise, but his nights were dark and terrible. Injun Joe haunted all his dreams, and Tom was too afraid to venture out and meet Huck as he used to do. Poor Huck was in the same state of terror.

The night before the jury was to hand down its decision, Tom had gone to see Muff Potter's attorney and had told him the whole story. Huck was disappointed with Tom for breaking their oath of secrecy, but Tom's conscience could not bear the heavy burden of what he had seen. Now, Tom and Huck were afraid Injun Joe would never be captured. They felt sure that they could never draw a safe breath again until that villain was dead and they had seen his corpse.

Rewards were offered for Injun Joe's capture, and a detective was even hired, but not a clue was uncovered.

The days drifted on, and eventually Tom and Huck began to relax more and more. Soon they were even ready to start on a new adventure.

One afternoon, Tom suggested to Huck that they try digging for buried treasure. Huck was doubtful, but Tom explained that there was treasure all over the place just waiting to be dug up. He described how robbers hid their stolen money under dead trees and in haunted houses. His descriptions were

A Reward for Injun Joe's Capture

so convincing that Huck finally agreed to join him on the hunt.

The boys gathered picks and shovels and began the long, three-mile walk up to Still-House Hill. When they reached the first dead tree, they began to dig. They worked and sweated for half an hour. No result. They toiled another hour. Still nothing.

"Do they always bury it as deep as this?" asked Huck.

"Sometimes, not always," answered Tom. "Maybe we just haven't got the right place."

So they found another dead tree and then another and dug some more, but there was no sign of any treasure. Eventually, the boys began to tire. It was at this point that Tom got another idea.

"Let's look in the haunted house on Cardiff Hill," he said.

Huck objected. The house was empty, so everyone assumed it was haunted, but no one

Digging for Buried Treasure

had ever dared to explore it. Tom finally convinced Huck that if any treasure was to be found, it would most likely be in the haunted house.

When they reached the house, there was something so weird and grisly about the silence, that they were afraid, for a moment, to venture in. Then they crept to the door and took a trembling peep. They saw a cobwebbed, floorless room overgrown with weeds. It had an old fireplace and open spaces where windows once were.

Tom and Huck entered on tiptoe, their ears alert to catch the slightest sound. When they heard nothing for several minutes, they relaxed and began to explore the place with interest. In one corner, they found a closet. What mystery did it contain? . . . They turned the knob, the closet squeaked open, and then . . . nothing! The closet was empty.

They were full of courage now and decided

The Haunted House

to explore the second floor. Just as they reached the top of the stairs . . .

"Sh!" said Tom.

"What is it?" whispered Huck.

"Sh! . . . There! . . . Hear it?"

"Yes! . . . Let's run!"

But they didn't dare make a sound by running. They stretched themselves out on the floor, glued their eyes to the knotholes in the rotting wood, and lay waiting in misery and fear.

Two men entered the room below. The boys recognized one as an old deaf-and-dumb beggar who had been around town lately. The other man, a ragged, unkempt creature with an unpleasant face, was someone they had never seen before. The two men began to talk.

"No, I thought it over," said the ragged man, "and I don't like it. It's too dangerous." His voice seemed vaguely familiar to the boys.

Tom and Huck Hear Voices Below.

"Dangerous?" grunted the deaf-and-dumb beggar. "It is not!"

Suddenly Tom and Huck began to shake. The deaf-and-dumb man could hear and speak! But even worse, they recognized the familiar voice. It was Injun Joe's! The boys froze, hardly daring to breathe.

The men talked about plans for another "job," then ate some lunch, and soon fell into a deep sleep.

Huck and Tom decided to take this chance to escape. They rose slowly and softly. But their first step made such a hideous creak on the rotted floor that they sank back down, dead with fright.

They lay there, counting the dragging moments until Injun Joe finally awoke. He kicked his partner in the ribs, and the two men began to count their money. They had nearly six hundred dollars which they decided to bury in the room until they were

Spying on Injun Joe and His Partner

eady to make their escape. So Injun Joe began to rip at the old wooden floor planks with his knife. Suddenly his knife struck something solid.

"What's this?" he muttered as he reached his hand in and pulled out an old rusty box.

The two men pried open the lid, and there before their eyes were hundreds of gold coins and stacks of bills that had to be worth thousands of dollars!

"This must be where old Vic Murrel's gang hid their loot," said Injun Joe.

"What luck!" shouted his companion. "Now you won't have to do that other job."

Injun Joe frowned. "You don't know me," he snapped. "That job isn't just robbery, it's revenge! I'll need your help, and when it's finished, we can leave for good."

Tom and Huck began to shake even more. *Revenge!* That could only mean that Injun Joe was still after them for giving testimony

154

Treasure!

at Muff Potter's trial.

"Let's hide the loot," said Injun Joe.

"I'll bury it at number two, under the cross," said the beggar.

Injun Joe agreed, and the two men left the house with shovels, picks, and their treasure.

Tom and Huck waited a long time before they dared come out of hiding. They had only two things on their minds—Injun's Joe's revenge and the treasure hidden at number two, under the cross.

"Let's Hide the Loot."

Planning Their Strategy

CHAPTER 14
Trembling on the Trail

The adventure of the day tormented Tom's dreams that night. Even his waking hours were filled with fantasies of the thousands of dollars he and Huck had seen. It was more money than either boy had ever believed possible. If they could only figure out what Injun Joe had meant by "number two, under the cross," the money would be theirs.

The next afternoon, Huck and Tom met down by the river to plan their strategy.

"Huck, I've been thinking," began Tom. "I think that 'number two' might be the numer of a room in a tavern."

Huck immediately agreed. This idea sounded reasonable, and since there were only two taverns in town, he decided to find out which one had a room called "number two."

Within an hour, Huck had returned with some information. The smaller tavern had a room which was kept locked at all times. Huck was sure this was the "number two" Injun Joe had mentioned in the haunted house. The boys agreed to stake out the tavern.

They met that night and hid in the alley by the tavern door. No one resembling Injun Joe or his partner entered or left. After several hours, the boys gave up and agreed to return again the next night.

The following evening, at the same hour, they resumed their watch. This time, Huck stood guard, while Tom ventured closer to the

Staking Out the Tavern

tavern and to the locked room.

Huck waited in silence for what seemed like hours. "Maybe Tom fainted," he thought. "Maybe he has been caught. What if he is dead?"

Suddenly, there was a flash of light, and Tom came tearing by him, shouting, "Run! Run for your life!"

Tom didn't need to repeat these words. Huck was practically flying after him. When the two boys reached the abandoned barn at the edge of the village, they relaxed. As soon as Tom got his breath, he explained, "Huck, it was awful! I tried two of my keys, just as soft as I could, but they wouldn't turn. Then I took hold of the knob, and the door opened. It wasn't even locked! As I walked in . . . I almost stepped onto Injun Joe's hand! He was lying there, sound asleep on the floor, with his arms spread out. Huck, I didn't wait to look around. I didn't see the box and I didn't

"Run for Your Life!"

see the cross. All I saw was a lot of bottles and Injun Joe—stone drunk!"

The boys agreed that it was too risky to return to the tavern that night. Instead, Huck promised to watch the place every night, and if Injun Joe or his partner ever left for a while, he would give Tom the signal.

The boys said good night. Tom returned home, and Huck found a deserted hayloft to sleep in.

That night, Tom lay awake thinking of Injun Joe and the treasure and later dreamed of them too. There was no escape from these thoughts!

Huck Finds a Deserted Hayloft.

Tom and Becky, Back Together

CHAPTER 15
Huck Saves the Widow

The next morning, the first thing Tom heard was a piece of good news. Becky Thatcher, who had been on vacation with her family, had just returned. Now, Injun Joe and the treasure sank into secondary importance and Becky took the chief place in Tom's interest.

He saw her, and they spent the afternoon talking and having a wonderful time together. Becky finally got permission to have the picnic she had planned months ago. The invitations were sent out before sunset, and

he next day promised to be a treat for every
boy and girl in town.

Tom's excitement kept him awake until a
pretty late hour. He had hopes of hearing
Huck's signal, but he was disappointed. No
signal came that night.

By twelve o'clock the next afternoon,
everyone was gathered in the Thatcher's yard
to set out for the picnic. They boarded a ferryboat and planned to spend the day picnick-
ing on the other side of the river.

Three miles below town, the ferryboat
stopped in a wooded cove and tied up. The
crowd swarmed ashore, and soon their laughter and shouts could be heard echoing
throughout the forest.

By and by somebody shouted, "Who's ready
for the cave?"

Everybody was. Bundles of candles were
collected, and everyone scampered up the
hillside to the mouth of the cave. It was an

"Who's Ready for the Cave?"

pening shaped like the letter "A." The inside f the cave was romantic and mysterious to xplore. People said that one could wander ays and nights through its intricate chambers and never get out. Nobody "knew" the ave. That was an impossible thing. Most of he young men knew a portion of it, but noody ever dared venture beyond this known ortion. So Tom knew as little of the cave as nyone did.

The crowd filed into the cave and began he exploration. Laughter and shouts echoed rom the walls for an hour. Then the clanging f the ferryboat alerted everyone to the time.

As the ferryboat's lights came glinting towards the wharf in town, one pair of eyes lanced at them in the cloudy, dark night. hose eyes had been glued to the tavern door or hours, but, by now, Huck Finn had just bout given up any hope of seeing Injun Joe. uddenly a noise fell upon his ear. He was

Exploring the Cave

all attention.

Two men brushed by him, and one seemed to have something under his arm. It must be the box! So they were going to move the treasure. Why call Tom now? It would take too much time, and the men would get away. Then the treasure would be lost forever. So Huck decided to follow them himself.

The men moved up the river street three blocks, then turned left up a hill. Huck followed them for what seemed like hours. Soon the men stopped. They were five steps away from the path which led to the Widow Douglas' house.

Huck crept up behind them and heard a very low voice saying, "Drat! Maybe she's got company. I can see lights."

The men began to plot and plan. A deadly chill went to Huck's heart. This was the "revenge" job! Injun Joe still held a grudge against the Widow's dead husband who had

Huck Discovers Injun Joe's Plan.

been a judge and had Injun Joe horsewhipped as a punishment for vagrancy. Now, even though the judge was dead, Injun Joe decided to take his revenge on the old woman. He described horrible tortures he was planning, and as he spoke, he polished his knife. Huck could hear the evil in his voice.

Huck's first thought was to run. Then he remembered that the Widow Douglas had been kind to him more than once. These men were actually planning to murder her! He wanted to warn her, but there was no way to do it without being seen.

Holding his breath, Huck silently slipped away and sped to the nearest house. It was the home of Bill Welsh and his sons. Huck banged at the door.

"What's going on out there? Who's banging? What do you want?" called Mr. Welsh.

Huck breathlessly blurted out the story and begged Mr. Welsh not to tell anyone that

Begging Mr. Welsh to Help

t was him who squealed. He urged the man and his sons to hurry.

Three minutes later, Mr. Welsh and his sons, all well-armed, were at the top of the hill. Huck accompanied them no farther. He hid behind a large boulder and listened. There was a lagging, anxious silence, and then all of a sudden there was an explosion of firearms and a cry.

Huck didn't wait for anything. He sprang away and sped down the hill as fast as his legs could carry him.

At dawn the next morning, Huck returned to the Welsh home. Mr. Welsh and his sons greeted him with a warm welcome and a hearty breakfast. Then he told Huck that the Widow had been saved, but the villains had escaped.

The Welshes Go to Save the Widow.

Lost!

CHAPTER 16
Lost in the Cave

All the while that Huck was following Injun Joe and his partner to the Widow Douglas' house, Tom and Becky were still on the other side of the shore exploring the cave. Neither knew that the picnic party had long since departed. And, in the excitement of boarding the boat, no one in the laughing, shouting crowd of young people had noticed that Tom and Becky were not with them.

Without realizing it, Tom and Becky had lost their way. They had started through a long corridor in the cave and, at each new opening, they glanced to see if it looked familiar. But every time, the path was strange to Tom. His confidence began to fail him, and soon he began turning off into new openings at random. Becky began to cry.

"We're lost, Tom! We'll never get out of here. The others have left, and we'll surely die here before anyone finds us."

Tom tried to cheer her up. He assured her that they would find a way out.

But after several hours, hunger and fatigue set in. They ate their last piece of cake, and Becky's legs refused to carry her another inch. So she and Tom sat down and rested. In the light of their last candle, they talked of home, its comfortable beds, and all their friends. When the candle finally flickered and went out, Becky cried, and Tom frowned in silence. He was frightened too.

Time passed. Tom and Becky fell asleep and woke up several times. They had no way

The Last Food

of knowing how many hours or even days were passing. Only the gnawing hunger in their stomachs reminded them that time was slowly going by.

"Tom, do you think they'll miss us and come and hunt for us?" Becky asked hopefully.

"Yes, they will! They certainly will!" Tom reassured her.

Tom and Becky both realized how worried and anxious their family and friends must be. Their conversation drifted off, and they became silent and thoughtful.

The hours passed, and hunger began to torment them again. They were getting too weak to even move when Tom suddenly gasped. "Sh! Did you hear that?"

They both held their breaths and listened. There was a sound like a faint, far-off shout.

Tom jumped up and quickly answered it. Then he helped Becky to her feet. Leading

"Now, Tom, haven't we always been friends?" pleaded Huck. "You wouldn't leave me out, would you?"

"Huck, I wouldn't want to, and I *don't* want to, but what would people say? Why, they'd say, 'Mph! Tom Sawyer's gang! Pretty low characters in it,' and they'd mean *you*, Huck. You wouldn't like that, and neither would I."

Huck was silent for a long time. He had been used to living his own way for so many years, but now everything was different. Both the Widow and Tom wanted him to change. Maybe it wouldn't be so bad after all.

"Well, I'll go back to the Widow for a month and tackle it and see if I can stand it, but only if you let me belong to the gang, Tom."

So Tom and Huck walked arm and arm towards the Widow's big house on the hill. And as they walked, they planned all sorts of new adventures.

Huck Refuses to Return to the Widow.

"Sh! Did You Hear That?"

her by the hand, he started groping down the corridor in the direction of the shouts. Every few minutes they stopped and listened again. Each time, the sound seemed to be getting closer and closer.

"It's them!" shouted Tom. "They've come for us! Becky, we're all right now!"

The joy of the prisoners was almost overwhelming. Their speed was slow, however, because large, deep pits were common in the cave, and they had to walk carefully. They shortly came to one pit and had to stop. It might be three feet deep, it might be a hundred. They could not pass it.

Tom got down on his stomach and reached down as far as he could. No bottom. They would have to stay there and wait until the searchers came. They listened for the shouts again, but the voices were becoming more and more distant. After a little while, they disappeared altogether.

A Bottomless Pit!

Tom and Becky were miserable. Tom shouted until he was hoarse, but it was no use. Still, he talked hopefully to Becky as they groped their way back to a spring of fresh water they had passed earlier. They lay down to rest there, and the weary time dragged on.

When Tom awoke and could think clearly, he realized that there were some side passages along the corridors. It would be better to explore some of them than to sit and do nothing. So he took a ball of kite string from his pocket, tied it to a rock jutting out from the cave wall, and he and Becky started off. Tom led the way, unwinding the line as he groped along. At the end of twenty steps, the corridor ended in a ledge. Tom got down on his knees and felt below and then as far around the corner as he could reach. The moment his head turned the corner, his heart

filled with joy. For not twenty yards away he saw a human hand holding a candle.

Tom stood up and began to shout. Instantly, that hand was followed by a body from behind a rock. Tom was paralyzed with fear when he recognized . . . *Injun Joe!*

But before Tom could grab Becky and run, Injun Joe fled into the darkness. He probably had not recognized Tom's voice because of the echoes in the cave.

Still, Tom's fright weakened every muscle in his body. He told himself that if he had strength enough to get back to the spring, he would stay there. Nothing would tempt him to risk meeting Injun Joe again. He did not want to alarm Becky by telling her what he had seen, so he explained that he had only shouted "for luck."

But hunger led Tom to try again. After a long sleep, he awoke, ready to explore the cave once more. Becky was very weak. She

Injun Joe!

had sunk into a half-conscious state and would not be roused to go with him. She mumbled that she would wait where she was and die—it would not be long. She told Tom to go with the kite string and explore if he wanted to, but she asked only that he return to stay by her and hold herhand until it was all over.

Tom choked back a sob and kissed her. He made a show of being confident of finding the searchers or an escape from the cave, but he was distressed with hunger and fear. Taking the kite string in his hand, he went groping down one of the passages on his hands and knees.

Mrs. Thatcher Is Very Ill.

CHAPTER 17
Escape!

Back in the village, everyone was i
mourning. It was Tuesday, and the childre
had been missing for three days. Most of the
searchers had given up and gone back to thei
everyday lives, certain that Tom and Becky
would never be found.

Mrs. Thatcher was very ill. People who vis
ited her said it was heartbreaking to hear he
call Becky's name, raise her head to listen fo
an answer, then collapse wearily with a
moan.

Aunt Polly had drooped into a depression

and her grey hair had turned almost white overnight.

On Tuesday, the townsfolk went to sleep, sad and forlorn, only to be awakened in the middle of the night by a wild peal from the village bells. Within moments, the streets were swarming with frantic, half-dressed people shouting, "They're found, they're found!"

Tin pans and horns were added to the din as the villagers gathered and moved toward the river. An open carraige drawn by shouting citizens delivered Tom and Becky into their arms.

The village was all lit up and alive with excitement. It was the greatest night the little town of St. Petersburg had ever seen! During the first half-hour, a procession of villagers filed through the Thatcher house, touching Tom and Becky, kissing them, and trying to speak. But nobody could. Everyone was crying

"They're Found, They're Found!"

with joy and relief.

Aunt Polly's happiness was complete, but Mrs. Thatcher had to get a message to her husband first. He was still out at the cave searching for the children.

Tom lay upon the sofa with an eager audience around him. He told the history of the wonderful adventure, putting in many extra little tidbits to make it even more exciting. He described how he had left Becky and gone on an exploring expedition; how he had followed two passages as far as his kite string would reach; how he had followed the third to the fullest stretch of the kite string; and how he had been about to turn back, when he suddenly glimpsed a far-off speck that looked like daylight. At that moment, he had dropped the string and groped towards the speck of light. Reaching it, he had pushed his head and shoulders through a small hole. And there was the broad Mississippi River below!

An Eager Audience Hears Tom's Story.

"Just think," Tom added, "if it had happened at night, I wouldn't have seen that speck of daylight, and I wouldn't have explored that passage any more. So, I went back to Becky and broke the good news to her, but she told me not to bother her with such stuff, for she was tired, and she knew she was going to die. I talked and talked until I finally convinced her that I'd found an opening. Then she almost died with joy when I led her to that blue speck of daylight.

"We climbed out and sat beside the cave, crying with happiness until some men came along. I hailed them and told them our story. At first, they didn't believe me. They said it was a wild tale, but they took us home, fed us, and let us sleep for a few hours before bringing us back home."

Three days of toil and hunger in the cave were not to be shaken off at once, as Tom and Becky soon discovered. They were bedridden

Leaving the Cave

all of Wednesday and Thursday and seemed to grow more and more tired and worn all the time. Tom moved about a little on Thursday, was downtown on Friday, and was nearly as good as new by Saturday. But Becky did not leave her room until Sunday, and then she looked as if she had passed through a wasting illness.

Tom learned that Huck, too, was ill and was staying with Mr. Welsh and his sons. He went to visit his friend and was warned to keep still, not to excite Huck, and not to mention the incident with the Widow Douglas. Tom had already been told of Huck's brave act and about the discovery of a body in the river—a body identified as Injun Joe's partner. The man had obviously been drowned while trying to escape from the Welshes.

About two weeks after Tom's rescue from the cave, he stopped off to see Becky. Mr. Thatcher and some friends asked Tom if he

Tom Visits Huck.

wouldn't mind returning to the cave some-
time. Tom said he thought he wouldn't mind
it. It was then that Mr. Thatcher explained
to Tom, "To prevent anyone else getting lost
in the cave, I had the place sealed up and
triple locked two weeks ago."

Tom turned white as a sheet.

"What's the matter, boy?" cried Mr.
Thatcher. "Run, somebody! Get a glass of
water!"

The water was brought and thrown into
Tom's face.

"What's the matter?" repeated Mr. Thatcher.

"Injun Joe's in the cave!" whispered Tom.

"What's the Matter, Boy?"

Finding Injun Joe's Body

CHAPTER 18
Buried Treasure

Within minutes, the news had sprea[d]
around town, and dozens of men were on thei[r]
way to the cave with Tom and Mr. Thatcher[.]
When the cave door was unlocked, a sor[-]
rowful sight presented itself in the dim twi[-]
light. Injun Joe lay stretched upon the ground[,]
dead, his face close to the crack of the door[.]
It seemed as if his last moments had been[?]
spent searching for light and cheer from th[e]
outside world.

Tom was touched, for he knew through hi[s]
own experience how this man must have suf[-]

...ered. Tom felt pity, but even more, he felt an incredible sense of relief and security. Injun Joe was dead. No longer would Tom's dreams be haunted by thoughts of Injun Joe's revenge. No longer would he tiptoe around, wondering when the man would seek him out for having saved Muff Potter's life.

Injun Joe's bowie knife lay close by. Its blade was broken in two from Injun Joe's unsuccessful attempts at chipping and hacking at the door which blocked the cave exit.

Ordinarily, one could find dozens of bits of candles left by tourists in the crevices of this path. But now there were none. Injun Joe must have searched them out and eaten them. He had probably also caught a few bats and had eaten them too, leaving only their claws. The man had starved to death.

The men in the search party buried Injun Joe near the mouth of the cave. People flocked there in boats and wagons from the

A Broken Bowie Knife

owns, villages, and farms for miles around. They brought their children and all sorts of ood, making it more of a picnic than a fu-neral.

The morning after the funeral, Tom and Huck went to their secret place on the hill to have an important talk. Huck had learned all about Tom's adventure from Mr. Welsh and the Widow Douglas, and now Huck wanted to explain to Tom all that had hap-pened to him.

"I was standing watch outside the tavern, Tom, just like we agreed, and I followed Injun Joe and his partner when they left. I over-heard their terrible plans for the Widow Douglas, so I ran to Mr. Welsh and begged him to save her."

"That was great, Huck!" said Tom. "But why didn't you want anyone to know how brave you were?"

"Because even though the Widow Douglas

People Come from Miles Around.

was saved, Injun Joe had escaped."

Tom nodded. He understood exactly how
Huck had felt. But that was done, and Tom
wanted to discuss the subject that had been
on his mind for weeks—the treasure.

"Huck," he said, "that money was never in
room number two at the tavern."

"What!" Huck searched his friend's face for
some sort of clue. "Tom, have you got on the
track of that money again?"

"Huck, it's in the cave!"

Huck's eyes blazed. "Say it again, Tom," he
cried.

"The money's in the cave."

"Tom, are you serious? Do you promise you
aren't kidding about this?"

"I'm serious, Huck. Will you go in the cave
with me and help get it out?"

"You bet I will! . . . That is, I will, if we
can do it without getting lost."

"Huck, we can do it without the least little

"The Money's in the Cave!"

it of trouble. I promise you that. We'll need some bread and meat, a few strong bags, and three balls of kite string. Also, plenty of matches."

The boys gathered their supplies and, a lit-le after noon, they got underway. When they were close to the opposite shore of the river, Tom pointed high up on the hillside and said, "Now you see this bluff? It looks like all the others, but there's a small white mark up here. See it, Huck? That's one of my marks. We'll get ashore now."

The boys pulled the raft on shore, and Tom showed Huck the tiny cave opening hidden behind a thick clump of bushes. Huck was impressed. The hole would have been impos-sible to find without Tom.

They climbed through the hole and entered the cave. Tom took the lead, and they made their way to the far end of the tunnel. As they passed the spring, Tom felt a shudder go

Going Ashore

through him. He showed Huck the fragment of candlewick perched on a lump of clay against the wall, and he described how he and Becky had sat there watching the flame struggle and die.

The boys continued on through another corridor, talking only in whispers, until they reached the ledge. Then Tom raised his candle high in the air and tugged at Huck's sleeve. "Now I'll show you something," said Tom. "Look as far around the corner as you can. Do you see that? There, on the big rock, written with ashes?"

"Tom, it's a cross!"

"Now, where's your number two? Under the cross, right?"

Huck stared at the cross a while, then said with a shaky voice, "Tom, let's get out of here!"

But Tom was the cool voice of reason. He slowly explained to Huck that there were no

"It's a Cross!"

ghosts in the cave. "Injun Joe is dead," he
reminded Huck, "and we've both suffered
enough looking for the treasure. Now that
we're so close, it's silly to be afraid." Tom
managed to convince Huck that the treasure
was rightfully theirs.

At the base of a rock, they saw signs of
activity—a blanket, some tools, and a piece
of bacon rind—but no metal treasure chest.

"He said under the cross," whispered Huck.

"Well, this comes nearest to being under the
cross. It can't be under the rock itself, because
that sets on solid clay ground."

They searched everywhere around the rock,
then sat down discouraged. Huck had no
ideas, but Tom was thinking and planning
all the while he sat.

"Look there, Huck! There's footprints and
some candle grease on the clay on one side
of this rock, but not on the other sides. Now
what's that for? I bet you the money *is* under

Footprints and Candle Grease

he rock. I'm going to dig in the clay."

They both began to scratch and dig, and after two hours they uncovered some boards. Once the boards were removed, they discovered a whole new corridor which led under the rock. They followed the path until it turned a curve.

Tom stopped suddenly and exclaimed, "Huck, I've found it! Here's the treasure."

It *was* the treasure box, sure enough. Tom lifted the lid, and Huck scooped up the tarnished coins with his clay-filled hands.

"We're rich, Tom! We really are!"

For a few moments, the boys just stood and looked at their treasure. Soon, they began putting the money into the bags and carrying it out of the cave.

When they emerged from the cave into the clump of bushes, they looked around to make sure all was clear. After a short rest for lunch, he boys loaded their raft and pushed out into

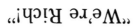

"We're Rich!"

the river. The sun was dipping toward the
horizon as they left the shore, and by the time
they landed, it was already dark.

"Now, Huck," said Tom, "we'll hide the
money in the loft of the Widow's woodshed.
I'll come up in the morning, and we'll count
it and divide it. Then we'll hunt up a place
out in the woods for it where it will be safe.
But for now, just you lay quiet here and watch
the stuff while I run and find a wagon. I'll
only be gone a minute."

Tom disappeared, but soon returned with
the wagon. They put the sacks of money into
it and started off, dragging their treasure
behind them.

As the boys passed Mr. Welsh's house, the
old man stepped out and called, "Is that you,
Huck . . . and you, Tom? Come along with
me. Everyone is waiting."

Mr. Welsh helped them pull the wagon a
short ways down the road, and they parked

Dragging the Treasure to a Safe Place

t outside the Widow Douglas' house. There
was a party going on inside. The Thatchers,
he Harpers, Aunt Polly, and just about
everybody of importance was there. The
Widow greeted the boys as heartily as anyone
could greet two such ragged, dirty-looking
young men who were covered with clay and
candle grease from their latest adventure.
Aunt Polly blushed and frowned, then shook
her head at Tom. But before she had a chance
o say a word, Mr. Welsh began explaining
now he had stumbled on Tom and Huck right
at his door. "So I just brought them along,"
ne added.

"And you did right," said the Widow.
"Come with me, boys." She took Tom and
Huck to a bedroom and added, "Now wash
and dress yourselves. Here are two new suits
of clothes with shirts and socks and everything you'll need. We'll wait for you downstairs. Come down when you're ready."

The Widow Douglas Greets the Boys.

Hucks Wants to Get Away.

CHAPTER 19
A Home for Huck

Huck looked at the clothes, then at Tom and said, "Tom, we can get out of here if we can find a rope. The window isn't too high up."

"What do you want to get away for?" asked Tom.

"Well, I'm not used to that kind of a crowd I can't stand it. I'm not going down there Tom."

"Oh, don't worry, Huck! It's nothing. I'll take care of you."

Then Sid entered the room and told Tom

THE ADVENTURES OF TOM SAWYER

and Huck that the party had been planned
for a special reason—Mr. Welsh intended to
tell everyone that it was Huck who had saved
the Widow's life. And then the Widow was
going to announce some secret.

"I don't know what the secret is," added
Sid, "but I do know that Mr. Welsh wants
Huck to be there to hear it."

Later, when the Widow's guests were at
the supper table and a dozen children were
propped up at little side tables, Mr. Welsh
rose to make his speech. He thanked the
Widow for the dinner she was giving in honor
of his sons and himself. "But," he added,
"there is another person whose modesty will
not permit him to reveal his part in this brave
rescue." Then, in his finest dramatic manner,
Mr. Welsh told the secret about Huck's share
in the adventure.

Widow Douglas heaped compliments and
thanks on Huck. Everyone was looking at

Mr. Welsh Praises Huck.

him, but poor Huck was just sitting there, squirming in his new and very uncomfortable suit.

Then the Widow announced that she meant to give Huck a home under her roof and have him educated. She added that when she could spare the money, she would start him in business in a modest way.

Tom saw that his chance had come. "Huck doesn't need money," he announced. "Huck is rich."

Only respect for the Widow stopped everyone from laughing out loud at Tom's foolish words. Huck, *rich?*

"Huck's got money," continued Tom. "Maybe you don't believe it, but he's got lots of it. Oh, you needn't smile. I guess I'll have to show you. Just wait a minute."

Tom ran outside. The guests looked at each other with a confused interest. Huck sat frozen to his seat. He couldn't bring himself to

Tom Displays the Treasure.

utter a word.

Tom entered, struggling with the weight of the sacks. He poured the mass of yellow coins onto the table and cried, "There! What did I tell you? Half of it's Huck's and half of it's mine!"

The spectacle took everyone's breath away. But in moments, they were all demanding an explanation.

Tom told the long, but interesting story, while everyone listened in silence. When he was finished, the money was counted. The sum amounted to a little over *twelve thousand dollars!* It was more money than anyone present had ever seen before.

"Huck Is Rich."

Tom and Huck Are Stars.

CHAPTER 20

Respectable Huck Joins the Gang

Tom and Huck's windfall caused quite a stir in the little town. It was talked about, gloated over, and glorified until the real story was pale and uninteresting compared to the myth created by the constant gossip.

Whenever Tom and Huck appeared, they were stared at and admired. They were stars. Everywhere they went, they were followed. Everything they said was listened to with sharp interest and repeated.

Widow Douglas put Huck's money in the bank for him, and Aunt Polly did the same with Tom's share. Each boy had an income now. Although it was only a dollar a day, to Tom and Huck it was a fortune.

Huck Finn's wealth and the fact that he was now under the Widow Douglas' protection introduced him to a whole new world. But for Huck, it was a world he wished he had never known. The Widow's servants kept him clean and neat, combed and brushed. He had to eat with a knife and fork, and he had to use a napkin, cup, and plate. The Widow even forced him to go to church.

Huck bravely bore these miseries for three weeks, and then one day he ran away. For three days, everyone hunted for him.

Early on the fourth morning, Tom wisely went poking around the abandoned slaughterhouse—one of Huck's earlier favorite hiding places. Sure enough, Huck was there. He was wearing his old rags and looked unkempt and uncombed.

Tom Finds Huck's Hiding Place.

When Tom told him how worried everyone was over his disappearance, Huck said, "Don't talk about it, Tom. I've tried that life, and it doesn't work. It isn't for me. The Widow was good to me, but I can't live like she does. She makes me dress and wash and do everything at a special time, and I'm just not used to living that way."

Tom tried to convince Huck that he would learn to like his new life, but it seemed hopeless. Then Tom thought of a plan to get Huck to stay with the Widow.

"Look here, Huck," he said. "We're going to form that gang we talked about back at the cave. But we can't let you join if you aren't respectable."

Huck was sad for a moment. "Can't you let me in, Tom?" he asked. "Didn't you let me play pirate?"

"Yes, but this is much more high-toned than a gang of pirates," said Tom.

❀❀

A PENNY A DAY

A
PENNY
A
DAY

BY

Walter de la Mare

Illustrated by
PAUL KENNEDY

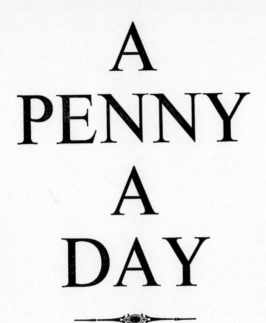

ALFRED·A·KNOPF   NEW YORK   1960

L. C. Catalog card number 60–13022

THIS IS A BORZOI BOOK,

PUBLISHED BY ALFRED A. KNOPF, INC.

CONTENTS

A Penny a Day   *3*

The Three Sleeping Boys of Warwickshire   *32*

The Lovely Myfanwy   *64*

The Dutch Cheese   *106*

Dick and the Beanstalk   *116*

The Lord Fish   *165*

❀❀

A PENNY A DAY

A PENNY A DAY

———◄●►———

Once upon a time, there lived
in a cottage that had been built out of the stones of a
ruinous Castle and stood within its very walls, an old
woman, and her granddaughter—whose name was
Griselda. Here they lived quite alone, being the only
two left of a family of farmers who had once owned
a wide track of land around them—fields, meadows,
heath and moorland—skirting the cliffs and the sea.

But all this was long ago. Now Griselda and her old
grandmother had little left but the roof over their heads
and a long garden whose apples and cherries and plum-
trees flowered in spring under the very walls of the Castle. Many birds nested in this quiet hollow; and the
murmur of the sea on the beach beyond it was never
hushed to rest.

The old woman tended the garden. And Griselda
had very little time wherein to be idle. After her day's
work in the farms and fields, she went so weary to bed
that however much she tried to keep awake in order to
enjoy the company of her own thoughts, she was usually
fast asleep before the wick of her tallow candle had
ceased to smoulder. Yet for reasons not known even to

herself she was as happy as she was good-natured. In looks she resembled a mermaid. Her fair face was unusually gentle and solemn, which may in part have come from her love and delight in gazing at and listening to the sea.

Whenever she had time to herself, which was very seldom, she would climb up by the broken weed-grown steps to the very top of the Castle tower, and sit there— like Fatima's sister—looking out over the green cliffs and the vast flat blue of the ocean. She sat as small as a manikin there. When the sea-winds had blown themselves out she would search the beach for driftwood— the only human creature to be seen—in the thin salt spray blown in on the wind. And the sea-birds would scream around her while the slow toppling Atlantic breakers shook the earth with their thunder. In still evenings, too, when storms had been raging far out over the ocean, and only a slow ground-swell poured in its heavy waters upon the shore, it seemed that sunken bells were ringing from a belfry submerged and hidden for ever in the deeps.

But no humans, except Griselda, were there to listen. It was seldom, even, that the people in the nearest village came down to the sea-strand; and never when night was falling. For the Castle was a place forbidden. It was the haunt, it was said, of the Strange Folk. On calm summer evenings unearthly dancers had been seen dancing between the dusk and the moonlight on the short green turf at the verge of the sands, where bugloss and sea-lavender bloomed, and the gulls had their meeting place, gabbling softly together as they preened their wings in the twilight.

Griselda had often heard these tales. But, as she had lived under the walls of the Castle, and had played alone in its ruins ever since she could remember anything at all, she listened to them with delight. What was there to be afraid of? She longed to see these dancers; and kept watch. And when the full moon was ablaze in the sky, she would slip out of her grandmother's cottage and dance alone in its dazzling light on the hard, sea-laid sands of the beach; or sit, half-dreaming, in some green knoll of the cliffs. She would listen to the voices of the sea among the rocks and in the caves; and could not believe that what she heard was only the lully and music of its waters.

Often, too, when sitting on her sun-warmed doorstep, morning or evening, mending her clothes, or peeling potatoes, or shelling peas, or scouring out some old copper pot, she would feel, all in an instant, that she was no longer alone. Then she would stoop her head a little lower over her needle or basin, pretending not to notice that anything was different. As you can hear the notes of an unseen bird or in the darkness can smell a flower past the finding, so it was with Griselda. She had company beyond hearing, touch, or sight.

Now and again, too, as she slid her downcast eyes to right or left, she had actually caught a fleeting glimpse of a shape, not *quite* real perhaps, but more real than nothing—though it might be half-hidden behind the bushes, or peering down at her from an ivy-shadowed hollow in the thick stone walls.

Such things did not alarm Griselda—no more than would the wind in the keyhole, or the cry of flighting swans at night. They were part of her life, just as the rarer birds and beetles and moths and butterflies are part of the Earth's life. And whatever these shadowy creatures were, she was certain they meant her no harm.

So the happy days went by, spring on to winter, though Griselda had to work nearly all her waking hours to keep herself and her old grandmother from want. Then, one day, the old woman fell ill. She had fallen on the narrow stairs as she was shuffling down in the morning, and there, at the foot of them, looking no more alive than a bundle of old clothes, Griselda found her when she came in with her driftwood.

She was old, and worn and weary, and Griselda knew well that unless great care was taken of her, she might get worse; and even die. The thought of this terrified her. 'Oh, Grannie, Grannie!' she kept whispering to herself as she went about her work, 'I'll do anything —anything in the world—I don't mind what happens —if only you'll promise not to *die!*' But she soon began to take courage again, and kept such a cheerful face that the old woman hadn't an inkling of how sick with care and foreboding Griselda's small head often was, or how near her heart came to despair.

She scarcely had time now to wash her face or comb her hair, or even to sleep and eat. She seldom sat down to a meal, and even when she did, there was but a minute or two in which to gobble it up. She was so tired she could scarcely drag her feet up the steep narrow staircase; the colour began to fade out of her cheeks, and her face to grow haggard and wan.

Still, she toiled on, still sang over her work, and simply refused to be miserable. And however sick and hungry and anxious she might feel, she never let her

grandmother see that she was. The old soul lay helpless
and in pain on her bed, and had troubles enough of her
own. So Griselda had nobody to share hers with; and
instead of their getting better they got worse.

And when—after a hot breathless night during
which she had lain between waking and dreaming
while the lightning flared at her window, and the thunder raved over the sea—when, next morning she came
down very early to find that the hungry mice had stolen
more than half of the handful of oatmeal she had left in
the cupboard, and that her little crock of milk had
turned sour, her heart all but failed her. She sat down
on the doorstep and she began to cry.

It was early in May; the flashing dark blue sea was
tumbling among the rocks of the beach, its surf like
snow. The sun blazed in the east, and all around her
the trees in their new leaves were blossoming, and the
birds singing, and the air was cool and fragrant with
flowers after the rain.

In a little while Griselda stopped crying—and very
few tears had trickled down from her eyes—and with
her chin propped on her hands, she sat staring out
across the bright green grass, her eyes fixed vacantly on
three butterflies that were chasing one another in the
calm sweet air. This way, that way, they glided, flut-
tered, dipped and soared; then suddenly swooped up
into the dazzling blue of the sky above the high broken
wall and vanished from sight.

Griselda sighed. It was as if they had been mocking
her misery. And with that sigh, there was no more
breath left in her body. So she had to take a much
deeper breath to make up for it. After that she sighed

no more—since she had suddenly become aware again
that she was being watched. And this time she knew by
what. Not twelve paces away, at the top of a flight of
tumbledown stone steps that corkscrewed up to one of
the Castle turrets, stood what seemed to be an old wizened pygmy hunched-up old man.

He was of the height of a child of five; he had
pointed ears, narrow shoulders, and a hump on his
back. And he wore a coat made of a patchwork of
moleskins. He stood there—as stock-still as the stones
themselves—his bright colourless eyes under his moleskin cap fixed on her, as if Griselda was as outlandish
an object to him as he was to Griselda.

She shut her own for a moment, supposing he might

have come out of her fancy; then looked again. But already, his crooked staff in his hand, this dwarf had come rapidly shuffling along over the turf towards her. And yet again he stayed—a few paces away. Then, fixing his small bright gaze on her face, he asked her in a shrill, cracked, rusty voice why she was crying. In spite of their lightness, his eyes were piercingly sharp in his dried-up face. And Griselda, as she watched him, marvelled how any living creature could look so old.

Gnarled, wind-shorn trees—hawthorn and scrub oak—grew here and there in the moorland above the sea, and had stood there for centuries among the yellow gorse and sea-pinks. He looked older even than these. She told him she had nothing to cry about, except only that the mice had been at her oatmeal, the milk had turned sour, and she didn't know where to turn next. He asked her what she had to do, and she told him that too.

At this he crinkled up his pin-sharp eyes, as if he were thinking, and glanced back at the turret from which he had come. Then, as if he had made up his mind, he shuffled a step or two nearer and asked Griselda what wages she would pay him if he worked for her for nine days. 'For three days, and three days, and three days,' he said, 'and that's all. How much?'

Griselda all but laughed out loud at this. She told the dwarf that far from being able to pay anyone to work for her, there wasn't a farthing in the house—and not even food enough to offer him a taste of breakfast. 'Unless', she said, 'you would care for a cold potato. There's one or two of *them* left over from supper.'

'Ay, nay, nay,' said the dwarf. 'I won't work without

wages, and I can get my own food. But hark now: if you'll promise to give me a penny a day for nine days, I will work here for you from dawn to dark. Then you yourself will be able to be off to the farms and the fields. But it must be a penny a day and no less; it must be paid every evening at sunset before I go to my own parts again; and the old woman up there must never see me, and shall hardly know that I have come.'

Griselda sat looking at him—as softly and easily as she could; but she had never in all her days seen any human being like this before. Though his face was wizened and cockled up like a winter apple, yet it seemed as if he could never have been any different. He looked as old as the stones around him and yet no older than the snapdragons that grew in them. To meet his eyes was like peering through a rusty keyhole into a long empty room. She expected at any instant he would vanish away, or be changed into something utterly different—a flowering thistle or a heap of stones!

Long before this very morning, indeed, Griselda had often caught sight of what looked like living shapes and creatures—on the moorland or the beach—which, when she had looked again, were clean gone; or, when she had come close, proved to be only a furze-bush, or a rock jutting out of the turf, or a scangle of sheep's wool caught on a thorn. This is the way of these strangers. While then she was not in the least afraid of the dwarf, she felt uneasy and bewildered in his company.

But she continued to smile at him, and answered that though she could not promise to pay him a penny until she had a penny to pay, she would do her best to earn some. Now nothing was left. And she had already made up her mind to be off at once to a farm along the sea-cliffs, where she would be almost sure to get work. If the dwarf would wait but one day, she told him, she would ask the farmer to pay her her wages before she came home again. 'Then I *could* give you the penny,' she said.

Old Moleskins continued to blink at her. 'Well,' he said, 'be off then now. And be back before sunset.'

But first Griselda made her grandmother a bowl of water-porridge, using up for it the last pinch of meal she had in the house. This she carried up to the old woman, with a sprig of apple blossom in a gallipot to put beside it and make it taste better. Since she had so promised him, and felt sure he meant no harm, she said nothing to her grandmother about the dwarf. She tidied the room, tucked in the bedclothes, gave the old woman some water to wash in, beat up her pillow, pinned a shawl over her shoulders, and, having made her as comfortable as she could manage, left her to herself, promising to be home again as soon as she could.

'And be sure, Grannie,' she said, 'whatever happens, not to stir from your bed.'

By good fortune, the farmer's wife whom she went off to see along the sea-cliffs was making butter that morning. The farmer knew Griselda well, and when she had finished helping his wife and the dairymaid with the churning, he not only paid her two pennies for her pains, but a third, 'For the sake,' as he said, 'of your goldilocks, my dear; and *they're* worth a king's ransom! . . . What say you, Si?' he called to his son, who had just come in with the calves. Simon, his face all red, and he was a good deal uglier (though pleasant in face) than his father, glanced up at Griselda, but the gold must have dazzled his eyes, for he turned away and said nothing.

At this moment the farmer's wife came bustling out into the yard again. She had brought Griselda not only a pitcher of new milk and a couple of hen's eggs to take to her grandmother, but some lardy-cakes and a jar of honey for herself. So Griselda, feeling ten times happier than she had been for many a long day, hurried off home.

Now there was a duck-pond under a willow on the way she took home, and there, remembering what the farmer had said, she paused, stooped over, and looked at herself in the muddy water. But the sky was of the brightest blue above her head; and there were so many smooth oily ripples on the surface of the water made by the ducks as they swam and preened and gossiped together that Griselda couldn't see herself clearly, or be sure from its reflection even if her hair was still gold! She got up, laughed to herself, waved her hand to the ducks and hastened on.

When, carrying her pitcher, she had come in under the high snapdragon-tufted gateway of the Castle, and so home again, a marvel it was to see. The kitchen was as neat as a new pin. The table had been scoured; the fire-irons twinkled like silver; the crockery on the dresser looked as if it had been newly painted; a brown jar of wallflowers bloomed sweet on the sill, and even the brass pendulum of the cuckoo-clock, that hadn't ticked for years, shone round as the sun at noonday, and was swinging away as if it meant to catch up before nightfall all the time it had ever lost.

Beside the hearth, too, lay a pile of broken drift-wood, a fire was merrily dancing in the grate, there was a fish cooking in the pan in the brick oven, the old iron kettle hung singing from its hook; and a great sauce-pan, brimful of peeled potatoes, sat in the hearth beneath it to keep it company. And not only this, for there lay on the table a dish of fresh-pulled salad—lettuces, radishes, and young sorrel and dandelion leaves. But of Old Moleskins, not a sign.

Griselda herself was a good housewife, but in all her days she had never seen the kitchen look like this. It was as fresh as a daisy. And Griselda began to sing— to keep the kettle company. Having made a custard out of one of the eggs and the milk she had brought home with her, she climbed upstairs again to see her grand-mother.

'Well, Grannie,' she said, 'how are you now? I've been away and come back. I haven't wasted a moment; but you must be nearly starving.'

The old woman told her she had spent the morning between dozing and dreaming and looking from her bed out of the window at the sea. This she could do because immediately opposite her window was the broken opening of what had once been a window in the walls of the Castle. It was a kind of spy-hole into the world for the old woman.

'And what else were you going to tell me, Grannie?' said Griselda.

The old woman spied about her from her pillow as if she were afraid she might be overheard. Then she warned Griselda that next time she went out she must make sure to latch the door. Some strange animal must have been prowling about in the house, she said. She had heard it not only under her open window, but even stirring about in the room below. 'Though I must say,' she added, 'I had to listen pretty hard!'

Griselda glanced up out of the lattice window and, since her head was a good deal higher than her grandmother's pillow, she could see down into the green courtyard below. And there stood Old Moleskins, looking up at her.

An hour or two afterwards, when the sun was dipping behind the green hills beyond the village, and Griselda sat alone, beside the fire, her sewing in her lap, she heard shuffling footsteps on the cobbles outside, and the dwarf appeared at the window. Griselda thanked him with all her heart for what he had done for her, and took out of her grandmother's old leather purse one of the three pennies she had earned at the farm.

The dwarf eyed it greedily, then, pointing with his thumb at an old pewter pot that stood on the chimney-shelf, told Griselda to put the penny in it and to keep it safe for him until he asked for it.

'Nine days,' he said, 'I will work for you—three and three and three—and no more, for the same wages. And then you must pay me all you owe me. And I will come every evening to see it into the pot.'

So Griselda tiptoed on the kitchen fender, put the penny in the pot, and shut down the lid. When she turned round again Old Moleskins was gone.

Before she went to bed that night, she peeped out of the door. There was no colour left in the sky except the dark blue of night; but a slip of moon, as thin as an egg-shell, hung in the west above the hill, and would soon be following the sun beyond it. Griselda solemnly bowed to the moon seven times, and shook the old purse in her pocket.

When she came down the next morning, the kitchen had been swept, a fire was dancing up the chimney, her mug and plate and spoon had been laid on the table, and a smoking bowl of milk-porridge was warming itself on the hearth. When Griselda took the porridge up to her grandmother, the old woman's eyes nearly popped out of her head, for Griselda had been but a minute gone. She took a sup of the porridge, smacked her lips, tasted it again, and asked Griselda what she had put in it to flavour it. It was a taste she had never tasted before. And Griselda told the old woman it was a secret.

That day the farmer gave Griselda some old gold-brown Cochin-China hens to pluck for market. 'They've seen better days, but will do for the pot,' he said. And having heard that her grandmother was better, he kept her working for him till late in the afternoon. So Griselda plucked and singed busily on, grieved for the old hens, but happy to think of her wages. Then once more the farmer paid her her two-pence; and, once more, a penny over; this time not for the sake of her bright gold hair, but for her 'glass-grey eyes.' So now there was fivepence in her purse, and as yet there had been no need, beyond last night's penny for the dwarf, to spend any of them.

When Griselda came home, not only was everything in the kitchen polished up brighter than ever, but a pot of broth was simmering on the hob, which, to judge by the savour of it, contained not only carrots and onions and pot-herbs but a young rabbit. Besides which, a strip of the garden had been freshly dug; three rows of brisk young cabbages had been planted, and, as Griselda guessed, two more each of broad beans and peas. Whatever the dwarf had set his hand to was a job well done.

Sharp to his time—the sun had but that a very moment dipped beneath the hills—he came to the kitchen door for his wages. Griselda smiled at him, thanked him, and took out a penny. He gazed at it earnestly; then at her. And he said, 'Put that in the pot, too,' So now there were two pennies in his pewter pot and four pennies in Griselda's purse.

And so the days went by. Her grandmother grew steadily better, and on the next Sunday—muffled up in a shawl like an old tortoiseshell cat—she sat up a little while beside her window. On most mornings Griselda had gone out to work at the farm or in the village; on one or two she had stayed in the house and sat with her grandmother to finish her sewing and mending or any other work she had found to do.

While she was in the cottage she never saw the dwarf, though he might be hidden away in the garden. But still her grandmother talked of the strange stirrings and noises she heard when Griselda was away. 'You'd have thought,' the old woman said, 'there was a whole litter of young pigs in the kitchen, and the old sow, too!'

On the eighth day, the farmer not only gave Griselda her tuppence for her wages and another for the sake of 'the dimple in her cheek,' but the third penny had a hole in it. 'And that's for luck,' said the farmer. She went home rejoicing. And seeing no reason why she shouldn't share her luck with the dwarf, she put the penny with the hole in it into the pewter pot when he came that evening. And as usual he said not a word. He merely watched Griselda's face with his colourless eyes while she thanked him for what he had done, and then watched her put his penny into the pot. Then in an instant he was gone.

'That maid Griselda, from the Castle yonder,' said the farmer to his wife that night as, candlestick in hand, the two of them were going to bed, 'she seems to me as willing as she's neat and pretty. And if she takes as good care of the pence as she seems to, my dear, there's never a doubt, I warrant, but as she will take as good care of the pounds!'

And he was right. Griselda had taken such good care of the pence that at this very moment she was sitting alone in the kitchen in the light of her solitary candle and slowly putting down on paper every penny that she had been paid and every penny that she had spent:

Acounts

receeved		Spent	
from Farmer for		oatmeel	2
wages	10	bones for soop	2
prezants	5	shuger	2
wages for Missus		hair ribon	1
Jakes	2	wole	1
wages for piggs	1	doll	1
	—	money for Moalskins	8
	18		—
			17

The doll had been a present for the cowman's little daughter. And though Griselda had made many mistakes before she got her sum right, it was right *now;* and here was the penny over in her purse to prove it.

The next evening, a little before sunset, Griselda sat waiting for the dwarf to come. Never had she felt so happy and lighthearted. It was the last of his nine days; she had all his nine pennies ready for him—one in her purse and eight in the pewter pot; the farmer had promised her as much work as she could manage; her old grandmother was nearly well again; the cupboard was no longer bare, and she was thankful beyond all words. It seemed as if her body could not possibly contain her happiness.

The trees stood in the last sunshine of evening as though they had borrowed their green coats from Paradise; the paths were weeded; the stones had a fresh coat of whitewash; there was not a patch of soil without its plants or seedlings. From every clump of ivy on the old walls of the Castle a thrush seemed to be singing; and every one of them seemed to be singing louder than the rest.

Her sewing idle in her lap, Griselda sat on the doorstep, drinking everything in with her clear grey eyes, and at the same time she was thinking too. Not only of Moleskins and of all he had done for her, but of the farmer's son also, who had come part of the way home with her the evening before. And then she began to day-dream.

But it seemed her spirit had been but a moment gone out of her body into this far-away when the tiny sound of stone knocking on stone recalled her to herself

again, and there—in the very last beam of the setting
sun—stood the dwarf on the cobbles of the garden
path. He told Griselda that his nine days' work for her
was done, and that he had come for his wages.

Griselda beckoned him into the kitchen, and there
she whispered her thanks again and again for all his
help and kindness. She took her last penny out of her
purse and put it on the table, then tiptoeing, reached up
to the chimney-shelf and lifted down the pewter pot.
Even as she did so, her heart turned cold inside her. Not
the faintest jingle sounded when she shook it. It seemed
light as a feather. With trembling fingers she managed
at last to lift the lid and look in. 'Oh!' she whispered.
'Someone . . .' A dark cloud came over her eyes. The
pot was empty.

The dwarf stood in the doorway, his eager cold
bright eyes fixed on her face. 'Well,' he croaked. 'Where
is my money? Why am I to be kept waiting, young
woman? Answer me that!'

Griselda could only stare back at him, the empty pot
in her hand. His eyebrows began to jerk up and down
as if with rage, like an orang-outang's. 'So it's gone, eh?
My pennies are all gone, eh? So you have cheated me!
Eh? Eh? *Cheated* me?'

Nothing Griselda could say was of any avail. He refused to listen to her. The more she entreated him only
to have patience and she would pay him all she owed
him, the more sourly and angrily he stormed at her.
And to see the tears rolling down her cheeks on either
side of her small nose only worsened his rage.

'I will give you one more day,' he bawled at last.
'One! I will come back to-morrow at sunset, and every

single penny must be ready for me. What I do, I can undo! What I make, I can break! Hai, hai! we shall see!' With that he stumped out into the garden and was gone.

Griselda was so miserable and her mind was in such a whirl that she could do nothing for a while but sit, cold and vacant, staring out of the open door. Where could the pennies have gone to? Mice don't eat pennies. Had she been walking in her sleep? Who could have stolen them? And how was she to earn as many more in only one day's work?

And while she sat brooding, there came a *thump, thump, thump* on the floor over her head. She sprang to her feet, lit a candle by the fire-flames, dabbed her eyes in the bucket of cold water that Old Moleskins had brought in from the well, and took up her grandmother's supper.

'Did you hear any noises in the house to-day, Grannie?' she asked cautiously as she put the bowl of broth into her skinny old hands. At this question the old woman, who was very hungry, fell into a temper. Every single evening, she told Griselda, she had warned her that some strange animal had come rummaging into the house below when she was away working at the farm. 'You never kept watch, you never even answered me,' she said. 'And now it's too late. To-day I have heard nothing.'

It was all but dark when, having made the old woman comfortable for the night, Griselda hastened down into the kitchen again. She could not bear to wait until morning. She had made up her mind what to do. Leaving her grandmother drowsy after her broth and

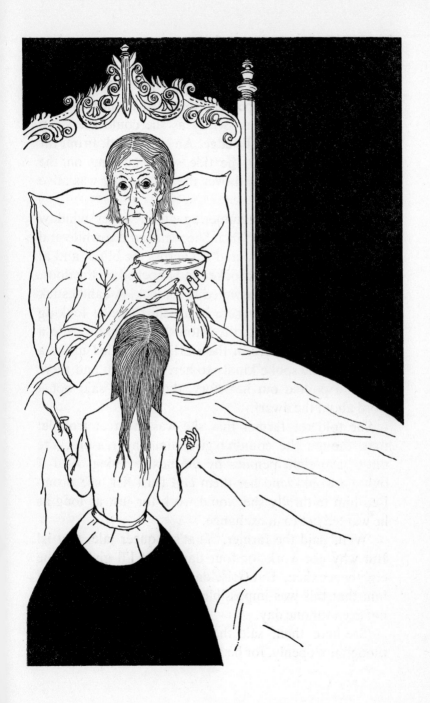

nodding off to sleep, she stole out of the house and shut the door gently behind her. Groping her way under the ivied walls into the open she hastened on in the quiet moonlight, climbing as swiftly as she could the steep grassy slope at the cliff's edge. An owl called. From far below she could hear the tide softly gushing on the stones of the beach; and over the sea the sky was alive with stars.

A light was still glimmering at an upper window when she reached the farm. She watched it a while and the shadows moving to and fro across the blind, and at last timidly lifted the knocker and knocked on the door. The farmer himself answered her knock. A candlestick in his hand, he stood there in his shirt sleeves looking out at her over his candle, astonished to find so late a visitor standing there in the starlight, muffled up in a shawl. But he spoke kindly to her. And then and there Griselda poured out her story, though she said not a word about the dwarf.

She told the farmer that she was in great trouble; that, though she couldn't give him any reasons, she must have eight pennies by the next evening. And if only he would lend her them and trust her, she promised him faithfully she would work for just as long as he wanted her to in exchange.

'Well,' said the farmer. 'That's a queer tale, *that* is! But why not work for four days, and I'll give 'ee the eightpence then.' But Griselda shook her head. She told him that this was impossible; that she could not wait, not even for one day.

'See here, then,' said the farmer, smiling to himself, though not openly, for he was curious to know what use

she was going to make of the money. 'I can't give you
any work to-morrow, nor be sure of the next day. But
supposing there's none for a whole week, if you promise to cut off that gold hair of yours and give me that
then, you shall have the eight pennies now—this very
moment—and no questions asked.'

Griselda stood quite still in the doorway, her face
pale and grave in the light of the farmer's candle. It
seemed that every separate hair she had was stirring
upon her head. This all came, she thought, of admiring
herself in the duck-pond; and not being more careful
with her money; and doing what the dwarf told her to
do and not what she thought best. But as it seemed that
at any moment the farmer might run in and fetch a pair
of shears to cut off her hair there and then, she made
her promise; and he himself went back laughing to his
wife, and told her what had happened. 'She turned as
white as a sheet,' he said. 'And what I'd dearly like to
know is what's worriting the poor dear. She's as gentle as
the day is long, and her word's as good as her bond.
Well, well! But I'll see to it. And we'll have just one lock
of that hair, my dear, if only for a keepsake.'

'It looks to *me,*' said the farmer's wife, *'that'*ll be for
our Simon to say.'

When Griselda reached home again—and a sad and
solitary walk it had been through the dewy fields above
the sea—she went to an old wooden coffer in which she
kept her few 'treasures.' Many of them were remem-
brances of her mother. And she took out a net for the
hair that her mother herself had worn when she was a
girl of about the same age as Griselda. Then she sat
down in front of a little bare square of looking-glass,

braided her hair as close as she could to her head, and
drew the net tightly over it. Then she put her purse with
the nine pennies in it under her pillow, said her prayers,
and got into bed.

For hours she lay listening to the breakers on the
shore, solemnly drumming the night away, and
watched her own particular star as moment by moment
it sparkled on from diamond pane to pane across her
lattice window. But when at last she fell asleep, her
dreams were scarcely less sorrowful than her waking.

She stayed at home the next day in case the dwarf
should come early, but not until sunset did she hear the
furtive clatter of his shoes as usual on the stones. She
took out her purse to pay him the pennies. He asked
her where they had come from. 'And why,' said he,
'have you braided your hair so close and caged it up in
a net? Are you frightened the birds will be after it?'

Griselda laughed at this in spite of herself. And she
told him that she had promised her hair to a friend, and
that she had wound it up tight to her head in order to
remind herself that it was not her own any longer, and
to keep it safe. At this Old Moleskins himself burst out
laughing under the green-berried gooseberry bush—
for Griselda had taken him out into the garden lest her
grandmother should hear them talking.

'A pretty bargain *that* was!' he said. 'But *I* know one
even better!' And he promised Griselda that if she
would let him snip off but one small lock of hair he
would transport her into the grottoes of the Urchin People under the sea. 'And *there*,' he said, 'if you will work
for us for only one hour a day for seven days, you shall
have seven times the weight of all your hair in fine solid

gold. If, after that, I mean,' and he eyed her craftily, 'you will promise to come back and stay with us always. And then you shall have a basket of fruit from our secret orchards.'

Griselda looked at the dwarf, and then at the small green ripening gooseberries on the bush, and then stared a while in silence at the daisies on the ground. Then she told the dwarf she could not give him a lock of her hair because that was all promised. Instead, she would work for him every day for nine days, free. It was the least she could do, she thought, in return for what he had done for her.

'Well then,' said Moleskins, 'if it can't be hair it must be an eyelash. Else you will never see the grottoes. An eyelash for your journey-money!'

To this she agreed, and knelt down beside the gooseberry bush, shutting her eyes tight so that he might more easily pluck out one of the lashes that fringed their lids. She felt his stumpy earthy fingers brush across them, and nothing beside.

But when she opened them, and looked out of her body, a change had come upon the scene around her— garden, cottage, castle walls and ruined turrets, cliffs, sea and caves—all had vanished. No evening ray of sun shone here, not the faintest sea-breeze stirred the air. It was a place utterly still, and lay bathed in a half-light pale and green, rilling in from she knew not where. And around her, and above her head, faint colours shimmered in the quarried quartz of the grottoes. And the only sound to be heard was a distant sighing, as of the tide.

There were many trees here, too, in the orchards of

the Urchin People, their slim stems rooted in sands as fine and white as hoarfrost. And their branches were laden with fruits of as many colours as there are precious stones. And there was a charm of birds singing, though Griselda could see none. The very air seemed thin and fine in this dim and sea-green light: the only other sound to be heard was a faint babbling of water among the rocks, water which lost itself in the sands of the orchard.

The dwarf had brought out some little rush baskets, and told Griselda what she must do. 'Gather up the fallen fruit,' he said, 'but pick none from the branches, and sort it out each according to its kind and colour, one colour into each of the baskets. But be sure not to climb into the trees or shake them. And when your hour is finished I will come again.'

Griselda at once set to work. Though the branches overhead were thick with fruit, there were as yet not many that had fallen, and it seemed at first it would take her but a few moments to sort them out into their baskets. But the thin air and twilight of the grotto made her drowsy, and as she stooped again and yet again to pick up the fruit, her eyelids drooped so heavily that at any moment she feared she would fall asleep. And if once she fell asleep what might not happen then? Would she ever win back to earth again? Was this all nothing but a dream? She refreshed her eyes in the trickle of snow-cold water rilling down from the rocks; and now she fancied she heard a faint metallic noise as of knocking and hammering and small voices in the distance. But even when all the fallen fruits had been sorted out into her baskets, emerald-green, orange, amethyst, crystal and blue, her work was not done. For the moment she sat down to rest, yet another of the fruits would plump down softly as an apple into deep grass upon the sand beneath it, and she had to hasten away to put it into its basket.

When the dwarf came back he looked about him to see that no fruits had been left lying in the sand. He squinnied here, he squinnied there, and even turned over the fruits in the baskets to see that they had been sorted right. 'Well, Griselda,' he said at last, and it was the first time he had used her name, 'what's well done is done for good. And here's the penny for your wages.'

There was a stealthy gleam in his eyes as he softly fumbled with his fingers in the old moleskin pouch that hung at his side, and fetched out his penny. Griselda held out her hand, and he put the penny into its palm, still watching her. She looked at it—and looked again. It was an old, thick, battered penny, and the king's image on it had been worn very faint. It had a slightly crooked edge, too, and there was a hole in it. There could be no doubt of it—this was the penny the farmer had given her, 'for luck.' Until now Griselda had not realized that she had for a moment suspected it might be Old Moleskins himself who had stolen his pennies out of the pewter pot. Now she was sure of it. She continued to stare at the penny, yet said nothing. After all, she was thinking to herself, the money in the pot belonged to him. He had a right to it. You cannot steal what is yours already! But then, a lie is almost as bad as stealing. Perhaps he hadn't meant it to be a lie. Perhaps he merely wanted to see what she might say and do. That would still be a lie but not such a wicked lie.

Perhaps since he wasn't *quite* human he couldn't in any case tell *quite* a lie. Perhaps it was only a dwarf lie, though his kindness to her had certainly not been only dwarf kindness! She smiled to herself at this; lifted up her face again, and seeing the dwarf still watching her, smiled at him also. And she thanked him.

At this he burst out laughing, till the roof and walls of the grotto echoed with the cackle of it, and at least half a dozen of the grotto fruits dropped from their twigs and thumped softly down into the sand. 'Aha,' he cried, 'what did I tell you? Weep no more, Griselda. That is one penny, and here are the others.' He took them out of his pouch, and counted them into her hand, and the eight pennies too that she had given him but a little while before; and as he did so, he sang out in a high quavering voice like a child's:

> '*Never whatever the* humans *say*
> *Have the Urchin Folk worked for any man's pay.*

Ah, Griselda,' he said, 'if we could keep you, you would scarcely ever have to work at all. No churning and weeding, no sewing and scrubbing, no cooking or polishing, sighing or sobbing; you should be for ever happy and for ever young. And you wouldn't have to scissor off a single snippet of your silk-soft hair!'

Griselda looked at him in the still green light and faintly shook her head. But she made a bargain with him none the less that every year she would work in the grottoes for the Urchin People—if he would come to fetch her—for one whole summer's day. So this was the bargain between them.

And he took out of his breeches' pocket a thick gold piece, about the size of an English crown-piece, and put it into her hand. On the one side of it the image of a mermaid was stamped, on the other a little fruit tree growing out of a mound of sand and knobbed with tiny fruits. 'That's for a keepsake,' he said. And he himself took one of each kind of the orchard fruits out of their baskets and put them into another. 'And since "no pay" is *no* pay,' he went on, 'stoop, Griselda, and I'll give you your eyelash back again.'

Griselda knelt down in the sand, and once more the earthy fingers brushed over her eyelids. The next instant all was dark; and a thin chill wind was stirring on her cheek. She opened her eyes to find herself alone again under the night-sky, and—as though she had been overtaken by the strangeness of a dream—kneeling on the dew-damped mould of her familiar garden under the stars. But for proof that what had happened was no dream, the gold piece stamped wth the images of the mermaid and the leafy tree was still clasped in her hand, and in the other was the basket of fruits.

As for the eyelash, since Griselda had never counted how many she had before Old Moleskins plucked one out, she could never tell for certain if it had been put back. But when she told Simon, the farmer's son, that there *might* be one missing—and she could tell him no more because of her promise to the dwarf—he counted them over again and again. And though he failed to make the total come to the same number twice, he assured Griselda that there couldn't possibly ever have been room for another. And Griselda gave him the green one of the grotto fruits she had brought him for a present from out of the dwarf's basket. This too was for a keepsake. 'It's as hard as a stone,' he said. 'Do we eat it, Griselda?' But hard though it was, there must have been a curious magic in it, for as they sat there together under the willow tree by the duck-pond, it was as if they had been transported not into the grottoes of the Urchin People under the sea, but clean back into the Garden of Eden.

As for Griselda's hair, there it shone as thick as ever on her head. And as for the farmer, he refused every single penny of the eightpence.

'It's a queer thing to me, mother,' he was saying to his wife at this very moment, as they sat together on either side of the kitchen fire—just as they were accustomed to sit even in the height of summertime—'it's a queer thing to me that this very farm of ours once belonged to that young woman's great-great-grandfather!' He took a long whiff of his pipe. 'And what *I* says is that them who once had, when they gets again, should know how to *keep*.'

'Ay, George,' said she, and she said no more.

✿✿

THE THREE SLEEPING BOYS
OF WARWICKSHIRE

In a long, low-ceiled, white-
washed room on the upper floor of a red-brick building in Pleasant Street, Cheriton, ranged there in their
glazed cases, is a collection of shells, conchs, seaweeds,
sea-flowers, corals, fossils, goggling fish, stuffed birds
—sea and land—and 'mermaids.' Coffers, chests and
anchors, and old guns, and lumps of amber and ore
and quartz. All sorts of outlandish oddities, too, curiosities and junk. And there for years and years—the
narrow windows, with their carved brick fruits and
flowers and old leaden gutters, showering the day's
light upon their still retreat—there for years and years
slumbered on in their great glass case the Three Sleeping Boys of Warwickshire. The tale of them goes a long
way back. But so, too, do most tales, sad or merry, if
only you will follow them up.

About the year 1600, when Queen Elizabeth was
sixty-seven, and William Shakespeare was writing his
play called 'Julius Caesar,' there died, twenty-four
miles from Stratford-on-Avon, a rich miller—John
James Nollykins by name. His was the handsomest

mill in Warwickshire. But none of his neighbours—or none at least of his poorer neighbours—could abide the sight of him. He was a morose, close-fisted, pitiless old man. He cheated his customers and had no mercy for those whom he enticed into his clutches.

As he grew older he had grown ever more mean and churlish until at last he had even begun to starve his own horses. Though he died rich, then, few of his neighbours mourned him much. And as soon as he was gone his money began to go too. His three sons gobbled up what he had left behind him, as jackals gobble up a lion's left supper-bones. It slipped through their fingers like sand through a sieve. They drank, they diced, they gambled high and low. They danced, and capered and feasted in their finery; but they hardly knew offal from grain. Pretty soon they began to lose not only their father's trade but also all his savings. Their customers said that there was not only dust but stones in the flour; and tares too. It was fusty; it smelt mousy. What cared they? They took their terriers rat-hunting, but that was for the sake of the sport and not of the flour. Everything about the Mill got shabbier and shabbier—went to rack and ruin. The sails were patched. They clacked in the wind. The rain drove in. There were blossoming weeds in the millstream and dam where should have been nothing but crystal water. And when their poorer customers complained, they were greeted with drunken jeers and mockery.

At length, three or four years after the death of the miller's last poor half-starved mare, his sons were ruined. They would have been ruined just the same if, as one foul windy night they sat drinking and singing together in the Mill-house, the youngest of them had not knocked over the smoking lamp on the table, and so burned the Mill to the ground.

The eldest—with what he could pick up—went off to Sea, and to foreign parts, and died of yellow fever in Tobago. The second son was taken in by an uncle who was a goldsmith in London. But he was so stupid and indolent that he broke more than he mended; and at last, by swallowing an exquisitely carved peach stone from China, which had been brought back to Italy by Marco Polo, so enraged his master that he turned him off then and there. He went East and became a fish-monger in Ratcliff Highway, with a shop like a booth, and a long board in front of it. But he neglected this trade too, and at last became a man-of-all-work (or of none) at the old Globe Theatre in Southwark, where he saw Shakespeare dressed up as the ghost in 'Hamlet' and was all but killed as if by accident while taking the part of the Second Murderer in 'Macbeth.'

The youngest son, named Jeremy, married the rich widow of a saddler. She was the owner of a fine gabled house in the High Street of the flourishing town of Cheriton—some eight miles from Bishops Hitching-worth. He had all the few good looks of the family, but he was sly and crafty and hard. The first thing he did after he came home from his honeymoon was to paint in a long red nose to the portrait of the saddler. The next thing he did was to drown his wife's cat in the water-butt, because he said the starveling had stolen the cheese. The third thing he did was to burn her best Sun-day bonnet, then her wig—to keep it company. How she could bear to go on living with him is a mystery. Nevertheless she did.

This Jeremy had three sons: Job, John and (another) Jeremy. But he did not flourish. Far from it. The family went 'down the ladder,' rung by rung, until at long last it reached the bottom. Then it began to climb up again. But Jeremy's children did best. His youngest daughter married a well-to-do knacker, and *their* only son (yet another Jeremy), though he ran away from home because he hated water-gruel and suet pudding, went into business as assistant to the chief sweep in Cheriton. And, at last, having by his craft and cunning and early rising and hard-working inherited his master's business, he bought his great-uncle's fine gabled house, and became Master Chimney-Sweep and 'Sweep by Appointment,' to the Mayor and Corporation and the Lords of three neighbouring Manors. And *he* never married at all. In spite of his hard childhood, in spite of the kindness shown him by his master, in spite of his good fortune with the three Lords of the Manor, he was a skinflint and a pick-halfpenny. He had an enormous brush over his door, a fine brass knocker, and—though considering all things, he had mighty few friends—he was the best, as well as the richest master-sweep in those parts.

But a good deal of his money and in later years most of his praise was due to his three small orphan 'prentices—Tom, Dick and Harry. In those days, hearths and fireplaces were as large as little rooms or chambers, or at any rate, as large as large cupboards or closets. They had wide warm comfortable ingle-nooks, and the chimneys were like deep wells running up to the roof, sometimes narrowing or angling off towards the top. And these chimneys were swept by hand.

Jeremy's 'prentices, then, had to climb up and up, from sooty brick to brick with a brush, and sweep till they were as black as blackest blackamoors, inside and out. Soot, soot, soot! Eyes, mouth, ears and nose. And now and then the bricks were scorching hot, and their hands got blistered. And now and then they were all but suffocated in the narrow juts. And once in a while were nearly wedged there, to dry like mummies in the dark. And sometimes, in the midst of the smother, a leg would slip, and down they would come tumbling like apples out of a tree or hailstones out of a cloud in April.

And Jeremy Nollykins, after tying up all the money they brought him in fat canvas and leather bags, served them out water-gruel for supper, and water-gruel for breakfast. For dinner on Tuesdays and Thursdays he gave them slabs of suet-pudding with lumps of suet in it like pale amber beads; what he called soup on Mondays and Wednesdays and Fridays; and a bit of cats-meat (bought cheap from his second cousin) on Sundays. But then you can't climb chimneys on *no* meat. On Saturdays they had piping-hot pease-pudding and pottage: because on Saturdays the Mayor's man might look in.

You would hardly believe it: but in spite of such poor mean living, in spite of their burns and their bruises, and the soot in their eyes and lungs and in their close lint-coloured hair, these three small boys, Tom, Dick and Harry, managed to keep their spirits up. They even rubbed their cheeks rosy after the week's soot had been washed off under the pump on a Saturday night.

They were like Tom Dacre in the poem:

... There's little Tom Dacre, who cried when his head
That curled like a lamb's back was shav'd: so I said
'Hush, Tom! never mind it for when your head's bare
You know that the soot cannot spoil your white hair.'

And so he was quiet, and that very night
As Tom was a-sleeping, he had such a sight!
That thousands of sleepers, Dick, Joe, Ned, and Jack
Were all of them lock'd up in coffins of black. . . .

Still, they always said 'Mum' to the great ladies and 'Mistress' to the maids, and they kept their manners even when some crabbed old woman said they were owdacious, or imperent, or mischeevious. And sometimes a goodwife would give them a slice of bread pudding, or a mug of milk, or a baked potato, or perhaps a pocket-full of cookies or a slice of white bread (which did not remain white for very long). And now and then, even a sip of elderberry wine. After all, even half-starved sparrows sometimes find tit-bits, and it's not the hungry who enjoy their victuals least.

When they *could* scuttle away too, they would bolt off between their jobs to go paddling in the river, or bird-nesting in the woods, or climbing in an old stone quarry not very far from the town. It was lovely wooded country thereabouts—near ancient Cheriton.

Whether they played truant or not, Jeremy Nollykins the Fourth—Old Noll, as his neighbours called him—used to beat them morning, noon and night. He believed in the rod. He spared nobody, neither man nor

beast. Tom, Dick and Harry pretty well hated old Noll: and that's a bad thing enough. But, on the other hand, they were far too much alive and hearty and happy when they were not being beaten, and they were much too hungry even over their water-gruel to *think* or to brood over how much they hated him: which would have been very much worse.

In sober fact—with their bright glittering eyes and round cheeks and sharp white teeth, and in spite of their skinny ribs and blistered hands, they were a merry trio. As soon as ever their teeth stopped chattering with the cold, and their bodies stopped smarting from Old Noll's sauce, and their eyes from the soot, they were laughing and talking and whistling and champing, like grasshoppers in June or starlings in September. And though they sometimes quarrelled and fought together, bit and scratched too, never having been taught to fight fair, they were very good friends. Now and again too they shinned up a farmer's fruit-trees to have a taste of his green apples. Now and again they played tricks on old women. But what lively little chimney-sweeps wouldn't?

They were three young ragamuffins, as wild as colts, as nimble as kids, though a good deal blacker. And, however hard he tried, Old Noll never managed to break them in. Never. And at night they slept as calm and deep as cradled babies—all three of them laid in a row up in an attic under the roof on an immense wide palliasse or mattress of straw, with a straw bolster and a couple of pieces of old sacking for blankets each.

Now Old Noll, simply perhaps because he was— both by nature as well as by long practice—a mean old

curmudgeonly miser, hated to see anybody merry, or
happy, or even fat. There were moments when he
would have liked to skin his three 'prentices alive. But
then he wanted to get out of them all the work he could.
So he was compelled to give them *that* much to eat. He
had to keep them alive—or the Mayor's man would ask
why. Still, it enraged him that he could not keep their
natural spirits down; that however much he beat them
they 'came up smiling'. It enraged him to know in his
heart (or whatever took its place) that though—when
they had nothing better to do, or were smarting from
his rod in pickle—they detested him, they yet had never
done him an ill-turn.

Every day he would gloat on them as they came clattering down to their water-gruel just as Giant Despair
gloated on Faithful and Christian in the dungeon. And
sometimes at night he would creep up to their bare
draughty attic, and the stars or the moon would show
him the three of them lying there fast asleep on their
straw mattress, the sacking kicked off, and on their
faces a faint far-away smile as if their dreams were as
peaceful as the swans in the Islands of the Blest. It enraged him. What could the little urchins be dreaming
about? What made ugly little blackamoors grin even in
their sleep? You can thwack a wake boy, but you can't
thwack a dreamer; not at least while he *is* dreaming. So
here Old Noll was helpless. He could only grind his
teeth at the sight of them. Poor Old Noll.

He ground his teeth more than ever when he first
heard the music in the night. And he might never have
heard it at all if hunger hadn't made him a mighty
bad sleeper himself. A few restless hours was the most

he got, even in winter. And if Tom, Dick and Harry had ever peeped in on *him* as he lay in his four-post bed, they would have seen no smile on his old sunken face, with its long nose and long chin and straggling hair— but only a sort of horrifying darkness. They might even have pitied him, stretched out there, with nightmare twisting and contorting his sharp features, and his bony fingers continually on the twitch.

Because, then, Old Noll could not sleep of nights, he would sometimes let himself out of his silent house to walk the streets. And while so walking, he would look up at his neighbours' windows, glossily dark beneath the night-sky, and he would curse them for being more comfortable than he. It was as if instead of marrow he had malice in his bones, and there is no fattening on that.

Now one night, for the first time in his life, except when he broke his leg at eighteen, Old Noll had been unable to sleep at all. It was a clear mild night with no wind, and a fine mild scrap of a moon was in the West, and the stars shone bright. There was always a sweet balmy air in Cheriton, borne in from the meadows that then stretched in within a few furlongs of the town; and so silent was the hour you could almost hear the rippling of the river among its osiers that far away.

And as Old Nollykins was sitting like a gaunt shadow all by himself on the first milestone that comes into the town—and he was too niggardly even to smoke a pipe of tobacco—a faint easy wind came drifting along the street. And then on the wind a fainter music —a music which at first scarcely seemed to be a music at all. None the less it continued on and on, and at last so rilled and trembled in the air that even Old Nolly-kins, who was now pretty hard of hearing, caught the strains and recognized the melody. It came steadily nearer, that music—a twangling and tootling and a horning, a breathing as of shawms, waxing merrier and merrier in the quick mild night October air:

Girls and boys, come out to play!
The moon doth shine as bright as day;
Leave your supper, and leave your sleep,
And come with your playfellows into the street! . . .

Girls and boys come out to play: on and on and on, now faint now shrill, now in a sudden rallying burst of sound as if it came from out of the skies. Not that the moon just then was shining as bright as day. It was but barely in its first quarter. It resembled a bent bit of intensely shining copper down low among the stars: or a gold basin, of which little more than the edge showed, resting a-tilt. But little moon or none, the shapes that were now hastening along the street, running and hopping and skipping and skirring and dancing, had heard the summons, had obeyed the call. From by-lane and alley, court, porch and house-door the children of Cheriton had come pouring out like water-streams in spring-time. Running, skipping, hopping, dancing, they kept time to the tune. Old Noll fairly gasped with astonishment as he watched them. What a dreadful tale to tell—and all the comfortable and respectable folks of Cheriton fast asleep in their beds! To think such innocents could be such wicked deceivers! To think that gluttonous and grubby errand and shop and boot-and-shoe and pot boys could look so clean and nimble and happy and free. He shivered; partly because of his age and the night air, and partly with rage.

But real enough though these young skip-by-nights appeared to be, there were three queer things about them. First, there was not the faintest sound of doors opening or shutting, or casement windows being thrust open with a squeal of the iron rod. Next, there was not the faintest rumour of footsteps even, though at least half the children of Cheriton were now bounding along the street, like autumn leaves in the wind, and all with their faces towards the East and the water-meadows. And last, though Noll could see the very eyes in their faces in the faint luminousness of starshine and a little moon, not a single one of that mad young company turned head to look at him, or showed the least sign of knowing that he was there. Clockwork images of wood or wax could not have ignored him more completely.

Old Noll, after feeling at first startled, flabbergasted, a little frightened even, was now in a fury. His few old teeth began to grind together as lustily as had the millstones of Jeremy the First when he was rich and prosperous. Nor was his rage diminished when, lo and behold, even as he turned his head, out of his own narrow porch with its three rounded steps and fluted shell of wood above it, came leaping along who but his own three half-starved 'prentices, Tom, Dick and Harry— now seemingly nine-year-olds as plump and comely to see as if they had been fed on the fat of the land, as if they had never never in the whole of their lives so much as tasted rod-sauce. Their mouths were opening and shutting, too, as if they were whooping calls one to the other and to their other street-mates, though no sound came from them. They snapped their fingers in the air. They came cavorting and skirling along in their naked feet to the strains of the music as if bruised elbows, scorched shins, cramped muscles and iron-bound clogs had never once pestered their young souls. Yet not a sound, not a whisper, not a footfall could the deaf old man hear—nothing but that sweet, shrill and infuriating music.

In a few minutes the streets were empty, a thin fleece of cloud had drawn across the moon, and only one small straggler was still in sight, a grandson of the Mayor. He was last merely because he was least, and had nobody to take care of him. And Old Noll, having watched this last night-truant out of sight, staring at him with eyes like marbles beneath his bony brows, hobbled back across the street to his own house, and after pausing awhile at the nearest doorpost to gnaw his beard and think what next was to be done, climbed his three flights of shallow oak stairs until he came to the uppermost landing under the roof. There at last with infinite caution he lifted the pin of the door of the attic and peered in on what he supposed would be an empty bed. Empty! Not a bit of it! Lying there asleep, in the dim starlight of the dusty dormer window, he could see as plain as can be the motionless shapes of his three 'prentices, breathing on so calmly in midnight's deepmost slumber that he even ventured to fetch in a tallow candle in a pewter stick in order that he might examine them more closely.

In its smoky beams he searched the three young

slumbering faces. They showed no sign that the old skinflint was stooping as close over them as a bird-snarer over his nets. There were smears of soot even on their eye-lids and the fine dust of it lay thick on the flaxen lambs'-wool of their close-shorn heads. They were smiling away, gently and distantly as if they were sitting in their dreams in some wonderful orchard, supping on strawberries and cream; as though the spirits within them were untellably happy though their bodies were as fast asleep as humming-tops or honey-bees in winter.

Stair by stair Old Nollykins crept down again, blew out his candle, and sat down on his bed to think. He was a cunning old miser, which is as far away from being generous and wise as the full moon is from a far-thing dip. His fingers had itched to wake his three sleeping chimney-boys with a smart taste of his rod, just to 'larn them a lesson.' He hated to think of the quiet happy smile resting upon their faces while the shadow-shapes or ghosts of them were out and away, pranking and gallivanting in the green water-meadows beyond the town. How was he to know that his dimming eyes had not deluded him? Supposing he went off to the Mayor himself in the morning and told his midnight tale, who would believe it? High and low, everybody hated him, and as like as not they would shut him up in the town jail for a madman, or burn his house about his ears supposing him to be a wizard. 'No, no, no!' he muttered to himself. 'We must watch and wait, friend Jeremy, and see what we *shall* see.'

Next morning his three 'prentices, Tom, Dick and Harry, were up and about as sprightly as ever, a full

hour before daybreak. You might have supposed from their shining eyes and apple cheeks that they had just come back from a long holiday on the blissful plains of paradise. Away they tumbled—merry as frogs—to work, with their brushes and bags, still munching away at their gritty oatcakes—three parts bran to one of meal.

So intent had Old Noll been on watching from his chimney-corner what he could see in their faces at breakfast, and on trying to overhear what they were whispering to each other, that he forgot to give them their usual morning dose of stick. But not a word had been uttered about the music or the dancing or the merry-making at the water-meadows. They just chattered their usual scatter-brained gibberish to one another—except when they saw that the old creature was watching them; and he was speedily convinced that whatever adventures their dream-shapes may have had in the night-hours, these had left no impression on their waking minds.

Poor Old Noll. An echo of that music and the sight he had seen kept him awake for many a night after, and his body was already shrunken by age and by his miserly habits to nothing much more substantial than a bag of animated bones. And yet all his watching was in vain. So weary and hungry for sleep did he become, that when at last the hunter's moon shone at its brightest and roundest over the roofs of Cheriton, he nodded off in his chair. He was roused a few hours afterwards by a faint glow in his room that was certainly not moonlight, for it came from out of the black dingy staircase passage. Instantly he was wide awake—but too late.

For, even as he peeped through the door-crack, there flitted past his three small 'prentices—just the ghosts or the spirits or the dream-shapes of them—faring happily away. They passed him softer than a breeze through a willow tree and were out of sight down the staircase before he could stir.

The morning after the morning after that, when Tom, Dick and Harry woke up at dawn on their mattress, there was a wonderful rare smell in the air. They sniffed it greedily as they looked at one another in the creeping light of daybreak. And sure enough, as soon as they were in their ragged jackets and had got down to their breakfast, the old woman who came to the house every morning to do an hour or two's charing for Old Nollykins, came waddling up to the kitchen table with a frying-pan of bacon frizzling in its fat.

'There, me boys,' said Old Noll, rubbing his hands together with a cringing smile, 'there's a rasher of bacon for ye all, and sop in the pan to keep the cold out, after that long night-run in the moonlight.'

He creaked up his eyes at them finger on nose; but all three of them, perched up there on their wooden stools the other side of the table, only paused an instant in the first polishing up of their plates with a crust of bread to stare at him with such an innocent astonishment on their young faces that he was perfectly sure they had no notion of what he meant.

'Aha,' says he, 'do ye never dream, me boys, tucked up snug under the roof in that comfortable bed of yours? D'ye never dream?—never hear a bit of a tune calling, or maybe see what's called a nightmare?

Lordee, when I was young there never went a night but had summat of a dream to it.'

'Dream!' said they, and looked at one another with their mouths half open. 'Why, if you ax me, Master,' says Tom, 'I dreamed last night it was all bright moonshine, and me sitting at supper with the gentry.'

'And I,' says Dick, 'I dreamed I was dancing under trees and bushes all covered over with flowers. And I could hear 'em playing on harps and whistles.'

'And me,' says Harry, 'I dreamed I was by a river, and a leddy came out by a green place near the water and took hold of my hand. I suppose, Master, it must have been my mammie, though I never seed her as I knows on.'

At all this the cringing smile on Old Nollykins' face set like grease in a dish, because of the rage in his mind underneath. And he leaped up from where he sat beside the skinny little fire in the immense kitchen hearth.

' "Gentry"! "Harps"! "Mammie"!' he shouted, 'you brazen, ungrateful, greedy little deevils. Be off with ye, or ye shall have such a taste of the stick as will put ye to sleep for good and all.'

And almost before they had time to snatch up their bags and their besoms, he had chased them out of the house. So there in the little alley beside the garden, sheltering as close to its wall as they could from the cold rain that was falling, they must needs stand chattering together like drenched jackdaws, waiting for the angry old man to come out and to send them about the business of the day.

But Old Nollykins' dish of bacon fat had not been

altogether wasted. He knew now that the young rap-
scallions only *dreamed* their nocturnal adventures, and
were not in the least aware that they themselves in ac-
tual shadow-shape went off by night to the trysting-
place of all Cheriton's children to dance and feast and
find delight. But he continued to keep watch, and
would again and again spy in on his three 'prentices
lying asleep together on their mattress up in the attic,
in the hope of catching them in the act of stealing out.
But although at times he discerned the same gentle
smile upon their faces, shining none the less serenely
for the white gutter-marks of tears on their sooty
cheeks, for weeks together he failed to catch any repeti-
tion of the strains of the strange music or the faintest
whisper of their dream-shapes coming and going on the
wooden stairs.

Nevertheless, the more he brooded on what he had
seen, the more he hated the three urchins, and the more
bitterly he resented their merry ways. The one thing he
could not decide in his mind was whether when next,
if ever, he caught them at their midnight tricks, he
should at once set about their slumbering bodies with
his stick or should wait until their dream-wraiths were
safely away and then try to prevent them from coming
back. Then indeed they might be at his mercy.

Now there was an old crone in Cheriton who was
reputed to be a witch. She lived in a stone hovel at the
far end of a crooked alley that ran beside the very walls
of Old Nollykins' fine gabled house. And Old Nollykins, almost worn to a shadow, knocked one dark evening at her door. She might have been the old man's

grandmother as she sat there, hunched up in her corner beside the great iron pot simmering over the fire. He mumbled out his story about his three 'thieving, godless little brats', and then sat haggling over the price he should pay for her counsel. And even then he hoped to cheat her. At last he put his crown in her shrunken paw.

Waken a sleeper, she told him, before his dream-shape can get back into his mortal frame, it's as like as not to be sudden death. But keep the wandering dream-shape out *without* rousing his sleeping body, then he may for ever more be your slave, and will never grow any older. And what may keep a human's dream-shape out—or animal's either—she said, is a love-knot or iron the wrong way up or a rusty horseshoe upside down, or a twisted wreath of elder and ash fastened up with an iron nail over the keyhole—and every window shut. Brick walls and stone and wood are nothing to such wanderers. But they can't abide iron. And what she said was partly true and partly false; and it was in part false because the foolish old man had refused to pay the crone her full price.

He knew well, and so did she, that there was only a wooden latch to his door, because he had been too much of a skinflint to pay for one of the new iron locks to be fixed on. He had no fear of thieves, because he had so hidden his money that no thief on earth would be able to find it, not if he searched for a week. So he asked the old woman again, to make doubly sure, how long a natural human creature would live and work if his dream-shape never came back. 'Why, that,' she cheepered, leering up at him out of her wizened old face, 'that depends how young they be; what's the blood, and what's the heart. Take 'em in the first bloom,' she said, 'and so they keeps.' She had long ago seen what the old man was after, and had no more love for him than for his three noisy whooping chimney-sweeps.

Very unwillingly he dropped another piece of money into her skinny palm and went back to his house, not knowing that the old woman, to avenge herself on his skinflint ways, had told him only half the story. That evening his three 'prentices had a rare game of hide-and-seek together in the many-roomed old rat-holed house; for their master had gone out. The moment they heard his shuffling footsteps in the porch they scampered off to bed, and were to all appearance fast asleep before he could look in on them.

He had brought back with him a bundle of switches of elder and ash, a tenpenny nail, a great key, and a cracked horseshoe. And, strange to say, the iron key which he had bought from a dealer in broken metal had once been the key of the Mill of rich old Jeremy the First at Stratford-on-Avon! He pondered half that night on what the old woman had said, and 'surely', said he to himself, 'their blood's fresh enough, my old stick keeps them out of mischief, and what is better for a green young body than a long day's work and not too much to eat, and an airy lodging for the night?' The cunning old creature supposed indeed, that if only by this sorcery and hugger-mugger he could keep their wandering dream-shapes from their bodies for good and all, his three young 'prentices would never age, never weary, but stay lusty and nimble perhaps for a century. Ay, he would use them as long as he wanted them, and sell them before he died. *He'd* teach them to play truant at night, when honest folk were snoring in their beds. For the first time for weeks his mingy supper off a crust and a ham-bone and a mug of water had tasted like manna come down from the skies.

The very next day chanced to be St. Nicholas's Day. And those were the times of old English winters. Already a fine scattering of snow was on the ground, like tiny white lumps of sago, and the rivers and ponds were frozen hard as iron. Better still, there was all but a fine full moon that night, and the puddles in Cheriton High Street shone like Chinese crystal in the beams slanting down on them from between the eaves of the houses.

For five long hours of dark, after his seven o'clock supper, Old Nollykins managed to keep himself awake. Then, a little before midnight, having assured himself that his three 'prentices were sound asleep in their bed, he groped downstairs again, gently lifted the latch and looked out. There was never such a shining scene before. The snow on the roofs and gables and carved stonework of the houses gleamed white and smooth as the finest millers' meal. There was not a soul, not even a cat, to be seen in the long stretch of the lampless street. And the stars in the grey-blue sky gleamed like dewdrops on a thorn.

Sure enough, as soon as ever the last stroke of midnight had sounded from St. Andrew's tower, there came faintly wreathing its way out of the distance the same shrill penetrating strains of the ancient tune. Lord bless me, if Old Nollykins had had but one sole drop of the blood of his own youth left in his veins he could not

have resisted dancing his old bones out of his body
down his steps and into the crudded High Street at the
sound of it:

Girls and boys, come out to play!
The moon doth shine as bright as day;
Leave your supper, and leave your sleep,
And come with your playfellows into the street! . . .

But, instead, he shuffled like a rat hastily back into
the house again; pushed himself in close under the staircase; and waited—leaving the door ajar.

Ho, ho, what's that? Faint flitting lights were now
showing in the street, and a sound as of little unhuman
cries, and in a minute or two the music loudened so
that an old glass case on a table near by containing
the model of a brig which had belonged to Old Nollykins' wicked grandfather who had died in Tobago,
fairly rang to the marvellous stirrings on the air. And
down helter-skelter from their bed, just as they had
slipped in under its sacking—in their breeches and rags
of day-shirts, barefoot, came whiffling from stair to
stair the ghosts of his three small 'prentices. Old Nollykins hardly had time enough to see the wonderful smile
on them, to catch the gleam of the grinning white teeth
beneath their parted lips, before they were out and
away.

Shivering all over, as if with the palsy, the old man
hastened up the staircase, and in a minute or two the
vacant house resounded with the strokes of his hammer as he drove in the tenpenny nail into the keyhole
above the attic door, and hung up key and horseshoe

by their strings. This done, he lowered his hammer and listened. Not the faintest whisper, sigh or squeak came from within. But in dread of what he might see he dared not open the door.

Instead, curiosity overcame him. Wrapping a cloak round his skinny shoulders he hurried out into the street. Sure enough, here, there, everywhere in the snow and hoarfrost were footprints—traces at any rate distinct enough for *his* envious eyes, though they were hardly more than those of the skirring of a hungry bird's wing on the surface of the snow. And fondly supposing in his simplicity that he had now safely cheated his 'prentices, that for ever more their poor young empty bodies would be at his beck and call, Old Noll determined to follow away out of the town and into the water-meadows the dream-shapes of the children now all of them out of sight. On and on he went till his breath was whistling in his lungs and he could scarcely drag one foot after the other.

And he came at last to where, in a loop of the Itchen, its waters shining like glass in the moon, there was a circle of pollard and stunted willows. And there, in the lush and frosty grasses was a wonderful company assembled, and unearthly music ascending, it seemed, from out of the bowels of a mound near by, called Caesar's Camp. And he heard a multitude of voices and singing from within. And all about the meadow wandered in joy the sleep-shapes not only of the children from Cheriton, but from the farms and cottages and gipsy camps for miles around. Sheep were there too, their yellow eyes gleaming in the moon as he trod past them. But none paid any heed to the children or to the 'strangers' who had called them out of their dreams.

Strange indeed were these strangers: of middle height, with garments like spider-web, their straight hair of the colour of straw falling gently on either side their narrow cheeks, so that it looked at first glimpse as if they were grey-beards. And as they trod on their narrow feet, the frozen grasses scarcely stirring beneath them, they turned their faces from side to side, looking at the children. And then a fairness that knows no change showed in their features, and their eyes were of a faint flame like that of sea-water on nights of thunder when the tide gently lays its incoming ripples on some wide flat sandy strand of the sea.

And at sight of them Old Nollykins began to be mortally afraid. Not a sign was there of Tom, Dick or Harry. They must have gone into the sonorous mound —maybe were feasting there, if dream-shapes feast. The twangling and trumpeting and incessant music made his head spin round. He peered about for a hiding-place, and at length made his way to one of the old gnarled willows beside the icy stream. There he might have remained safe and sound till morning, if the frost, as he dragged himself up a little way into the lower branches of the tree, had not risen into his nostrils and made him sneeze. There indeed he might have remained safe and sound if he had *merely* sneezed, for an old man's sneeze is not much unlike an old sheep's wheezy winter cough. But such was this poor old man's alarm and terror at the company he had stumbled into that he cried, 'God bless us!' after his sneeze—just as his mother had taught him to do.

That was the end of wicked old Nollykins; as it was

his first step on the long road of repentance. For the next thing he remembered was opening his eyes in the half-light of stealing dawn and finding himself perched up in the boughs of a leafless willow-tree, a thin mist swathing the low-lying water-meadows, the sheep gently browsing in the grasses, leaving green marks in the frosty grass as they munched onwards. And such an ache and ague was in Old Noll's bones as he had never, since he was swaddled, felt before. It was as if every frosty switch of every un-polled willow in that gaunt fairy circle by the Itchen had been belabouring him of its own free will the whole night long. His heart and courage were gone. Sighing and groaning, he lowered himself into the meadow, and by the help of a fallen branch for staff made his way at last back into the town.

It was early yet even for the milkmaids, though cocks were crowing from their frosty perches, and the red of the coming sun inflamed the eastern skies. He groped into his house and shut the door. With many rests on the way from stair to stair he hoisted himself up, though every movement seemed to wrench him joint from joint, until at last he reached the attic door. He pressed his long ear against the panel and listened a moment. Not a sound. Then stealthily pushing it open inch by inch, he thrust forward his shuddering head and looked in.

The ruddy light in the East was steadily increasing, and had even pierced through the grimy panes of the dormer window as though to light up the slumbers of his small chimney-sweeps. It was a Sunday morning and their fair skins and lamb's-wool heads showed no trace of the week's soot. But while at other times on spying in at them it looked to Old Nollykins as if their smiling faces were made of wax, now they might be of alabaster. For each one of the three—Tom, Dick, and Harry —was lying on his back, their chapped, soot-roughened hands with the torn and broken nails resting on either side of their bodies. No smile now touched their features, but only a solemn quietude as of images eternally at rest. And such was the aspect of the three children that even Old Nollykins dared not attempt to waken them because he knew in his heart that no earthly rod would ever now bestir them out of this slumber. Not at least until their spirits had won home again. And the soured old crone was not likely to aid him in that.

He cursed the old woman, battering on her crazy door, but she paid him no heed. And at last, when the Cheriton Church bells began ringing the people to morning service, there was nothing for it, if there was any hope of saving his neck, but to go off to the Mayor's man, dragging himself along the street on a couple of sticks, to tell him that his 'prentices were dead.

Dead they were not, however. The Mayor's man fetched a doctor, and the doctor, after putting a sort of wooden trumpet to their chests, asseverated that there was a stirring under the cage of their ribs. They were fallen into a trance, he said. What is called a *catalepsy*. It was a dreamlike seizure that would presently pass away. But though the old midwife the doctor called in heated up salt, for salt-bags, and hour by hour put a hot brick fresh from the fire to each 'prentice's stone-cold feet, by not a flutter of an eyelid nor the faintest of sighs did any one of the three prove that he was alive or could heed.

There they lay, on their straw pallet, motionless as mummies, still and serene, lovely as any mother might wish, with their solemn Sunday-morning soap-polished cheeks and noses and foreheads and chins, and as irresponsive as cherubs made of stone.

And the Mayor of the Town, after listening to all Old Nollykins could say, fined him Five Bags of Guineas for allowing his three 'prentices to fall into a catalepsy for want of decent food and nourishment. And what with the pain of his joints and the anguish of having strangers trampling all over his house, and of pleading with the Mayor, and of seeing his money fetched out from its hiding-places and counted out on the table, the miserable old man was so much dazed and confused that he never thought to take down the wreath of ash and elder and the horseshoe and the key. That is why, when a week or two had gone by and no sign had shown how long this trance would continue, the Mayor and Councillors decided that as Tom, Dick and Harry could be of no further use to the town as chimney-sweeps, they might perhaps earn an honest penny for it as the 'Marvels of the Age.'

So the Mayor's man with a flowing white muslin band round his black hat, and his two mutes—carrying bouquets of lilies in their hands—came with his hand-cart and fetched the three bodies away. A roomy glass case had been made for them of solid Warwickshire oak, with a fine chased lock and key. And by the time the Waits had begun to sing their Christmas carols in the snow, the three children had been installed in this case on the upper floor of the Cheriton Museum, and there lay slumbering on and on, quiet as Snow-White in the dwarfs' coffin, the gentle daylight falling fairly on their quiet faces—though during the long summer days a dark blind was customarily drawn over the glass whenever the sun shone in too fiercely at the window.

News of this wonder spread fast, and by the following Spring visitors from all over the world—even from cities as remote as Guanojuato and Seringapatam—came flocking into Warwickshire merely to gaze a while at the sleeping Chimney-Sweeps: at 6d. a time. After which a fair proportion of them went on to Stratford to view the church where lie William Shakespeare's honoured bones. Indeed Mrs. Giles, the old woman who set up an apple and ginger-bread stall beside the Museum, in a few years made so much money out of her wares that she was able to bring up her nine orphaned grandchildren all but in comfort, and to retire at last at the age of sixty to a four-roomed cottage not a hundred yards from that of Anne Hathaway's herself.

In course of time the Lord-Lieutenant and the Sheriffs and the Justices of the Peace and the Bishop and the mayors of the neighbouring towns, jealous no doubt of this fame and miracle in their midst, did their utmost to persuade and compel the Mayor and Corporation of Cheriton to remove the Boys to the county-town—the Earl himself promising to lodge them in an old house not a stone's-throw distant from the lovely shrine of his ancestors, Beauchamp Chapel. But all in vain. The people of Cheriton held tight to their rights: and the Lord Chief Justice after soberly hearing both sides at full length wagged his wigged head in their favour.

For fifty-three years the Sleeping Boys slept on. During this period the Town Council had received One Hundred and Twenty Three Thousand, Five Hundred and Fifty-Five sixpences in fees alone (i.e. £3,088 17s. 6d.). And nearly every penny of this vast sum was almost clear profit. They spent it wisely too—widened their narrow chimneys, planted lime trees in the High Street and ash and willow beside the river, built a fountain and a large stone dove-cot, and set apart a wooded meadowland with every comfort wild creatures can hope to have bestowed on them by their taskmaster, Man.

Then, one fine day, the curator—the caretaker—of the Museum, who, for forty years had never once missed dusting the 'prentices' glass case first thing in the morning, fell ill and had to take to his bed. And his niece, a pretty young thing, nimble and high-spirited, came as his deputy for a while, looked after the Museum, sold tickets, and kept an eye on the visitors in his stead. She was only seventeen; and was the very first person who had ever been heard to sing in the Museum —though of course it was only singing with her lips all but closed, and never during show-hours.

And it was Summer-time, or rather the very first of May. And as each morning she opened the great door of the Museum and ascended the wide carved staircase and drew up the blinds of the tall windows on the upper floor, and then turned—as she always turned—to gaze at the Three Sleepers (and not even a brass farthing to pay), she would utter a deep sigh as if out of the midst of a happy dream.

'You lovely things!' she would whisper to herself. 'You lovely, lovely things!' She had a motherly heart; and the wisps of her hair were as transparent as the E-string of a fiddle in the morning light. And the glance of her blue eyes rested on the glass case with such compassion and tenderness that if mere looking could have awakened the children they would have been dancing an Irish jig with her every blessed morning.

Being young, too, she was inclined to be careless, and had even at times broken off a tiny horn of coral, or a half-hidden scale from the mermaid's tail for a souvenir of Cheriton to any young stranger that particularly took her fancy. Moreover, she had never been told anything about the magicry of keys or horseshoes or iron or ash or elder, having been brought up at a School where wizardry and witchcraft were never so much as mentioned during school hours. How could she realize then that the little key of the glass case and the great key of the Museum door (which, after opening both, she had dropped out of her pocket by accident plump into the garden well) could keep anybody or anything out, or in, even when the doors were wide open? Or that water can wash even witchcraft away?

That very morning there had been such a pomp of sunshine in the sky, and the thrushes were singing so shrilly in the new-leafed lime trees as she came along to her work, that she could resist her pity and yearning no longer. Having drawn up the blinds on the upper floor, in the silence she gently raised the three glass lids of the great glass case and propped them back fully open. And one by one—after first listening at their lips as steadily as if in hope of hearing what their small talk

might be in their dreams—she kissed the slumbering
creatures on their stone-cold mouths. And as she kissed
Harry she fancied she heard a step upon the stair. And
she ran out at once to see.

No one. Instead, as she stood on the wide staircase
listening, her young face tilted and intent, there came
a waft up it as of spiced breezes from the open spaces
of Damascus. Not a sound, no more than a breath, faint
and yet almost unendurably sweet of Spring—straight
across from the bird-haunted, sheep-grazed meadows
skirting the winding river: the perfume of a whisper. It
was as if a distant memory had taken presence and
swept in delight across her eyes. Then stillness again,
broken by the sounding as of a voice smaller than the
horn of a gnat. And then a terrible sharp crash of
glass. And out pell-mell came rushing our three young
friends, the chimney-sweeps, their dream-shapes home
at last.

Now Old Nollykins by this time had long been laid in
his grave. So even if anyone had been able to catch
them, Tom, Dick, and Harry would have swept no more
chimneys for him. Nor could even the new Mayor manage it. Nor the complete Town Council. Nor the Town
Crier, though he cried twice a day to the end of
the year: 'O-yess! O-yess!! O-yess!!! Lost, stolen, or
strayed: Three World-Famous and Notorious Sleeping
Boys of Warwickshire.' Nor even the Lord-Lieutenant.
Nor even the mighty Earl.

As for the mound by the pollard willows—well, what
clever Wide-awake would ever be able to give any news
of that?

THE LOVELY MYFANWY

*In an old castle under the for-*ested mountains of the Welsh Marches there lived long ago Owen ap Gwythock, Lord of Eggleyseg. He was a short, burly, stooping man with thick black hair on head and face, large ears, and small restless eyes. And he lived in his great castle alone, except for one only daughter, the lovely Myfanwy.

Lovely indeed was she. Her hair, red as red gold, hung in plaits to her knees. When she laughed, it was like bells in a faraway steeple. When she sang, Echo forgot to reply. And her spirit would sit gently looking out of her blue eyes like cushats out of their nest in an ivy bush.

Myfanwy was happy, too—in most things. All that her father could give her for her ease and pleasure was hers—everything indeed but her freedom. She might sing, dance, think and say; eat, drink, and delight in whatsoever she wished or willed. Indeed her father loved her so dearly that he would sit for hours together merely watching her—as you may watch wind over wheat, reflections in water, or clouds in the heavens. So long as she was safely and solely his all was well.

But ever since Myfanwy had been a child, a miserable foreboding had haunted his mind. Supposing she should some day leave him? Supposing she were lost or decoyed away? Supposing she fell ill and died? What then? The dread of this haunted his mind day and night. His dark brows loured at the very thought of it. It made him morose and sullen; it tied up the tongue in his head.

For this sole reason he had expressly forbidden Myfanwy even to stray but a few paces beyond the precincts of his castle; with its battlemented towers, its galleries and corridors and multitudinous apartments, its high garden and courtyard, its alleys, fountains, fish-pools and orchards. He could trust nobody. He couldn't bear her out of his sight. He spied, he watched, he walked in his sleep, he listened and peeped; and all for fear of losing Myfanwy.

So although she might have for company the doves and swans and peacocks, the bees and butterflies, the swallows and swifts and jackdaws and the multitude of birds of every song and flight and feather that haunted the castle; humans, except her father, she had none. The birds and butterflies could fly away at will wherever their wings could carry them. Even the fishes in the fish-pools and in the fountains had their narrow alleys of marble and alabaster through which on nimble fin they could win back to the great river at last. Not so Myfanwy.

She was her father's unransomable prisoner; she was a bird in a cage. She might feast her longing eyes on the distant horizon beyond whose forests lay the sea, but knew she could not journey thither. While as for the neighbouring township, with its busy streets and marketplace—not more than seven country miles away—she had only dreamed of its marvels and dreamed in vain. A curious darkness at such times came into her eyes, and her spirit would look out of them not like a dove but as might a dumb nightingale out of its nest—a nightingale that has had its tongue cut out for a delicacy to feed some greedy prince.

How criss-cross a thing is the heart of man. Solely because this lord loved his daughter so dearly, if ever she so much as sighed for change or adventure, like some stubborn beast of burden he would set his feet together and refuse to budge an inch. Beneath his heavy brows he would gaze at the brightness of her unringleted hair as if mere looking could keep that gold secure; as if earth were innocent of moth and rust and change and chance, and had never had course to dread and tremble at sound of the unrelenting footfall of Time.

All he could think of that would keep her his own was hers without the asking: delicate raiment and meats and strange fruits and far-fetched toys and devices and pastimes, and as many books as would serve a happy scholar a long life through. He never tired of telling her how much he loved and treasured her. But there is a hunger of the heart no *thing* in the world can ever satisfy. And Myfanwy listened, and sighed.

Besides which, Myfanwy grew up and grew older as a green-tressed willow grows from a sapling; and now that she had come to her eighteenth spring she was lovelier than words could tell. This only added yet another and sharper dread and foreboding to her father's mind.

It sat like a skeleton at his table whenever he broke
bread or sipped wine. Even the twittering of a happy
swallow from distant Africa reminded him of it like a
knell. It was this: that some day a lover, a suitor, would
come and carry her off.

Why, merely to *see* her, even with her back turned—
to catch a glimpse of her slim shoulders, of her head
stooping over a rosebush would be enough. Let her but
laugh—two notes—and you listened! Nobody—prince
nor peasant, knight nor squire—brave, foolish, young
or weary, would be able to resist her. Owen ap Gwythock knew it in his bones. But one look, and instantly the looker's heart would be stolen out of
his body. He would fall in love with her—fall as deep
and irrevocably as the dark sparkling foaming water
crashing over into the gorge of Modwr-Eggleyseg,
scarcely an arrow's flight beyond his walls.

And supposing any such suitor should *tell* Myfanwy
that he loved her, might she not—forgetting all his
own care and loving-kindness—be persuaded to flee
away and leave him to his solitude? Solitude—now
that old age was close upon him! At thought of this, for
fear of it, he would sigh and groan within: and he
would bid the locksmiths double their locks and bolts
and bars; and he would sit for hours watching the highroad that swept up past his walls, and scowling at sight
of every stranger who passed that way.

He even at last forbade Myfanwy to walk in the garden except with an immense round mushroom hat on
her head, a hat so wide in the brim that it concealed
from any trespasser who might be spying over the wall
even the glinting of her hair—everything of her indeed

except her two velvet shoes beneath the hem of her dress as they stepped in turn—and softly as moles—one after the other from blossoming alley to alley and from lawn to lawn.

And because Myfanwy loved her father almost as dearly as he loved her, she tried her utmost to be gay and happy and not to fret or complain or grow pale and thin and pine. But as a caged bird with a kind mistress may hop and sing and flutter behind its bars as if it were felicity itself, and yet be sickening at heart for the wild wood and its green haunts, so it was with Myfanwy.

If only she might but just once venture into the town, she would think to herself; but just to see the people in the streets, and the pedlars in the market-place, and the cakes and sweetmeats and honey-jars in the shops, and strangers passing to and fro, and the sunshine in the high gables, and the talking and the laughing and the bargaining and the dancing—the horses, the travellers, the bells, the starshine.

Above all, it made her heart ache to think her father should have so little faith in her duty and love for him that he would not consent to let her wander even a snail's journey out of his sight. When, supper over, she leaned over his great chair as he sat there in his crimson —his black hair dangling on his shoulders, his beard hunched up on his chest—to kiss him good night, this thought would be in her eyes even if not on the tip of her tongue. And at such times he himself—as if he knew in his heart what he would never dare to confess —invariably shut down his eyelids or looked the other way.

Now servants usually have long tongues, and gossip

flits from place to place like the seeds of thistledown. Simply because Myfanwy was never seen abroad, the fame of her beauty had long since spread through all the countryside. Minstrels sang of it, and had even carried their ballads to countries and kingdoms and principalities far beyond Wales.

Indeed, however secret and silent men may be concerning rare beauty and goodness, somehow news of it sows itself over the wide world. A saint may sit in his cave or his cell, scarcely ever seen by mortal eye, quiet as sunshine in a dingle of the woods or seabirds in the hollows of the Atlantic, doing his deeds of pity and loving-kindness, and praying his silent prayers. And he may live to be a withered-up, hollow-cheeked old man with a long white beard, and die, and his body be shut up in a tomb. But nevertheless, little by little, the fame of his charity, and of the miracles of his compassion will spread abroad, and at last you may even chance on his image in a shrine thousands of leagues distant from the hermitage where he lived and died, and centuries after he has gone on his way.

Like this it was with the loveliness and gentleness of Myfanwy. That is why, when the Lord of Eggleyseg himself rode through the streets of the neighbouring town, he perceived out of the corner of his eye strangers in outlandish disguise who he suspected at once must be princes and noblemen from foreign climes come thither even if merely to set eyes on his daughter. That is why the streets were so full of music and singing that of a summer evening you could scarcely hear the roar of its cataracts. That is why its townsfolk were enter-

tained with tumblers and acrobats and fortune-tellers
and soothsayers and tale-tellers almost the whole year
long. Ever and again, indeed, grandees visited it *without* disguise. They lived for weeks there, with their reti-
nues of servants, their hawks and hounds and tasselled
horses in some one of its high ancient houses. And their
one sole hope and desire was to catch but a glimpse of
the far-famed Myfanwy.

But as they came, so they went away. However they
might plot and scheme to gain a footing in the castle—
it was in vain. The portcullis was always down; there
were watchmen perpetually on the look-out in its turrets; and the gates of the garden were festooned with
heavy chains. There was not in its frowning ancient
walls a single window less than twenty feet above the
ground that was not thickly, rustily, and securely
barred.

None the less, Myfanwy occasionally found herself
in the garden alone. Occasionally she stole out if but for
one breath of freedom, sweeter by far to those who pine
for it than that of pink, or mint, or jasmine, or honey-
suckle. And one such early evening in May, when her
father—having nodded off to sleep, wearied out after
so much watching and listening and prying and peering
—was snoring in an arbour or summerhouse, she came
to its western gates, and having for a moment lifted the
brim of her immense hat to look at the sunset, she
gazed wistfully a while through its bars out into the
green woods beyond.

The leafy boughs in the rosy light hung still as pictures in deep water. The skies resembled a tent of silk,

blue as the sea. Deer were browsing over the dark turf;
and a wonderful charm and carolling of birds was rising out of the glades and coverts of the woods.

But what Myfanwy had now fixed her dark eyes on
was none of these, but the figure of a young man leaning there, erect but fast asleep, against the bole of a
gigantic tree, not twenty paces distant from the gate at
which she stood. He must, she fancied, have been keeping watch there for some little time. His eyelids were
dark with watching; his face pale. Slim and gentle
does were treading close beside him; the birds had
clean forgotten his presence; and a squirrel was crack-
ing the nut it held between its clawed forepaws not a
yard above his head.

Myfanwy had never before set eyes on a human
stranger in this valley beyond the gates. Her father's
serving men were ancients who had been in his service
in the castle years before she was born. This young man
looked, she imagined, like a woodman, or a forester, or
a swine-herd. She had read of them in a handwritten
book of fantastic tales which she had chanced on
among her mother's belongings.

And as Myfanwy, finger on brim of her hat, stood intently gazing, a voice in her heart told her that whoever and whatever this stranger might be, he was someone she had been waiting for, and even dreaming about,
ever since she was a child.

All else vanished out of her mind and her memory.
It was as if her eyes were intent on some such old
story itself, and one well known to her. This uncon-
scious stranger was that story. Yet he himself—stiff
as a baulk of wood against the beech-trunk, as if

indeed he had been nailed to its bark—slumbered on.

So he might have continued to do, now so blessedly asleep, until she had vanished as she had come. But at that moment the squirrel there, tail for parasol immediately above his head, having suddenly espied Myfanwy beyond the bars of the gate, in sheer astonishment let fall its nut, and the young man—as if at a tiny knock on the door of his mind—opened his eyes.

For Myfanwy it was like the opening of a door into a strange and wonderful house. Her heart all but ceased to beat. She went cold to her fingertips. And the stranger too continued to gaze at Myfanwy—as if out of a dream.

And if everything could be expressed in words, that this one quiet look between them told Myfanwy of things strange that yet seemed more familiar to her than the pebbles on the path and the thorns on the rose-bushes and the notes of the birds in the air, then it would take a book ten times as long as this in which to print it.

But even as she gazed Myfanwy suddenly remembered her father. She sighed; her fingers let fall the wide brim of her hat; she turned away. And oddly enough, by reason of this immense ridiculous hat, her father who but a few moments before had awakened in his arbour and was now hastening along the path of the rosery in pursuit of her, caught not a single glimpse of the stranger under the beech-tree. Indeed, before the squirrel could scamper off into hiding, the young man had himself vanished round the trunk of the tree and out of sight like a serpent into the grass.

In nothing except in this, however, did he resemble a serpent. For that very evening at supper her father told Myfanwy that yet another letter had been delivered at the castle, from some accursed Nick Nobody, asking permission to lay before him his suit for her hand. His rage was beyond words. He spilt his wine and crumbled his bread—his face a storm of darkness; his eyes like smouldering coals.

Myfanwy sat pale and trembling. Hitherto, such epistles though even from princes of renowned estate and of realms even of the Orient, had carried much less meaning to her heart than the cuckooing of a cuckoo, or the whispering of the wind. Indeed, the cuckoo of those Welsh mountains and the wind from over their seas were voices of a language which, though secret, was not one past the heart's understanding. Not so these pompous declarations. Myfanwy would laugh at them—as though at the clumsy gambollings of a bear. She would touch her father's hand, and smile into his face, to assure him they had no meaning, that she was still as safe as safe could be.

But *this* letter—not for a single moment had the face of the young stranger been out of her mind. Her one sole longing and despair was the wonder whether she would ever in this world look upon him again. She sat like stone.

'Ay, ay, my dear,' said her father at last, laying his thick, square hand on hers as she sat beside him in her high-backed velvet chair—'ay, ay, my gentle one. It shows us yet again how full the world is of insolence and adventurers. This is a *cave,* a warning, an *alarum,* my dear—maledictions on his bones! We must be ten

times more cautious; we must be wary; we must be
lynx and fox and Argus—all eyes! And remember, my
all, my precious one, remember this, that while I, your
father, am alive, no harm, no ill can approach or touch
you. Believe only in my love, beloved, and all is well
with us.'

Her cold lips refused to speak. Myfanwy could find
no words with which to answer him. With face averted
she sat in a woeful daydream, clutching her father's
thumb, and only vaguely listening to his transports of
fury and affection, revenge and adoration. For her
mind and heart now welled over with such a medley of
thoughts and hopes and fears and sorrows that she
could find no other way but this dumb clutch of express-
ing that she loved her father too.

At length, his rage not one whit abated, he rose from
his chair, and having torn the insolent letter into thirty-
two tiny pieces he flung them into the huge log fire
burning in the stone chimney. 'Let me but lay a finger
on the shameless popinjay,' he muttered to himself;
'I'll—I'll cut his tongue out!'

Now the first thing Myfanwy did when the chance
offered was to hasten off towards the Western Gate if
only to warn the stranger of her father's rage and men-
aces, and bid him go hide himself away and never,
never, never come back again.

But when once more she approached its bars the
deer were still grazing in the forest, the squirrel was
nibbling another nut, the beech had unfolded yet a few
more of its needle-pointed leaves into the calm evening
light; but of the stranger—not a sign. Where he had
stood was now only the assurance that he was indeed

gone forever. And Myfanwy turned from the quiet scene, from the forest, its sunlight faded, all its beauty made forlorn. Try as she might in the days that followed to keep her mind and her thoughts fixed on her needle and her silks, her lute and her psalter, she could see nothing else but that long look of his.

And now indeed she began to pine and languish in body, haunted by the constant fear that her stranger might have met with some disaster. And simply because her father loved her so jealously, he knew at once what worm was in her mind, and he never ceased to watch and spy upon her, and to follow her every movement.

Now Myfanwy's bed-chamber was in the southern tower of this lord's castle, beneath which a road from the town to the eastward wound round towards the forests and distant mountains. And it being set so high above the ground beneath, there was no need for bars to its windows. While then, from these window-slits Myfanwy could see little more than the tops of the wayfarers' heads on the turf below, they were wide and lofty enough to let the setting sun in its due hour pour in its beams upon her walls and pictures and curtained Arabian bed. But the stone walls being so thick, in order to see out of her chamber at all, she must needs lie along a little on the cold inward sill, and peer out over the wide verdant countryside as if through the port-hole of a ship.

And one evening, as Myfanwy sat sewing a seam—and singing the while a soft tune to herself, if only to keep her thoughts from pining—she heard the murmur of many voices. And, though at first she knew not why, her heart for an instant or two stopped beating. Laying her slip of linen down, she rose, stole over the mats on the flagstones, and gently pushing her narrow shoulders onwards, peeped out and down at last through the window to look at the world below. And this was what she saw. In an old velvet cloak, his black hair dangling low upon his shoulders, there in the evening light beneath her window was a juggler standing, and in a circle round and about him was gathered a throng of gaping country-folk and idlers and children, some of whom must even have followed him out of the town. And one and all they were lost in wonder at his grace and skill.

Myfanwy herself indeed could not have imagined such things could be, and so engrossed did she become in watching him that she did not catch the whisper of a long-drawn secret sigh at her keyhole; nor did she hear her father as he turned away on tip-toe to descend the staircase again into the room below.

Indeed one swift glance from Myfanwy's no longer sorrowful eyes had pierced the disguise—wig, cloak, hat, and hose—of the juggler. And as she watched him she all but laughed aloud. Who would have imagined that the young stranger, whom she had seen for the first time leaning dumb, blind, and fast asleep against the trunk of a beech-tree could be possessed of such courage and craft and cunning as this!

His head was at the moment surrounded by a halo of glittering steel—so fast the daggers with which he was juggling whisked on from hand to hand. And suddenly the throng around him broke into a roar, for in glancing up and aside he had missed a dagger. It was falling—falling: but no, in a flash he had twisted back the sole of his shoe, and the point had stuck quivering in his heel, while he continued to whirl its companions into the golden air.

In that instant, however, his upward glance had detected the one thing in the world he had come out in hope to see—Myfanwy. He flung his daggers aside and fetched out of his travelling box a netful of coloured balls. Holloing out a string of outlandish gibberish to the people, he straightaway began to juggle with these. Higher and higher the seven of them soared into the mellow air, but one of the colour of gold soared on ever higher and higher than any. So high, indeed, that at last the people could watch it no longer because of the dazzle of the setting sun in their eyes. Presently, indeed, it swooped so loftily into the air that Myfanwy need but thrust out her hand to catch it as it paused for a breath of an instant before falling, and hung within reach of her stone window-sill.

And even as she watched, enthralled, a whispering voice within her cried, 'Take it!' She breathed a deep breath, shut her eyes, paused, and the next instant she had stretched out her hand into the air. The ball was hers.

Once more she peeped down and over, and once more the juggler was at his tricks. This time with what appeared to be a medley of all kinds of varieties of fruits; pomegranates, quinces, citrons, lemons, oranges and nectarines, and soaring high above them, nothing more unusual than an English apple. Once again the whisperer in Myfanwy's mind cried, 'Take it!' And she put out her hand and took the apple too.

Yet again she peeped and peered over, and this time it seemed that the juggler was flinging serpents into the air, for they writhed and looped and coiled around him as they whirled whiffling on from hand to hand. There was a hissing, too, and the people drew back a little, and a few of the timider children ran off to the other side of the highroad. And now, yet again, one of the serpents was soaring higher and higher above the rest. And Myfanwy could see from her coign of vantage that it was no live serpent but a strand of silken rope. And yet again and for the third time the whisperer whispered, 'Take it!' And Myfanwy put out her hand and took that too.

And, it happening that a little cloud was straying across the sun at this moment, the throng below had actually seen the highestmost of the serpents thus mysteriously disappear and they cried out as if with one voice, 'Gone!' 'Vanished!' 'Vanished!' 'Gone!' 'Magician, magician!' And the coins that came dancing into the juggler's tambourine in the moments that followed were enough to make him for that one minute the richest man in the world.

And now the juggler was solemnly doffing his hat to the people. He gathered his cloak around him more closely, put away his daggers, his balls, his fruits, his serpents, and all that was his, into a long green narrow box. Then he hoisted its strap over his shoulder, and doffing his cap once more, he clasped his tambourine under his elbow and seizing his staff, turned straight from the castle tower towards the hazy sun-bathed mountains. And, it beginning to be towards nightfall, the throng of people soon dispersed and melted away;

the maids and scullions, wooed out by this spectacle from the castle, returned to their work; and the children ran off home to tell their mothers of these marvels and to mimic the young juggler's tricks as they gobbled up their supper-crusts and were hastily packed off to bed.

In the stillness that followed after the juggler's departure, Myfanwy found herself kneeling in her chamber in the tranquil golden twilight beside a wooden chair, her hands folded in her lap and her dark eyes fixed in wonderment and anxiety on the ball, and the apple and the rope; while in another such narrow stone chamber only ten or twelve stone steps beneath, her father was crouching at his window shaken with fury, and seeing in his imagination these strange gifts from the air almost as clearly as Myfanwy could see them with her naked eye.

For though the sun had been as much a dazzle to himself as to the common people in the highway, he had kept them fastened on the juggler's trickeries none the less, and had counted every coloured ball and every fruit and every serpent as they rose and fell in their rhythmical maze-like network of circlings in the air. And when each marvellous piece of juggling in turn was over, he knew that in the first place a golden ball was missing, and that in the second place a fruit like an English apple was missing, and that in the third place a silken cord with a buckle-hook to it like the head of a serpent had been flung into the air but had never come down to earth again. And at the cries and the laughter and the applause of the roaring common people and children beneath his walls, tears of rage and despair had burst from his eyes. Myfanwy was deceiving him. His dreaded hour was come.

But there again he was wrong. The truth is, his eyes were so green with jealousy and his heart so black with rage that his wits had become almost useless. Not only his wits either, but his courtesy and his spirit; for the next moment he was actually creeping up again like a thief from stair to stair, and presently had fallen once more on to his knees outside his beloved Myfanwy's chamber door and had fixed on her one of those green dark eyes of his at its little gaping cut-out pin-hole. And there he saw a strange sight indeed.

The evening being now well advanced, and the light of the afterglow too feeble to make more than a glimmer through her narrow stone window-slits, Myfanwy had lit with her tinder box (for of all things she loved light) no less than seven wax candles on a seven-branched candlestick. This she had stood on a table beside a high narrow mirror. And at the moment when the Baron fixed his eye to the pin-hole, she was standing, a little astoop, the apple in her hand, looking first at it, and then into the glass at the bright-lit reflected picture of herself holding the apple in her hand.

So now there were two Myfanwys to be seen—herself and her image in the glass. And which was the lovelier not even the juggler could have declared. Crouching there at the door-crack, her father could all but catch the words she was softly repeating to herself as she gazed at the reflected apple: 'Shall I, shan't I? Shall I, shan't I?' And then suddenly—and he dared not stir or cry out—she had raised the fruit to her lips and had nibbled its rind.

What happened then he could not tell, for the secret
and sovereign part of that was deep in Myfanwy herself. The sharp juice of the fruit seemed to dart about in
her veins like flashing fishes in her father's crystal fountains and water-conduits. It was as if happiness had begun gently to fall out of the skies around her, like dazzling flakes of snow. They rested on her hair, on her
shoulders, on her hands, all over her. And yet not snow,
for there was no coldness, but a scent as it were of
shadowed woods at noonday, or of a garden when a
shower has fallen. Even her bright eyes grew brighter;
a radiance lit her cheek; her lips parted in a smile.

And it is quite certain if Myfanwy had been the
Princess of Anywhere-in-the-World-at-All, she would
then and there—like Narcissus stooping over his lilied
water-pool—have fallen head over ears in love with
herself! 'Wonder of wonders!' cried she in the quiet;
'but if this is what a mere nibble of my brave juggler's
apple can do, then it were wiser indeed to nibble no
more.' So she laid the apple down.

The Baron gloated on through the pin-hole—watching her as she stood transfixed like some lovely flower
growing in the inmost silent solitude of a forest and
blossoming before his very eyes.

And then, as if at a sudden thought, Myfanwy turned
and took up the golden ball, which—as she had suspected and now discovered—was no ball, but a small
orb-shaped box of rare inlaid woods, covered with
golden thread. At touch of the tiny spring that showed
itself in the midst, its lid at once sprang open, and Myfanwy put in finger and thumb and drew out into the
crystal light a silken veil—but of a gossamer silk so

finely spun that when its exquisite meshes had wreathed themselves downward to the floor the veil looked to be nothing more than a silvery grey mist in the candlelight.

It filmed down from her fingers to the flagstones beneath, almost as light as the air in which it floated. Marvellous that what would easily cover her, head to heel, could have been packed into so close a room as that two-inch ball! She gazed in admiration of his exquisite handiwork. Then, with a flick of her thumb, she had cast its cloudlike folds over her shoulders.

And lo!—as the jealous lord gloated on—of a sudden there was nothing to be seen where Myfanwy had stood but seven candles burning in their stick, and seven more in the mirror. She had vanished.

She was not gone very far, however. For presently he heard—as if out of nowhere—a low chuckling childlike peal of laughter which willy-nilly had broken from her lips at seeing that this Veil of Invisibility had blanked her very glass. She gazed steadily on into its clear vacancy, lost in wonder. Nothing at all of her whatsoever was now reflected there!—not the tip of her nose, not a thumb, not so much as a button or a silver tag. Myfanwy had vanished; and yet, as she well knew, here she truly was in her own body and no other, though tented in beneath the folds of the veil, as happy as flocks on April hills, or mermaids in the deep blue sea. It was a magic thing indeed, to be there and yet not there; to hear herself and yet remain transparent as water.

Motionless though she stood, her thoughts were at the same time flitting about like quick and nimble birds in her mind. This veil, too, was the gift of the juggler; her young sleeping stranger of the beech-tree in a strange disguise. And she could guess in her heart what use he intended her to make of it, even though at thought of it that heart misgave her. A moment after and as swiftly as she had gone, she had come back again—the veil in her fingers. Laughing softly to herself she folded and refolded it and replaced it in its narrow box. Then turning, she took up from the chair the silken cord, and as if in idle fancy twined it twice about her slender neck. And it seemed the cord took life into itself, for lo, showing there in the mirror, calm now as a statue of coloured ivory, stood Myfanwy; and couched over her left temple the swaying head of the Serpent of Wisdom, whispering in her ear.

Owen ap Gwythock could watch no more. Groping his way with trembling fingers through the thick gloom of the staircase he crept down to the Banqueting Hall where already his Chief Steward awaited his coming to announce that supper was prepared.

To think that his Lovely One, his pearl of price, his gentle innocent, *his* Myfanwy—the one thing on earth he treasured most, and renowned for her gentleness and beauty in all countries of the world—had even for an instant forgotten their loves, forgotten her service and duty, was in danger of leaving and forsaking him for ever! In his jealousy and despair tears rolled down his furrowed cheeks as he ground his teeth together, thinking of the crafty enemy that was decoying her away.

Worse still; he knew in his mind's mind that in certain things in this world even the most powerful are powerless. He knew that against true love all resistance, all craft, all cunning at last prove of no avail. But in this grief and despair the bitterest of all the thoughts that were now busy in his brain was the thought that Myfanwy should be cheating and deceiving him, wantonly beguiling him; keeping things secret that should at once be told.

A dark and dismal mind was his indeed. To distrust one so lovely!—*that* might be forgiven him. But to creep about in pursuit of her like a weasel; to spy on her like a spy; to believe her guilty before she could prove her innocence! Could *that* be forgiven? And even at this very moment the avenger was at his heels.

For here was Myfanwy herself. Lovely as a convolvulus wreathing a withered stake, she was looking in at him from the doorpost, searching his face. For an instant she shut her eyes as if to breathe a prayer, then she advanced into the room, and, with her own hand, laid before him on the oak table beside his silver platter, first the nibbled apple, next the golden ball, and last the silken cord. And looking at him with all her usual love in her eyes and in her voice, she told him how these things had chanced into her hands, and whence they had come.

Her father listened; but durst not raise his eyes from his plate. The scowl on his low forehead grew blacker and blacker; even his beard seemed to bristle. But he heard her in silence to the end.

'So you see, dear father,' she was saying, 'how can I but be grateful and with all my heart to one who takes so much thought for me? And if you had seen the kindness and courtesy of his looks, even you yourself could not be angry. There never was, as you well know, any-

body else in the whole wide world whom I wished to
speak to but to you. And now there is none other than
you except this stranger. I know nothing but that. Can
you suppose indeed he meant these marvellous gifts for
me? And why for me and no other, father dear? And
what would you counsel me to do with them?'

Owen ap Gwythock stooped his head lower. Even
the sight of his eyes had dimmed. The torches faintly
crackled in their sconces, the candles on the table
burned unfalteringly on.

He turned his cheek aside at last like a snarling dog.
'My dear,' he said, 'I have lived long enough in this
world to know the perils that beset the young and fair.
I grant you that this low mountebank must be a creature of infinite cunning. I grant you that his tricks, if
harmless, would be worth a charitable groat. If, that is,
he were only what he seems to be. But that is not so. For
this most deadly stranger is a Deceiver and a Cheat. His
lair, as I guess well, is in the cruel and mysterious East,
and his one desire and stratagem is to snare you into his
company. Once within reach of his claws, his infamous
slaves will seize on you and bear you away to some evil
felucca moored in the river. It seems, beloved, that your
gentle charms are being whispered of in this wicked
world. Even the beauty of the gentlest of flowers may be
sullied by idle tongues. But once securely in the hands
of this nefarious mountebank, he will put off to Bar-
bary, perchance, or to the horrid regions of the Turk,
perchance, there to set you up in the scorching market-
place and to sell you for a slave. My child, the danger,
the peril is gross and imminent. Dismiss at once this evil
wretch from your mind and let his vile and dangerous

devices be flung into the fire. The apple is pure delu-
sion; the veil which you describe is a mere toy; and the
cord is a device of the devil.'

Myfanwy looked at her father, stooping there, with
sorrow in her eyes, in spite of the gladness sparkling
and dancing in her heart. Why, if all that he was saying
he thought true—why could he not lift his eyes and
meet her face to face?

'Well then, that being so, dear father,' she said softly
at last, 'and you knowing ten thousand times more of
God's world than I have ever had opportunity of knowing, whatever my desire, I must ask you but this one
small thing. Will you promise me not to have these
pretty baubles destroyed at once, before, I mean, you
have thought once more of *me?* If I had deceived you,
then indeed I should be grieved beyond endurance. But
try as I may to darken my thoughts of him, the light
slips in, and I see in my very heart that this stranger
cannot by any possibility of nature or heaven be all that
you tell me of him. I have a voice at times that whispers
me yes or no: and I obey. And of him it has said only
yes. But I am young, and the walls of this great house
are narrow, and you, dear father, as you have told me
so often, are wise. Do but then invite this young man
into your presence! Question him, test him, gaze on him,
hearken to him. And that being done, you will believe in
him as I do. As I know I am happy, I know he is honest.
It would afflict me beyond all telling to swerve by a
hair's-breadth from my dear obedience to you. But,
alas, if I never see him again, I shall wither up and die.
And that—would it not——' she added smilingly—
'that would be a worse disobedience yet? If you love

me, then, as from my first hour in the world I *know* you
have loved me, and I have loved you, I pray you think
of me with grace and kindness—and in compassion
too.'

And with that, not attempting to brush away the
tears that had sprung into her eyes, and leaving the juggler's three gifts amid the flowers and fruit of the long
table before him, Myfanwy hastened out of the room
and returned to her chamber, leaving her father alone.

For a while her words lay like a cold refreshing dew
on the dark weeds in his mind. For a while he pondered
them, even; while his own gross fables appeared in all
their ugly falseness.

But alas for himself and his pride and stubborn-
ness, these gentler ruminations soon passed away. At
thought once more of the juggler—of whom his spies
had long since brought him far other tidings than he
had expressed—rage, hatred and envy again boiled up
in him and drowned everything else. He forgot his courtesy, his love for Myfanwy, his desire even to keep her
love for him. Instead, on and on he sipped and sipped,
and sat fuming and plotting and scheming with but one
notion in his head—by hook or by crook to defeat this
juggler and so murder the love of his innocent Myfanwy.

'Lo, now,' broke out at last a small shrill voice inside
him. 'Lo, now, if thou taste of the magic apple, may it
not be that it will give thee courage and skill to contend
against him, and so bring all his hopes to ruin? Remember what a marvel but one merest nibble of the outer
rind of it wrought in thy Myfanwy!'

And the foolish creature listened heedfully to this

crafty voice, not realizing that the sole virtue of the apple was that of making any human who tasted it more like himself than ever. He sat there—his fist over his mouth—staring intently at the harmless-looking fruit. Then he tiptoed like a humpback across the room and listened at the entry. Then having poured out, and drained at a draught, yet another cup of wine, he cautiously picked up the apple by its stalk between finger and ringed thumb and once more squinted close and steadily at its red and green, and at the very spot where Myfanwy's small teeth had rasped away the skin.

It is in a *moment* that cities fall in earthquake, stars collide in the wastes of space, and men choose between good and evil. For suddenly—his mind made up, his face all turned a reddish purple—this foolish lord lifted the apple to his mouth and, stalk to dried blossom, bit it clean in half. And he munched and he munched and he munched.

He had chawed for but a few moments, however, when a dreadful and continuous change and transformation began to appear upon him. It seemed to him that his whole body and frame was being kneaded and twisted and wrung in much the same fashion as dough being made into bread, or clay in a modeller's fingers. Not knowing what these aches and stabbings and wrenchings meant, he had dropped as if by instinct upon his hands and knees, and thus stood munching, while gazing blankly and blindly, lost in some inward horror, into the great fire on the hearth.

And meanwhile, though he knew it not in full, there had been sprouting upon him grey coarse hairs—a full thick coat and hide of them—in abundance. There had come a tail to him with a sleek, dangling tassel; long hairy ears had jutted out upon his temples; the purple face turned grey, lengthening as it did so until it was at least full eighteen inches long with a great jawful of large teeth. Hoofs for his hands, hoofs where his feet used to be, and behold!—standing there in his own banqueting hall—this poor deluded Owen ap Gwythock, Lord of Eggleyseg, transmogrified into an ass!

For minutes together the dazed creature stood in utter dismay—the self within unable to realize the change that had come over its outer shape. But, happening to stretch his shaggy and unfamiliar neck a little outward, he perceived his own image in a scoured and polished suit of armour that stood on one side of the great chimney. He shook his head, the ass's head replied. He shook himself, the long ears flapped together like a wood-pigeon's wings. He lifted his hand—a hoof clawed at nowhere!

At this the poor creature's very flesh seemed to creep upon his bones as he turned in horror and dismay in search of an escape from the fate that had overtaken him. That ass *he?* he *himself?* His poor wits in vain endeavoured to remain calm and cool. A panic of fear all but swept him away. And at this moment his full, lustrous, long-lashed, asinine eyes fell by chance upon the golden ball lying ajar on the table beside his wine-cup —the Veil of Invisibility glinting like money-spider's web from within.

Now no ass is quite such a donkey as he looks. And this Owen ap Gwythock, though now completely shut up in this uncouth hairy body, was in his *mind* no more (though as much) of a donkey than he had ever been.

His one thought, then, was to conceal his dreadful condition from any servant that might at any moment come that way, while he himself could seek out a quiet secluded corner in the dark wherein to consider how to rid himself of his ass's frame and to regain his own usual shape. And there lay the veil! What thing sweeter could there be than to defeat the juggler with his own devices.

Seizing the veil with his huge front teeth, he jerked it out of the ball and flung it as far as he could over his shaggy shoulders. But alas, his donkey's muzzle was far from being as deft as Myfanwy's delicate fingers. The veil but half concealed him. Tail, rump and back legs were now vanished from view; head, neck, shoulders and fore-legs remained in sight. In vain he tugged; in vain he wriggled and wrenched; his hard hoofs thumping on the hollow flagstones beneath. One half of him stubbornly remained in sight; the rest had vanished. For the time being he was no more even than half an ass.

At last, breathless and wearied out with these exertions, trembling and shuddering, and with not a vestige of sense left in his poor donkey's noddle, he wheeled himself about once more and caught up with his teeth the silken cord. It was his last hope.

But this having been woven of wisdom—it being indeed itself the Serpent of Wisdom in disguise—at touch of his teeth it at once converted itself into a strong hempen halter, and, before he could so much as rear out of the way to escape its noose or even bray for help, it had tethered him to a large steel hook in his own chimneypiece.

Bray he did, none the less: 'Hee-haw! Hee-haw!! Hee-ee-ee-ee Haw-aw-aw!!!' His prolonged, see-saw, dismal lamentations shattered the silence so harshly and so hoarsely that the sound rose up through the echoing stone walls and even pierced into Myfanwy's own bedchamber, where she sat in the darkness at her window, looking out half in sorrow, half in unspeakable happiness, at the stars.

Filled with alarm at this dreadful summons, in an instant or two she had descended the winding stone steps; and a strange scene met her eyes.

There, before her, in the full red light of the flaming brands in the hearth and the torches on the walls, stood the forelegs, the neck, head, and ears of a fine, full-grown ass, and a yard or so behind them just nothing at all. Only vacancy!

Poor Myfanwy—she could but wring her hands in grief and despair; for there could be no doubt in her mind of who it was in truth now stood before her—her own dear father. And on his face such a look of rage, entreaty, shame and stupefaction as never man has seen on ass's countenance before. At sight of her the creature tugged even more furiously at his halter, and shook his shaggy shoulders; but still in vain. His mouth opened and a voice beyond words to describe, brayed out upon the silence these words: 'Oh, Myfanwy, see into what a pass your sorceries and deceits have reduced me!'

'Oh, my dear father,' she cried in horror, 'speak no more, I beseech you—not one syllable—or we shall be discovered. Or, if you utter a sound, let it be but in a whisper.'

She was at the creature's side in an instant, had flung her arms about his neck, and was whispering into his long hairy ear all the comfort and endearments and assurances that loving and tender heart could conceive. 'Listen, listen, dear father,' she was entreating him, 'I see indeed that you have been meddling with the apple, and the ball, and the cord. And I do assure you, with all my heart and soul, that I am thinking of nothing else but how to help you in this calamity that has overtaken us. Have patience. Struggle no more. All will be well. But oh, beloved, was it quite just to me to speak of my deceits?'

Her bright eyes melted with compassion as she looked upon one whom she had loved ever since she could remember, so dismally transmogrified.

'How can you hesitate, ungrateful creature?' the see-saw voice once more broke out. 'Relieve me of this awful shape, or I shall be strangled on my own hearthstone in this pestilent halter.'

But now, alas, footsteps were sounding outside the door. Without an instant's hesitation Myfanwy drew the delicate veil completely over the trembling creature's head, neck and forequarters and thus altogether concealed him from view. So—though it was not an instant too soon—when the Lord of Eggleyseg's Chief Steward appeared in the doorway, nothing whatever was changed within, except that his master no longer sat in his customary chair, Myfanwy stood solitary at the table, and a mysterious cord was stretched out between her hand and the hook in the chimney-piece.

'My father,' said Myfanwy, 'has withdrawn for a while. He is indisposed, and bids me tell you that even a whisper must disturb his rest. Have a hot posset prepared at once, and see that the room beneath is left vacant.'

The moment the Steward had gone to do her bidding Myfanwy turned at once to her father, and lifting the veil, whispered into the long hairy ear again that he must be of good cheer. 'For you see, dear father, the only thing now to be done is that we set out together at once in search of the juggler who, meaning no unkindness, presented me with these strange gifts. He alone can and will, I am assured, restore you to your own dear natural shape. So I pray you to be utterly silent— not a word, not a murmur—while I lead you gently forth into the forest. Once there I have no doubt I shall be able to find our way to where he is. Indeed he may be already expectant of my coming.'

Stubborn and foolish though the Baron might be, he realized, even in his present shape, that this was his only wisdom. Whereupon, withdrawing the end of the bridle from the hook to which it was tethered, Myfanwy softly led the now invisible creature to the door, and so, gently onward down the winding stone staircase, on the stones of which his shambling hoofs sounded like the hollow beating of a drum.

The vast room beneath was already deserted by its usual occupants, and without more ado the two of them, father and daughter, were soon abroad in the faint moonlight that now by good fortune bathed the narrow bridle-path that led into the forest.

Never before in all her years on earth had Myfanwy strayed beyond the Castle walls; never before had she stood lost in wonder beneath the dark emptiness of the starry skies. She breathed in the sweet fresh night air, her heart blossoming within her like an evening primrose, refusing to be afraid. For she knew well that the safety of them both—this poor quaking animal's and her own—depended now solely on her own courage and resource, and that to be afraid would almost certainly lead them only from one disaster into another.

Simply, however, because a mere ownerless ass wandering by itself in the moonlit gloom of the forest would be a spectacle less strange than that of a solitary damsel like herself, she once more drew down her father's ear to her lips and whispered into it, explaining to him that it was she who must now be veiled, and that if he would forgive her such boldness—for after all, he had frequently carried her pickaback when she was a child—she would mount upon his back and in this way they would together make better progress on their journey.

Her father dared not take offence at her words, whatever his secret feelings might be. 'So long as you hasten, my child,' he gruffed out in the hush, striving in vain to keep his tones no louder than a human whisper, 'I will forgive you all.' In a moment then there might be seen jogging along the bridle-path, now in moonlight, now in shadow, a sleek and handsome ass, a halter over its nose, making no stay to browse the dewy grass at the wayside, but apparently obeying its own whim as it wandered steadily onward.

Now it chanced that night there was a wild band of mountain robbers encamped within the forest. And when of a sudden this strange and pompous animal unwittingly turned out of a thicket into the light of their camp fire, and raised its eyes like glowing balls of emerald to gaze in horror at its flames, they lifted their voices together in an uproarious peal of laughter. And one of them at once started up from where he lay in the bracken, to seize the creature's halter and so make it his prize.

Their merriment, however, was quickly changed into dismay when the robbers saw the strange creature being guided, as was evident, by an invisible and mysterious hand. He turned this way, he turned that, with an intelligence that was clearly not his own and not natural even to his kind, and so eluded every effort made by his enemy to get a hold on his halter, his teeth and eyeballs gleaming in the firelight.

At this, awe and astonishment fell upon these outlaws. Assuredly sorcery alone could account for such ungainly and unasslike antics and manoeuvres. Assuredly some divine being must have the beast in keeping, and to meddle with it further might only prove their own undoing.

Fortunate indeed was it that Myfanwy's right foot, which by mischance remained uncovered by the veil, happened to be on the side of the animal away from the beams of the camp fire. For certainly had these malefactors seen the precious stones blazing in its buckle, their superstitions would have melted away like morning mist, their fears have given place to cupidity, and they would speedily have made the ass their own and held its rider to an incalculable ransom.

Before, however, the moon had glided more than a soundless pace or two on her night journey, Myfanwy and her incomparable ass were safely out of sight: and the robbers had returned to their carousals. What impulse bade her turn first this way, then that, in the wandering and labyrinthine glades and tracks of the forest, she could not tell. But even though her father—not daring to raise his voice in the deep silence—ever and again stubbornly tugged upon his halter in the belief that the travellers had taken a wrong turning and were irrevocably lost, Myfanwy kept steadily on her way.

With a touch of her heel or a gentle persuasive pat of her hand on his hairy neck she did her best to reassure and to soothe him. 'Only trust in me, dear father: I am sure all will be well.'

Yet she was haunted with misgivings. So that when at last a twinkling light, sprinkling its beams between the boughs, showed in the forest, it refreshed her heart beyond words to tell. She was reaching her journey's end. It was as if that familiar voice in the secrecy of her heart had murmured, 'Hst! He draws near!'

There and then she dismounted from off her father's hairy back and once more communed with him through that long twitching ear. 'Remain here in patience a while, dear father,' she besought him, 'without straying by a hair's-breadth from where you are; for everything tells me our Stranger is not far distant now, and no human being on earth, no living creature, even, must see you in this sad and unseemly disguise. I will hasten on to assure myself that the light which I perceive beaming through the thicket yonder is his, and no other's. Meanwhile—and this veil shall go with me in case of misadventure—meanwhile do you remain quietly beneath this spreading beech-tree, nor even stir unless you are over-wearied after our long night journey and you should feel inclined to rest a while on the softer turf in the shadow there under that bush of fragrant roses, or to refresh yourself at the brook whose brawling I hear welling up from that dingle in the hollow. In that case, return here, I pray you; contain yourself in patience, and be your tongue as dumb as a stone. For though you may *design* to speak softly, dearest father, that long sleek throat and those great handsome teeth will not admit of it.'

And her father, as if not even the thick hairy hide he wore could endure his troubles longer, opened his mouth as if to groan aloud. But restraining himself, he only sighed, while an owl out of the quiet breathed its mellow night-call as if in response. For having passed the last hour in a profound and afflicted reverie, this poor ass had now regained in part his natural human sense and sagacity. But pitiful was the eye, however asinine the grin, which he now bestowed as if in promise on Myfanwy who, with veil held delicately in her fingers stood there, radiant as snow, beside him in the moonlight.

And whether it was because of her grief for his own condition or because of the expectancy in her face at the thought of her meeting with the Stranger, or because maybe the ass feared in his despair and dejection that he might never see her again, he could not tell; but true it was that she had never appeared in a guise so brave and gay and passionate and tender. It might indeed be a youthful divinity gently treading the green sward beside this uncouth beast in the chequered light and shadow of that unearthly moonshine.

Having thus assured herself that all would be well until her return, Myfanwy kissed her father on his flat

hairy brow, and veil in hand withdrew softly in the di-
ection of the twinkling light.

Alas, though the Baron thirsted indeed for the chill
dark waters whose song rose in the air from the hollow
beneath, he could not contain himself in her absence,
but unmindful of his mute promise followed after his
daughter at a distance as she made her way to the light,
his hoofs scarce sounding in the turf. Having come
near, by peering through the dense bushes that encir-
cled the juggler's nocturnal retreat in the forest, he
could see and hear all that passed.

As soon as Myfanwy had made sure that this stranger sitting by his glowing watch-fire was indeed the juggler and no man else—and one strange leap of her
heart assured her of this even before her eyes could
carry their message—she veiled herself once more, and
so, all her loveliness made thus invisible, she drew
steathily near and a little behind him, as he crouched
over the embers. Then pausing, she called gently and in
a still low voice, 'I beseech you, Stranger, to take pity on
one in great distress.'

The juggler lifted his dreaming face, ruddied and
shadowed in the light of his fire, and peered cautiously
but in happy astonishment all around him.

'I beseech you, Stranger,' cried again the voice from
the unseen, 'to take pity on one in great distress.'

And at this it seemed to the juggler that now ice was
running through his veins and now fire. For he knew
well that this was the voice of one compared with whom
all else in the world to him was nought. He knew also
that she must be standing near, though made utterly
invisible to him by the veil of his own enchantments.

'Draw near, traveller. Have no fear,' he cried out softly into the darkness. 'All will be well. Tell me only how I may help you.'

But Myfanwy drew not a hair's-breadth nearer. Far from it. Instead, she flitted a little across the air of the glade, and now her voice came to him from up the wind towards the south, and fainter in the distance.

'There is one with me,' she replied, 'who by an evil stratagem has been transformed into the shape of a beast, and that beast a poor patient ass. Tell me this, sorcerer—how I may restore him to his natural shape, and mine shall be an everlasting gratitude. For it is my own father of whom I speak.'

Her voice paused and faltered on the word. She longed almost beyond bearing to reveal herself to this unknown one, trusting without the least doubt or misgiving that he would serve her faithfully in all she asked of him.

'But *that*, gentle lady,' replied the juggler, 'is not within my power, unless he of whom you speak draws near to show himself. Nor—though the voice with which you speak to me is sweeter than the music of harp-strings twangling on the air—nor is it within my power to make promises to a bodiless sound only. For how am I to be assured that the shape who utters the words I hear is not some dangerous demon of the darkness who is bent on mocking and deluding me, and who will bring sorcery on myself?'

There was silence for a while in the glade, and then 'No, no!' cried the juggler. 'Loveliest and bravest of all that is, I need not see thy shape to know thee. Thou art most assuredly the lovely Myfanwy, and all that I am, have ever been, and ever shall be is at thy service. Tell me, then, where is this poor ass that was once thy noble father?'

And at this, and at one and the same moment, Myfanwy, withdrawing the veil from her head and shoulders, disclosed her fair self standing there in the faint rosy glow of the slumbering fire, and there broke also from the neighbouring thicket so dreadful and hideous a noise of rage and anguish—through the hoarse and unpractised throat of the eavesdropper near by—that it might be supposed the clamour was not of one but of a chorus of demons—though it was merely our poor ass complaining of his fate.

'Oh, sir, sighed Myfanwy, 'my dear father, I fear, in his grief and anxiety has been listening to what has passed between us. See, here he comes.'

Galloping hoofs were indeed now audible as the Lord of Eggleyseg in ass's skin and shape drew near to wreak his vengeance on the young magician. But being at this moment in his stubborn rage and folly more ass than human, the glaring of the watch-fire dismayed his heavy wits, and he could do no else but paw with his fore-legs, lifting his smooth nose with its gleaming teeth into the night air, snuffing his rage and defiance some twenty paces distant from the fire.

The young magician, being of a nature as courteous as he was bold, did not so much as turn his head to scan the angry shivering creature, but once more addressed Myfanwy. She stood bowed down a little, tears in her eyes; in part for grief at her father's broken promise and the humiliation he had brought upon himself, in part for joy that their troubles would soon be over and that she was now in the very company of the stranger who unwittingly had been the cause of them all.

'Have no fear,' he said, 'the magic that has changed the noble Baron your father into a creature more blest in its docility, patience, and humbleness than any other in the wide world, can as swiftly restore him to his natural shape.'

'Ah then, sir,' replied the maid, 'it is very certain that my father will wish to bear witness to your kindness with any small gift that is in our power. For, as he well knows, it was not by any design but his own that he ate of the little green apple of enchantment. I pray you, sir, moreover, to forgive me for first stealing that apple, and also the marvellous golden ball, *and* the silken cord from out of the air.'

The juggler turned and gazed strangely at Myfanwy. 'There is only one thing I desire in all this starry universe,' he answered. 'But I ask it not of *him*—for it is not of his giving. It is for your own forgiveness, lady.'

'*I* forgive you!' she cried. 'Alas, my poor father!'

But even as she spoke a faint smile was on her face, and her eyes wandered to the animal standing a few paces beyond the margin of the glow cast by the watch-fire, sniffing the night air the while, and twitching dismally the coarse grey mane behind his ears. For now that her father was so near his deliverance her young heart grew entirely happy again, and the future seemed as sweet with promise as wild flowers in May.

Without further word the juggler drew from out of his pouch, as if he always carried about with him a little privy store of vegetables, a fine, tapering, ripe, red carrot.

'This, lady,' said he, 'is my only wizardry. I make no bargain. My love for you will never languish, even if I never more again refresh my sleepless eye with the vision of your presence in this solitary glade. Let your noble father the Lord of Eggleyseg draw near without distrust. There is but little difference, it might be imagined, between a wild apple and a carrot. But then, when all is said, there is little difference in the long sun between any living thing and another in this strange world. There are creatures in the world whose destiny it is in spite of their gentleness and humility and lowly duty and obedience to go upon four legs and to be in service of masters who deserve far less than *they* deserve, while there are men in high places of whom the reverse might truly be said. It is a mystery beyond my unravelling. But now all I ask is that you bid the ass who you tell me is hearkening at this moment to all that passes between us to nibble of this humble but useful and wholesome root. It will instantly restore him to his proper shape. Meanwhile, if you bid, I will myself be gone.'

Without further speech between them, Myfanwy accepted the magic carrot, and returned once more to the ass.

'Dear father,' she cried softly, 'here is a root that seems to be only a carrot; yet nibble of it and you will be at once restored, and will forget you were ever an— as you are. For many days to come, I fear, you will not wish to look upon the daughter that has been the unwilling cause of this night's woeful experience. There lives, as I have been told, in a little green arbour of the forest yonder, a hermit. This young magician will, I am truly certain, place me in his care a while until all griefs are forgotten between us. You will of your kindness consent, dear father, will you not?' she pleaded.

A long prodigious bray resounded dolefully in the hollows of the far-spread forest's dells and thickets. The Lord of Eggleyseg had spoken.

'Indeed, father,' smiled Myfanwy, 'I have never before heard you say "Yes" so heartily. What further speech is needed?'

Whereupon the ass, with more dispatch than gratitude, munched up the carrot, and in a few hours Owen ap Gwythock, once more restored to his former, though hardly his more appropriate shape, returned in safety to his Castle. There for many a day he mourned his woeful solitude, but learned, too, not only how true and faithful a daughter he had used so ill, but the folly of a love that is fenced about with mistrust and suspicion and is poisoned with jealousy.

And when May was come again, a prince, no longer in the disguise of a wandering juggler, drew near with his adored Myfanwy to the Lord of Eggleyseg's ancient castle. And Owen ap Gwythock, a little older but a far wiser man, greeted them with such rejoicings and entertainment, with such feastings and dancing and minstrelsy and jubilations as had never been heard of before. Indeed he would have been ass unadulterated if he had done else.

THE DUTCH CHEESE

Once—once upon a time there lived, with his sister Griselda, in a little cottage near the Great Forest, a young farmer whose name was John. Brother and sister, they lived alone, except for their sheep-dog, Sly, their flock of sheep, the numberless birds of the forest, and the 'fairies.' John loved his sister beyond telling; he loved Sly; and he delighted to listen to the birds singing at twilight round the darkening margin of the forest. But he feared and hated the fairies. And, having a very stubborn heart, the more he feared, the more he hated them; and the more he hated them, the more they pestered him.

Now these were a tribe of fairies, sly, small, gay-hearted and mischievous, and not of the race of fairies noble, silent, beautiful and remote from man. They were a sort of gipsy-fairies, very nimble and of aery and prankish company, and partly for mischief and partly for love of her they were always trying to charm John's dear sister Griselda away, with their music and fruits and trickery. He more than half believed it was they who years ago had decoyed into the forest not only his poor old father, who had gone out faggot-cutting in his sheepskin hat with his ass; but his mother too, who soon after had gone out to look for him.

But fairies, even of this small tribe, hate no man. They mocked him and mischiefed him; they spilt his milk, rode astraddle on his rams, garlanded his old ewes with sow-thistle and briony, sprinkled water on his kindling wood, loosed his bucket into the well, and hid his great leather shoes. But all this they did, not for hate—for they came and went like evening moths about Griselda—but because in his fear and fury he shut up his sister from them, and because he was sullen and stupid. Yet he did nothing but fret himself. He set traps for them, and caught starlings; he fired his blunderbuss at them under the moon, and scared his sheep; he set dishes of sour milk in their way, and sticky leaves and brambles where their rings were green in the meadows; but all to no purpose. When at dusk, too, he heard their faint, elfin music, he would sit in the door blowing into his father's great bassoon till the black forest re-echoed with its sad, solemn, wooden voice. But that was of no help either. At last he grew so surly that he made Griselda utterly miserable. Her cheeks lost their scarlet and her eyes their sparkling. Then the fairies began to plague John in earnest—lest their lovely, loved child of man, Griselda, should die.

Now one summer's evening—and most nights are cold in the Great Forest—John, having put away his mournful bassoon and bolted the door, was squatting, moody and gloomy, with Griselda, on his hearth beside the fire. And he leaned back his great hairy head and stared straight up the chimney to where high in the heavens glittered a host of stars. And suddenly, while

he lolled there on his stool moodily watching them
there appeared against the dark sky a mischievous elv-
ish head secretly peeping down at him; and busy fingers
began sprinkling dew on his wide upturned face. He
heard the laughter too of the fairies miching and gam-
bolling on his thatch, and in a rage he started up, seized
a round Dutch cheese that lay on a platter, and with all
his force threw it clean and straight up the sooty chimney at the faces of mockery clustered above. And after
that, though Griselda sighed at her spinning wheel, he
heard no more. Even the cricket that had been whistling all through the evening fell silent, and John supped
on his black bread and onions alone.

Next day Griselda woke at dawn and put her head
out of the little window beneath the thatch, and the day
was white with mist.

"Twill be another hot day,' she said to herself, comb-
ing her beautiful hair.

But when John went down, so white and dense with
mist were the fields, that even the green borders of the
forest were invisible, and the whiteness went to the sky.
Swathing and wreathing itself, opal and white as milk,
all the morning the mist grew thicker and thicker about
the little house. When John went out about nine o'clock
to peer about him, nothing was to be seen at all. He
could hear his sheep bleating, the kettle singing, Griselda sweeping, but straight up above him hung only,
like a small round fruit, a little cheese-red beamless sun
—straight up above him, though the hands of the clock
were not yet come to ten. He clenched his fists and
stamped in sheer rage. But no one answered him, no
voice mocked him but his own. For when these idle,

mischievous fairies have played a trick on an enemy they soon weary of it.

All day long that little sullen lantern burned above the mist, sometimes red, so that the white mist was dyed to amber, and sometimes milky pale. The trees dripped water from every leaf. Every flower asleep in the garden was neckleted with beads; and nothing but a drenched old forest crow visited the lonely cottage that afternoon to cry: 'Kah, Kah, Kah!' and fly away.

But Griselda knew her brother's mood too well to speak of it, or to complain. And she sang on gaily in the house, though she was more sorrowful than ever.

Next day John went out to tend his flocks. And wherever he went the red sun seemed to follow. When at last he found his sheep they were drenched with the clinging mist and were huddled together in dismay. And when they saw him it seemed that they cried out with one unanimous bleating voice:

'O ma-a-a-ster!'

And he stood counting them. And a little apart from the rest stood his old ram Soll, with a face as black as soot; and there, perched on his back, impish and sharp and scarlet, rode and tossed and sang just such another fairy as had mocked John from the chimney-top. A fire seemed to break out in his body, and, picking up a handful of stones, he rushed at Soll through the flock. They scattered, bleating, out into the mist. And the fairy, all-acockahoop on the old ram's back, took its small ears between finger and thumb, and as fast as John ran, so fast jogged Soll, till all the young farmer's stones were thrown, and he found himself alone in a quagmire so sticky and befogged that it took him till

afternoon to grope his way out. And only Griselda's singing over her broth-pot guided him at last home.

Next day he sought his sheep far and wide, but not one could he find. To and fro he wandered, shouting and calling and whistling to Sly, till, heartsick and thirsty, they were both wearied out. Yet bleatings seemed to fill the air, and a faint, beautiful bell tolled on out of the mist; and John knew the fairies had hidden his sheep, and he hated them more then ever.

After that he went no more into the fields, brightly green beneath the enchanted mist. He sat and sulked, staring out of the door at the dim forests far away, glimmering faintly red beneath the small red sun. Griselda could not sing any more, she was too tired and hungry. And just before twilight she went out and gathered the last few pods of peas from the garden for their supper.

And while she was shelling them, John, within doors in the cottage, heard again the tiny timbrels and the distant horns, and the odd, clear, grasshopper voices calling and calling her, and he knew in his heart that, unless he relented and made friends with the fairies, Griselda would surely one day run away to them and leave him forlorn. He scratched his great head, and gnawed his broad thumb. They had taken his father, they had taken his mother, they might take his sister—but he *wouldn't* give in.

So he shouted, and Griselda in fear and trembling came in out of the garden with her basket and basin and sat down in the gloaming to finish shelling her peas.

And as the shadows thickened and the stars began to shine, the malevolent singing came nearer, and presently there was a groping and stirring in the thatch, a tapping at the window, and John knew the fairies had come—not alone, not one or two or three, but in their company and bands—to plague him, and to entice away Griselda. He shut his mouth and stopped up his ears with his fingers, but when, with great staring eyes, he saw them capering like bubbles in a glass, like flames along straw, on his very doorstep, he could contain himself no longer. He caught up Griselda's bowl and flung it—peas, water and all—full in the snickering faces of the Little Folk! There came a shrill, faint twitter of laughter, a scampering of feet, and then all again was utterly still.

Griselda tried in vain to keep back her tears. She put her arms round John's neck and hid her face in his sleeve.

'Let me go!' she said, 'let me go, John, just a day and

a night, and I'll come back to you. They are angry with us. But they love me; and if I sit on the hillside under the boughs of the trees beside the pool and listen to their music just a little while, they will make the sun shine again and drive back the flocks, and we shall be as happy as ever. Look at poor Sly, John dear, he is hungrier even than I am.' John heard only the mocking laughter and the tap-tapping and the rustling and crying of the fairies, and he wouldn't let his sister go.

And it began to be marvellously dark and still in the cottage. No stars moved across the casement, no water-drops glittered in the candleshine. John could hear only one low, faint, unceasing stir and rustling all around him. So utterly dark and still it was that even Sly woke from his hungry dreams and gazed up into his mistress's face and whined.

They went to bed; but still, all night long, while John lay tossing on his mattress, the rustling never ceased. The old kitchen clock ticked on and on, but there came no hint of dawn. All was pitch-black and now all was utterly silent. There wasn't a whisper, not a creak, not a sigh of air, not a footfall of mouse, not a flutter of moth, not a settling of dust to be heard at all. Only desolate silence. And John at last could endure his fears and suspicions no longer. He got out of bed and stared from his square casement. He could see nothing. He tried to thrust it open; it would not move. He went downstairs and unbarred the door and looked out. He saw, as it were, a deep, clear, green shade, from behind which the songs of the birds rose faint as in a dream.

And then he sighed like a grampus and sat down, and knew that the fairies had beaten him. Like Jack's beanstalk, in one night had grown up a dense wall of peas. He pushed and pulled and hacked with his axe, and kicked with his shoes, and buffeted with his blunderbuss. But it was all in vain. He sat down once more in his chair beside the hearth and covered his face with his hands. And at last Griselda, too, awoke, and came down with her candle. And she comforted her brother, and told him if he would do what she bade she would soon make all right again. And he promised her.

So with a scarf she bound tight his hands behind him; and with a rope she bound his feet together, so that he could neither run nor throw stones, peas or cheeses. She bound his eyes and ears and mouth with a napkin, so that he could neither see, hear, smell, nor cry out. And, that done, she pushed and pulled him like a great bundle, and at last rolled him out of sight into the chimney-corner against the wall. Then she took a small sharp pair of needlework scissors that her godmother had given her, and snipped and snipped, till at last there came a little hole in the thick green hedge of peas. And putting her mouth there she called softly through the little hole. And the fairies drew near the doorstep and nodded and nodded and listened.

And then and there Griselda made a bargain with them for the forgiveness of John—a lock of her golden hair; seven dishes of ewes milk; three and thirty bunches of currants, red, white and black; a bag of thistledown; three handkerchiefs full of lambs' wool; nine jars of honey; a peppercorn of spice. All these (except the hair) John was to bring himself to their secret places as soon as he was able. Above all, the bargain between them was that Griselda would sit one full hour

each evening of summer on the hillside in the shadow and greenness that slope down from the great forest towards the valley, where the fairies' mounds are, and where their tiny brindled cattle graze.

Her brother lay blind and deaf and dumb as a log of wood. She promised everything.

And then, instead of a rustling and a creeping, there came a rending and a crashing. Instead of green shade, light of amber; then white. And as the thick hedge withered and shrank, and the merry and furious dancing sun scorched and scorched and scorched, there came, above the singing of the birds, the bleatings of sheep— and behold sooty Soll and hungry Sly met square upon the doorstep; and all John's sheep shone white as hoarfrost on his pastures; and every lamb was garlanded with pimpernel and eyebright; and the old fat ewes stood still, with saddles of moss; and their laughing riders sat and saw Griselda standing in the doorway in her beautiful yellow hair.

As for John, tied up like a sack in the chimney-corner, down came his cheese again crash upon his head, and, not being able to say anything, he said nothing.

DICK AND THE BEANSTALK

*In the county of Gloucester-*shire there lived with his father, who was a farmer, a boy called Dick. Their farm was not one of the biggest of the Gloucestershire farms thereabouts. It was of the middle size, between large and small. But the old house had stood there, quiet and peaceful, for at least two hundred years, and it was built of sound Cotswold stone. It had fine chimney stacks and a great roof. From his window under one of its gables Dick looked out across its ploughland and meadows to distant hills, while nearer at hand its barns, stables and pigsties clustered around it, like chicks round a hen.

Dick was an only son and had no mother. His father —chiefly for company's sake—had never sent him to school. But being a boy pretty quick in his wits, Dick had all but taught himself, with his father's help, to read and write and figure a little. And, by keeping his eyes and his ears open wherever he went, by asking questions and, if need be, finding out the answers for himself, he had learned a good deal else besides.

When he was a child he had been sung all the old rhymes and told most of the country tales of those parts by his mother, and by an old woman who came to the farm when there was sewing to be done, sheets to be hemmed, or shirts to be made. She was a deaf, poring old woman, but very skilful with her needle; and he never wearied of listening to the tales she told him; though at times, and particularly on dark windy nights in the winter, he would at last creep off rather anxious and shuddering to bed.

These tales not only stayed in Dick's head, but *lived* there. He not only remembered them, but thought about them; and he sometimes dreamed about them. He not only knew almost by heart what they told, but would please himself by fancying what else had happened to the people in them after the tales were over or before they had begun. He could not only find his way about in a story-book, chapter by chapter, page by page, but if it told only about the inside of a house he would begin to wonder what its garden was like—and in imagination would find his way out into it and then perhaps try to explore even further. It was in this way, for example, that Dick had come to his own conclusions on which finger Aladdin wore his ring, and the colour of his uncle the Magician's eyes; on what too at last had happened to the old Fairy Woman in *The Sleeping Beauty*. After, that is, she had ridden off on her white ass into the forest when the magic spindle had begun to spread the deathly slumber over her enemies that was not to be broken for a hundred years. *He* knew why she didn't afterwards come to the Wedding!

And as for Blue-beard's stone-turreted and many-windowed castle, with its chestnut gallery to the east, and its muddy moat with its carp, under the cypresses,

Dick knew a good deal more about *that* than ever Fatima did! So again, if he found out that Old Mother Hubbard had a *cat,* he could tell you the cat's name. And he could describe the crown that Molly Whuppie was crowned with when she became Queen, even to its last emerald. He was what is called a *lively* reader.

Dick often wished he had been born the youngest of three brothers, for then he would have gone out into the world early to seek his fortune. And in a few years, and after many adventures, he would have come back again, his pockets crammed with money, a magic Table on his back or a Cap of Invisibility in his pocket, and lived happily with his father ever afterwards. He had long been certain too that if only he could spruce up his courage and be off if but a little way, even if only into one of the next counties, Warwickshire or Wiltshire, Monmouthshire or Somerset, adventures would be sure to come. He itched to try his luck.

But there was a hindrance. His father would hardly let him out of his sight. And this was natural. Poor man, he had no daughters, so Dick was his only child as well as his only son. And his mother was dead. Apart then from his farm, the farmer had but one thought in the world—Dick himself. Still, he would at times give him leave to jog off alone to the nearest market town on an errand or two. And going alone for Dick was not the same thing as *not* going alone.

Sometimes Dick went further. He had an uncle, a very fat man, who was a mason at Moreton-in-the-Marsh, and an old widowed aunt who had a windmill and seven cats at Stow-on-the-Wold. He would visit *them.* He had also been to the Saffron Fair at Cirencester; and had stayed till the lights came out and the flares of the gingerbread stalls and Merry-go-rounds. But as for the great cities of Gloucestershire—Gloucester itself, or Bristol; or further still, Exeter, or further the other way, London (where his old friend and namesake Dick Whittington had been Lord Mayor three-and-a-half times)—Dick had never walked the streets of any of them, except in his story-books or in dreams. However, those who wait long enough seldom wait in vain.

On his next birthday after the one on which he had gone to the Saffron Fair, his father bought him for a birthday present a rough-coated pony. It was hog-maned—short and bristly; it was docktailed, stood about eleven hands high, and was called Jock. His father gave Dick leave to ride about the country when his morning's work was done, 'just to see the world a bit,' as he said, and to learn to fend for himself. And it was a bargain and promise between them that unless any mischance or uncommon piece of good fortune should keep him late, Dick would always be home again before night came down. Great talks of the afternoon's and evening's doings the two of them would have over their supper together in the farmhouse kitchen. His father began to look forward to them as much as Dick looked forward to them himself. Very good friends they were together, Dick and his father.

Now one winter morning—in the middle of January—of the next year, Dick asked leave of his father to have the next whole fine day all to himself. The weather had been frosty, the evening skies a fine shepherd's red, and everything promised well. He told his father he

wanted to press on further afield than he had before—
'beyond those hills over there.' And as the days were
now short, he must be off early, since there were few
hours after noon before dark. His father gave him
leave, but warned him to be careful of what company
he got into and against any folly or foolhardiness.
'Don't run into mischief, my son,' he said, 'nor let mischief run into you!' Dick laughed and promised.

Next day, before dawn, while still the stars were shining, he got up, put on his clothes, crept downstairs, ate
a hurried breakfast and cut himself off a hunch of
bread and meat in the larder to put in his pocket. Then
he scribbled a few lines to his father to tell him that he
had gone, pinned the paper to the kitchen table, and
having saddled up his pony set out due north-west into
the morning.

There had been a very sharp frost during the night.
It was as though a gigantic miller had stalked over the
fields scattering his meal as he went. The farm ruts
were hard and sharp as stone, and, as they jogged
along, Jock's hoofs splintered the frozen puddles lying
between them as if they were fine thin glass. Soon the
sun rose, clear as a furnace, though with so little heat
yet that its beams were not strong enough even to melt
the rime that lay in the hollows and under the woods.

Now on the Friday before this, Dick had come to a
valley between two round hills, and had looked out beyond it. But it had been too late in the day to go further.
He reached this valley again about ten o'clock of the
morning, and pushed on, trotting steadily along between its wooded slopes, following a faint overgrown
grass-track until at last the track died away, and he

came out on the other side. Here was much emptier, flatter country, though not many miles distant snow-topped hills began again. These hills were strange to him, and he had no notion where he was.

The unploughed fields were larger here than any he was accustomed to, and were overgrown with weeds. In these a multitude of winter birds were feeding. The hedges were ragged and untended, and there was not a house to be seen. Dick got off Jock's back and took out his lunch. Uncommonly good it tasted in the sharp cold air. And as he ate—sitting on a green knoll in the thin pale sunshine—he looked about him. And he saw a long way off what at first sight he took to be a column of smoke mounting up into the sky. He watched it awhile, marvelling. But there was no show of fire or of motion in it. It hung still and glimmering between the frosty earth and the blue of space. If not smoke, what could it be? Dick pondered in vain.

Having hastily finished his bread and meat, and feeling much the better for it, he mounted again and set off as fast as Jock could carry him in its direction. About three o'clock in the afternoon he drew near. And he found himself at last in a hollow where was an old tumbledown cottage, its thatch broken, its chimney fallen, its garden run wild. And growing within a few paces of this old cottage—towering up high above it, its top beyond view—was a huge withered tangle of what looked like a coarse kind of withy-wind or creeper. It went twisting and writhing corkscrew-fashion straight up into the air and so out of sight. Dick could not guess how far, because the sunlight so dazzled his eyes. But when he examined this great growth closely, and its gigantic pods of dried-up seeds as big as large kidney-shaped pebble-stones that still clung to its stem, he decided that it must be beans.

Never had he seen anything to match these beans. Who could have planted them, and when, and for what purpose? And where was he gone to? And then, in a flash, Dick realised at last where he himself *was*, and what he was looking at. There could be no doubt in the world. This was *Jack's* old cottage. This was where Jack had lived with his mother—before he met the friendly butcher on his way to market. And this huge tangled ladder here—which must have sprung up again as mighty as ever after Jack had cut it down and the Giant had fallen headlong—was Jack's famous Beanstalk.

Poor old woman, thought Dick. Jack's mother must be dead and gone ages and ages ago. And Jack too. He spied through the broken wall where a window had been. The hearth was full of old nettles. The thatch was riddled with abandoned bird-nests and rat-holes. There was not a sound in earth or sky; nor any trace of human being. He sat down on a hummock in the sun not far from the walls, and once more gazed up at the Beanstalk; and down again; and in his mind Dick went through all Jack's strange adventures. He knew them by heart.

The turf at his foot had been nibbled close by rabbits. His seat, though smooth, was freckled with tiny holes, and it rounded up out of the turf like a huge grey stone. Near at hand, ivy and bramble had grown over it, but there showed another smaller hummock in the turf about three or four paces away. And as he eyed it he suddenly realised that he must be sitting on the big knuckle end of one of Jack's Giant's larger bones, probably his thigh bone, now partly sunken and buried and hidden in the ground. At thought of this he sprang to his feet again, and glanced sharply about him. Where, he wondered, lay the Giant's skull. Then he took another long look at the vast faded Beanstalk, and another at the bone. It was still early afternoon, but it was winter; and at about four o'clock, he reckoned, the sun would be set.

The more Dick looked at the Beanstalk, the more he itched to climb it—even if he got only as high as the cottage chimney. Farther up, much father up, he would be able to see for miles. And still farther, he might even, if his sight carried, catch a glimpse of Old Bowley—a lofty hill which on days when rain was coming he could see from his bedroom window.

And he began arguing with himself: 'Now, surely, my father would never forgive me if he heard that I had actually discovered Jack's Beanstalk, and had come away again without daring to climb an inch of it!' And his other self answered him: 'Aye, that's all very well, my friend! But an inch, if it bears you, will be as good as a mile. What of *that?*"

What of *that?* thought Dick. He went close and tugged with all his might at the tangle of stalks. A few hollow cockled-up bean seeds peppered down from out of their dry shucks. He ducked his head. Once more he tugged; the stalks were tough as leather. And he began to climb.

But he made slow progress. The harsh withered strands of the bean-vines not only cut into his hands but were crusted over with rime, and his hands and feet were soon numb with cold. He stayed breathless and panting, not venturing yet to look down. On he went, and after perhaps a full hour's steady climbing, he stayed again and gazed about him. And a marvellous scene now met his eyes. His head swam with the strangeness of it.

Low in the heavens hung the red globe of the sun, and beneath him lay the vast saucer of the world. And there, sure enough, was Old Bowley! Jack's cottage seemingly no bigger than a doll's house showed plumb under his feet. And an inch or so away from it stood Jock, no bigger than a mole, cropping the grass in Jack's mother's garden.

Having come so high, Dick could not resist climbing higher. So on he went. Bruised with the beans that continually rattled down on him, breathless and smoking hot though powdered white with hoarfrost, at last he reached the top of the Beanstalk. There he sat down to rest. He found himself in a country of low, smooth, but very wide hills and of wide gentle valleys. Here too a thin snow had fallen. In this clear blue light it looked much more like the strange kind of place he had sometimes explored in his dreams than anything he had ever seen down below. And, far, far to the north, rising dark and lowering in the distance above the blur and pallor of snow, showed the turrets of a Castle. Dick watched that Castle; and the longer he watched it, the less he liked the look of it.

Still, where Jack had led, Dick soon decided to follow. And best be quick! Thinking no more whether or not he would be able to get home that night, and believing his father would forgive him for not this time keeping to the bargain between them, since it was certain Dick would have plenty to tell him in the morning, he set off towards the Castle as fast as he could trudge. The frozen snow was scarcely an inch deep, but it was numbing cold up here in this high country; and the crystals being dry and powdery he could not get along fast.

Indeed, Dick did not reach the great Castle's gates under their cavernous, echoing, stone archway until a three-quarters moon had risen bright behind him. It shone with a dazzling lustre over the snow—on the square-headed iron nails in the gates, and on the grim bare walls of the Castle itself. A rusty bell-chain hung high over his head beside the gates. Dick stood there eyeing it, his heart thumping against his ribs as it had never thumped before. But having come so far he was ashamed to turn back. He gave a jump, clutched at the iron handle with both hands, and tugged with all his might.

He heard nothing, not a sound. But in a few minutes —and slow they seemed—a wicket that had been cut out of the timbers of the huge gate, turned on its hinges, and a leaden-faced woman, her head and shoulders muffled up in a shawl, and, to Dick's astonishment, only about nine feet high, looked out on him and asked him what he wanted.

Following Jack's example, Dick told her that he had lost his way—as indeed he had, though he had found Jack's! He said he was tired out and hungry, and afraid of perishing in the cold. He implored the woman to give him a drink of water and a crust of bread, and perhaps to let him warm himself if only for a few minutes by her fire. 'Else, ma'am,' he said, 'the only thing I can do is to lie down under the wall here and maybe die. I can go no further.'

Not the faintest change showed in the woman's long narrow bony face. She merely continued to peer down at him. Then she asked him his name. Dick told her his name, and at that her eyes sharpened as if she had expected it.

'Step out there into the moonlight a little,' she told him, 'so that I can see your face. So it's *Dick,* is it?' she repeated after him. ' "Dick"! And you have come begging, eh? I have heard that tale before. And how, pray, am I to tell that you aren't from the same place, wherever that may be, as that villainous *Jack* who came here years and years and years ago with just such a tale as you have told me, and then ran off, first with my great-grandfather's moneybags, then with his Little Hen, and last with his Harp? How am I to know *that?* Why!—from what I've heard—you look to me as like as two peas!'

Dick stared up in wonder into her face. Jack's Giant, he thought, could not have been nearly so far back as the story had made out if this woman was only his great-granddaughter. He himself would have guessed a round dozen of *greats* at least. It was a mystery.

'Jack?' he said, as if he were puzzled. 'And who was Jack, ma'am? There are so many Jacks where I come from. Nobody of mine. What became of him, then?'

'Ah,' said the woman, 'you may well ask that. If my great-grandfather had caught him he would have ground his bones to powder in his mortar, and made soup of what was left. He was in the flower of his age,

was my great-grandfather then, but he never came back. Never. And a kinder gentler soul never walked! *"And who was* JACK," says he!' she muttered to herself, and Dick little liked the sound of it.

'Well, I wonder!' said he, wishing he could hide his face from the glare of the moon. 'I mean, I wonder if your great-grandfather ever found his Harp again. Or his Little Hen either. There are plenty of hens where I come from. And harps too, as I have heard. It sounds a dreadful story, I mean; but what could that bad boy you mention have wanted with a harp?'

'Aye,' said the leaden-faced woman, blinking once but no more as she stared at him. 'What?'

'Anyhow,' said Dick, 'that must have been more years ago than I could count. And if I *were* Jack, ma'am, or even his great-grandson either, I couldn't be the size I am now. I should have grown a grey beard as long as your arm, and be dead and done with long ago. I am sorry about your great-grandfather. It is a sad story. And I don't know *what* end that Jack mustn't have come to. But if you would give me only a sip of water and a bit of bread and a warm by the fire, I wouldn't ask for *anything* more.'

'Nor did Jack, so they say,' said the woman sourly; and looked him over, top to toe again.

But she led him in none the less through the great gates of the Castle and down into the kitchen, where a fire was burning on the hearth. This kitchen, Dick reckoned, was about the size of (but not much bigger than) a little church. It was warm and cosy after the dark and cold. A shaded lamp stood burning on the table, and there were pewter candlesticks three feet high for fat tallow candles on the dresser. Dick looked covertly about him, while he stood warming his hands a few paces from the huge open hearth. Here, beside him, was the very cupboard in which in terror Jack had hidden himself. The shut oven door was like the door of a dungeon. Through a stone archway to the right of him he could spy out the copper. A chair stood beside the table. And on the table, as if waiting for somebody, was a tub-sized soup tureen. There was a bowl beside it, and a spoon to fit. And next the spoon was a hunch of bread of about the size of a quartern loaf. Even though he stood at some distance, it was only by craning his neck that Dick could spy out what was on the table.

He looked at all this with astonished eyes. He had fancied Jack's Giant's kitchen was a darker and gloomier place. But in Jack's day there was perhaps a fire less fierce burning in the hearth and no lamp alight; perhaps too in summer the shadows of the Castle walls hung coldly over its windows. Not that he felt very comfortable himself. Now that he had managed to get into the Castle, he began to be anxious as to what might happen to him before he could get out again. The ways and looks of this woman were not at all to his fancy and whoever was going to sup at that table might look even worse!

She had taken off her shawl now, and after rummaging in a high green cupboard had come back with a common-sized platter and an earthenware mug—mere dolls' china by comparison with the tureen on the table. She filled the mug with milk.

'Now get you up on to that stool,' she said to Dick,

bringing the mug and a platter of bread over to him. 'Sit you up there and eat and drink and warm yourself while you can. My husband will be home at any moment. Then you can tell him who you are, what you want, why you have come, and where from.'

Dick quaked in his shoes—not so much at the words, as at the woman's mouth when she said them. But he looked back at her as boldly as he dared, and climbed up on to the stool. There, clumsy mug in one hand and crust in the other, he set to on his bread and milk. It was pleasant enough, he thought to himself, to sit here in the warm eating his supper, though a scrape of butter would have helped. But what kind of dainty might not this woman's husband fancy for *his* when *he* came home!

So, as he sipped, he peeped about him for a way of escape. But except for the door that stood ajar, some great pots on the pot-board under the dresser, and a mouse's hole in the wainscot that was not much bigger than a fox's in a hedgerow, there was no crack or cranny to be seen. Besides, the woman was watching him as closely as a cat. And he decided that for the present it would be wiser to keep his eyes to himself, and to stay harmless where he was.

At last there came the sound of what Dick took for footsteps, from out of the back parts of the Castle. It was as if a man were pounding with a mallet on a tub. They came nearer. In a moment or two the kitchen door opened, and framed in the opening stood the woman's husband. Dick could not keep from squinting a little as he looked at him.

He guessed him to be about eighteen to twenty feet

high—not more. Apart from this, he was not, thought Dick, what you could call a fine or large-sized giant. He was lean and bony; his loose unbuttoned leather jacket hung slack from his shoulders; and his legs in his stockings were no thicker than large scaffolding poles. There was a long nose in his long pale face, and on either side of his flat hat dangled dingy straw-coloured hair, hanging down from the mop above it.

When his glance fell on Dick enjoying himself on his stool by the kitchen fire, his watery green-grey eyes looked as if they might drop at any moment from out of his head.

'Head and choker! what have we here, wife?' he said at last to the leaden-faced woman. 'What have we here! *Hm, hm.*'

Before she could answer, Dick spoke up as boldly as he knew how, and told the young giant (for though Dick could not be certain, he *looked* to be not above thirty)—he told the young giant how he had lost his way, and chancing on the withered Beanstalk had climbed to the top of it to have a look round him. He told him, too, how grieved he had been to hear that the woman's great-grandfather had never come back to the Castle after he had chased the boy called Jack away, and how much he wondered whether the Little Hen was buried, and what had become of the Harp. Dick went on talking because it was easier to do so than to keep silent, seeing that the two of them continued to stare at him, and in a far from friendly fashion.

'I expect it played its last tune,' he ended up, 'ages and ages before I was born.'

'Aye,' said the woman. 'That's all pretty enough. But

what *I* say is that unless the tale I have heard is all fable, this ugly imp here must be little short of the very spit of that wicked thief himself. Anywise, he looks to me as if he had come from the same place. What's more——' she turned on Dick, 'if you can tell us where that is, you shall take my husband there and show it him. And he can look for the grave of my great-grandfather. And perhaps,' and her thin dark lips went arch-shaped as she said it, 'perhaps if you find it, you shall learn to play a tune on his Harp!'

Dick, as has been said, liked neither the looks nor the sound of this woman. She was, he decided, as sly and perhaps as treacherous as a fox. 'I can show you where *I* came from easily enough,' he answered. 'But I know no more about Jack than I have—than I have heard.'

'Nor don't we,' said the woman. 'Well, well, well! When he has supped you shall take my husband the way you came, and we shall see what we *shall* see.'

Dick glanced at the giant, who all this while had been glinting at him out of his wide and almost colourless eyes. So, not knowing whether he followed his great-grandfather's habits, or how long his wife would remain with them, he thought it best to say no more. He smiled, first at one of them, and then at the other, took a sip of milk, and rank greasy goat's milk it was, and said, 'When you are ready, I am ready too.' The difficulty was to keep his tongue from showing how fast his heart was beating.

At this the giant sat down to table and began the supper his wife had prepared for him. Spoon in hand he noisily supped up his huge basin of soup, picking out gingerly with his fingers, and as greedily as a starling, the hot steaming lumps of meat in it. He ate like a grampus. His soup finished, he fell to work on what looked like a shepherd's pie that had been sizzling in the oven. Then having sliced off a great lump of greenish cheese, he washed it all down with what was in his mug. But whether wine, ale, cider, or water, Jack could not tell.

Having eaten his fill, the young giant sat back in his chair, as if to think his supper over. And soon he fell asleep. Not so did the woman. She had seated herself on the other side of the hearth in a great rocking-chair, a good deal closer to him than Dick fancied, and she had begun to knit. Like the clanking of fire-irons her needles sounded on and on in the kitchen, while the young giant his mouth wide open, now and again shuddered in his slumbers or began or ceased to snore. Whereas if Dick even so much as opened his mouth to yawn, or shifted his legs out of the blaze of the fire, the woman's slow heavy face turned round on him, and stared at him as if she had been made of stone.

At last, much to Dick's comfort, the young giant awoke and stretched himself. He seemed to be in a good humour after his nap, and not sulky or sharp as some people are. 'What *I* say,' he said with a laugh on seeing Dick again, 'what *I* say is, there's more than one kind of supper!'

'Ha, ha, ha!' echoed Dick, but not very merrily. The giant then fumbled for a great club of blackthorn that stood behind the kitchen door. He put on his flat hat again, wound a scarf of sheep's wool round his neck, and said he was ready. Never had Dick, inside a book or out, heard before of a giant that wore a scarf. He clambered down from his stool and stood waiting. Her hand over her mouth, and her narrow sallow face showing less friendly than ever, the woman took another long look at him. Then she turned to her husband, and looked him over too.

'Well, it's a cold night,' she said, 'but you will soon get warm walking, and won't need your sheepskins.' At mention of *cold* her husband stepped back and lifted the curtain that concealed the kitchen window. He screened his eyes with his hands and looked out.

'Cold!' he said. 'It's perishing. There's a moon like a lump of silver, and a frost like iron. Besides,' he grumbled, 'a nap's no sleep, and I don't stir a step until the morning.'

The two of them wrangled together for a while and Dick listened. But at last after drawing iron bars across the shutters and locking him in, leaving him nothing to make him comfortable, and only the flames of the fire for company, they left him—as Dick hoped, for good. But presently after, the woman came back again, dangling a chain in her hand.

'So and *so!*' she said, snapping together the ring at the end of it on his ankle. 'There! That kept safe my old Poll parrot for many a year, so it may keep even *you* safe until daybreak!'

She stooped to fix the other end of the chain round a leg of the great table. Then, 'Take what sleep you can, young man,' she said, 'while you can, and as best you can. You'll need all your wits in the morning.'

Her footsteps died away. But long afterwards Dick could hear the voices of the two of them, the giant and his wife, mumbling on out of the depths of the night overhead, though he himself had other things to think about. After striving in vain to free his leg from the ring of the chain, he examined as best he could with the help of his stool the locks and bolts of the shutters over the windows—stout oak or solid iron every one of them. He reckoned the walls of this kitchen must be twelve feet thick at least and the bolts were to match.

And while more and more anxiously he was still in search of a way out, he heard a sudden scuffling behind him, and a squeak as shrill as a bugle. He turned in a flash, and in the glow of the fire saw what he took to be a mouse that had come out of its hole, though it was an animal of queer shape, lean and dark, and half as large again as a full-sized English rat. Next moment, a score or more of these creatures had crept out of the wainscot. They gambolled about on the kitchen floor, disporting themselves and looking for supper.

By good fortune, when the squeak sounded, Dick had been standing on his stool by the window. He held his breath at sight of them, and perhaps had held it too long, or the giant's pepper had got into his nose, for he suddenly sneezed. At which a jubilee indeed went up in the kitchen. And if, in spite of his chain, by a prodigious leap from the stool to the table he had not managed to land on it safely, it might well have been the last of him. Luckily too, the margins of the table jutted out far beyond its legs, so that though the sharp-nosed hungry animals scrabbled up the legs in hopes to get him, they could climb no further.

Now and again, squatting there, through the long hours that followed—half-hidden between the giant's tureen and mug—Dick drowsed off, in spite of these greedy noisy rodents, and in spite too of the crickets in the outer cracks of the oven, which kept up a continuous din like a covey of willow-wrens. He was pestered also by the cunning and curiosity of a wakeful housefly, though others like it, straddling as big as cockroaches on the walls in the dusky light of the fire, remained asleep. It must be a fusty airless place, Dick thought, that had flies in winter. And so he passed a sorry night.

It was five by the clock when the giant and his wife came down again, Grackel still grumbling, and she pressing him to be gone. At last he was ready. She looked him up and down. 'What's to be done is best done quickly,' she said to him. 'You can get breakfast at a tavern maybe. And leave your aunt's watch behind you, husband. It will be safer at home.'

The giant sullenly did as his wife had bidden, drew out of his pocket a fine gold watch, its back embedded with what looked to Dick like sapphires and emeralds and other precious stones, and laid it on the table.

'That looks a fine watch,' said Dick, shivering in his breeches, for he was stiff and cold.

'Aye, so it is,' said the woman, and she put it away on a shelf in the cupboard. 'Now look you here, Grackel,' she added, when they had all three come together to the gates of the Castle, 'if you are not home before sundown the day after to-morrow, I shall send for your uncles, and they shall come and look for you.'

Dick raised his hat to the woman as he left her there by the Castle gates, but there was so much mistrust of him in her eye that he feigned he had done so only in order to scratch his head, and he couldn't manage even to say the Good-day that was in his mouth.

So he and the giant went off together into the snow, shining white in the light of the moon. The moon was still far from her setting. But they had not gone much above a mile—one of Dick's miles—before the giant began to be impatient at the slow pace he had to move in order that Dick might keep up with him, even though for every stride *he* took Dick trotted three. So at last he stooped down in the snow and told Dick to climb up over his back on to his shoulders. Up went Dick like a cat up a tree, clutched on to his coarse yellow hair, and away they went.

Perched up on high like this, a good twenty feet above the snow, and tossing along on Grackel's shoulders, the giant's great bony hand clutched round his knees, Dick thought he had never seen a more magical sight than these strange hills and valleys sparkling cold and still in the glare of the moonlight. No, not even in his dreams. He might have been an Arab on the hump of his camel in the desert of Gobi.

It was easy for the giant to find his way. For though there were many prints of wild creatures and of long-clawed birds in the snow, Dick's footmarks were clearer than any. Now and then they passed a great clump of trees—their bare twigs brushing the starry sky—which looked like enormous faggots of kindling wood. And in less than a quarter of the time that Dick had spent on his journey to the Castle, they came to the top of the Beanstalk. And Dick shouted in the giant's ear that he wanted to be put down.

'Here we are,' he shouted, when he was on his own feet again. The giant in the last few minutes had been ambling on very warily as if he knew he was on dangerous ground. As soon as Dick had stamped life into his legs again, he pointed to the huge tangle of frosty bine and withy that jutted high above the edge of the abyss. 'See there!' he shouted at the top of his voice, in the sharp frosty air. 'That's the Beanstalk. Down *there* is where I come from. But I doubt if it will bear *you*.'

He almost laughed out loud to see with what caution Grackel crept out on hands and knees to peer out over the brink at the world below. But the giant could see nothing in the sombre shadow of the moon except the dried-up Beanstalk twisting and writhing down below him into space. 'Hm, hm,' he kept stupidly muttering.

And Dick understood at last how it was that the Beanstalk had never been discovered before. These giants, it seemed, were by nature a stupid race. So scared was Grackel at last at sight of the abyss that his teeth began to chatter like millstones, and his face was as white as a sheet. Dick rejoiced. It seemed he would never dare even to set foot on the Beanstalk.

Grackel peered round at him. 'So this,' he said, 'is where my great-grandad climbed down when he was chasing after that thief and vagabond Jack! I can't see to the bottom of it!'

Dick shook his head. 'No, nor, I suppose, could he! Though why you should be so fond of your *wife's* grandad I can't think!'

'Aye,' said the giant leering at him, 'and supposing she and I are first cousins and he was grandad to both, what then?'

'Well,' said Dick, 'I know nothing of that. But Jack or no Jack, this is not only the only way down I know, but it's the way I climbed *up*. Once, I suppose, it must have been green and fresh and full of sap. Now it's all dried-up and withered away. And every yard I climbed I supposed it would come tumbling down over my head.'

'Aye,' said the giant. 'But what did you want to come *for?*'

'Oh, just to see,' said Dick, as airily as he could. The giant with a sigh rose to his feet.

'Well,' he said, 'I'm not so weighty as was my great-grandad, not at least according to his portrait in the gallery. And if he managed to climb down in safety when this ladder was young and green, what is there to prevent my doing the same, now that it is old and tough and dry?'

With that, he thrust his long lean arm over the edge and, clutching the tangle of withered shoots, violently shook the Beanstalk. It trembled like a spider's web in all its fibres, and Dick could hear the parched seeds clattering down from out of their pods towards the earth below.

'Well,' said he, looking up at the giant in the moonlight, 'what may be, may be. My only fear is that once down there, you may find it impossible to get back again. Or supposing it breaks in the middle?'

Grackel stared into his face, and then at the snow. 'He's thinking of the Little Hen,' thought Dick to himself, 'and the Harp.'

'Yes, it would be a dreadful thing,' Dick repeated, 'if it broke in the middle.'

'Aye,' leered the giant, 'and so it would! But what about my great-grandad? It didn't break in the middle with him.' Dick made no answer to this. He held his peace.

'We'll have no more words about it,' said the giant. 'I'm never so stupid as when folks talk at me. You shall go first, being no more than an atomy, and I will follow after. I'll wait no longer.'

And with that, he flung his cudgel over the edge and began to pull up his wristbands. Dick listened in vain to hear the crash of the cudgel on the earth below. He feared for poor Jock.

There was no help in waiting. So Dick began to climb down the Beanstalk, and the giant followed after him so close with his lank scissor-legs that Dick had to keep dodging his head to avoid his great shoes, with their shining metal hooks instead of laces. Beanseeds came scampering down over Dick's head and shoulders like hailstones. It was lucky for him they were hollow and dry.

'Now,' said Dick at last, when they reached the bottom and he had seen the cudgel sticking up out of the ground beyond the broken wall. 'Here we are. This is where I come from. This is England. And *you* will want to be off at once to look for your great-grandfather's grave. Now that way is the way you should go. I go this. My father is expecting me and I must get home as soon as I can.'

It was so he hoped to slip away. But Grackel was at least too crafty for that. He stood leaning his sharp elbows on the broken roof of the cottage, leering down at Dick so steadily that he was mortally afraid the giant might notice the bulge of his great-grandad's leg-bone in the rabbit-nibbled turf of the garden.

'No, no, my young master,' said he at last. 'Fair and easy! Good friends keep together. You have had bite and sup in my house, now you shall give me bite and sup in yours. And it may be your father has heard of that Jack. The cackling of my great-grandad's Hen, let alone the strumming of his Harp, must have reached a long way among stubby hills in a little country like this! England!'

The rose and grey of daybreak was stirring in the eastern sky. Dick, though angry, reasoned with the giant as best he could, but the great oaf could not be dissuaded from keeping him company. It was bitter cold in this early morning, and Dick longed to let his father know that nothing was amiss with him.

'Well,' he said at last, 'I have told you nine times over that no travellers come this way. It is over there the big cities are.' And he pointed west. 'But if come you must, why come! And I can only hope my father will be pleased to see you.'

He put two fingers into his mouth and whistled. There came an answering whinny. And from a lean-to or out-house behind the cottage where it had found shelter during the night and a bite or two of old hay to munch, Jock answered his summons. This time Grackel had no reason to complain of Dick's lagging behind. Jock cantered away up the valley with his young master on his back, and the giant like a gallows strode on beside them.

When they came at length to a drift of woodland near the farm, Dick dismounted; and, having pointed out the chimneys of the farmhouse in the hollow below, he told the giant to hide himself among the trees, while he went to prepare his father for the guest he had brought home with him. So Grackel edged down as best he could among the trees, and Dick, leading Jock by his bridle, went on to the house.

In spite of the cold, the back door was ajar, and on an old horsehair sofa beside the burnt-out fire Dick found his father fast asleep, the stable lantern with which he had been out in the night looking for his son still burning beside him. Dick called him softly and touched his hand. His father stirred, muttering in his dreams; then his eyes opened. And at sight of Dick a light came into them as if he had found an unspeakable treasure.

Safely come home again, Dick was soon forgiven for being so long away. As quickly as he could he told his father his adventures. But when the farmer heard that the giant was actually in hiding not more than a quarter of a mile away from the house, and greedy for bed and board, he opened his eyes a good deal wider.

'Is that so?' he said at last. 'Twenty-foot in his shoes and all! Lorramussy! Well, well! And his great-grandad and all! That don't seem so *very* far back, now do it? Still, if there he is, my son, why, there he *is;* and we must do the best we can. And I don't see myself,' he added, glancing at Dick's troubled face, 'being what and where you were, you could have done much else. But who'd have guessed it, now? Who *would?* That Beanstalk!'

'The worst of all, father,' said Dick, 'is that woman up there. She'd freeze your blood even to look at her. What *she* wants is the Little Hen. And if *she* came down . . . !'

'Fox or vixen, one thing at a time, my son,' said the farmer. 'Your friend out in the cold, if we keep him waiting, may get restless. So we'll be off at once to see what we can do to keep him quiet. The other must come after.'

The shining of the wintry sun lay all over the frosty fields when they went back together to the giant. And sour and fretful they found him. He only scowled at the farmer's polite Good-morning, grumbled that he was famished and wanted breakfast. 'And plenty of it!' he muttered, leering at Dick.

The farmer eyed him up and down for the twentieth time, and wished more than ever that Dick could have persuaded him to stay in his own country. He liked neither his pasty peevish face nor his manners. And his blood boiled to think of Dick tied up like a monkey to the leg of a table. Still, it had always been the farmer's rule in life to make the best of a bad job. With worry, what's wrong waxes worse, he would say. So he decided then and there to lodge the giant for the time being in his great barn; and to keep him in a good temper with plenty of victuals. The sooner they could pack him off the better. But they must be cautious.

So Dick and his father led the giant off to the barn, the sheep-dogs following behind them. They threw open the wide double doors, and stooping low, Grackel went in and stretched his long shins in the hay at the other end of it. After which they shut-to the doors again and hastened off to the farm to fetch him breakfast.

By good chance there was not only a side of green bacon but a cold roast leg of mutton in the larder that had been prepared for dinner the day before, though then the farmer had no stomach for it. With this, a tub of porridge, half a dozen loaves of bread, a basketful of boiled hens' eggs and a couple of buckets of tea, they went back to the barn. Two or three journeys the giant gave them before he licked the last taste out of his last broken honey-pot, wiped his mouth with the back of his hand, and said he had had enough. Indeed, he had gorged himself silly.

'My son tells me', bawled the farmer, 'that you have had a broken night. *His* friends are *my* friends. Maybe you'd enjoy a nap in the hay now. Make yourself easy; we'll be back anon.'

They closed behind them the great doors of the barn again, and went off themselves to breakfast, staying their talk and munching every now and again to listen to what sounded like distant thunder, but which, Dick explained to his father, was only the giant's snoring.

For the next day or two their guest was good-humoured and easy-going enough but, like some conceited people far less than half his size, he was by nature both crafty *and* stupid. And since he had now found himself in lodgings where he had nothing to do, no wife to make him mind and keep him busy, and he could eat and guzzle and sleep and idle the whole day long, he had little wish to be off in search of his great-grandfather, and none to go home again.

He knew well, the cunning creature, that even if his wife sent out his uncles in search of him and they discovered the Beanstalk, neither of them would venture to set foot on it. It would be certain death! For these were ordinary-sized giants, while he himself was laughed at in his own country for a weakling and nick-named Pygmy Grackel. But this Dick did not know till afterwards.

When evening came, and the farm hands had gone home from their work, Grackel would take a walk in the fields, though Dick's father, after once accompanying him, did not do so again. He had kept the great bumpkin out of the meadows and the turnips because it was lambing season. But it enraged him to see Grackel's clod-hopper footprints in his winter wheat, and the ricks in his stackyard ruined by Grackel's leaning upon them to rest. And it enraged him even more when the giant crept up to the farmhouse one midnight to stare in at him as he lay in his bed, and kicked over the water-butt on his way. The great lubber grew more and more mischievous.

In less than a week both Dick and his father were at their wits' end to know what to do with their guest. The good woman who cooked for them had to toil continually the best part of the day to prepare his food. A couple of ducks and three or four fat hens he accounted no more than a snack; he would gollop up half a roasted sheep for supper and ask for more. Indeed his appetite was far beyond his size, and he seemed to think of nothing but his belly.

Apart from this too, and the good home-brewed ale and cider they had to waste on him, he lay on their minds like a thunder cloud. And when he had eaten and guzzled to gluttony, as like as not he would grow sulky and malicious. He could do more damage in five minutes than an angry bull in half an hour. And when in a bad humour he would do it on purpose. Besides, tongues soon began to get busy about him in the villages round about. The shepherd complained that his lambs began to be missing; the ploughman's wife that her two small children had not been out of doors for a week. It was reported that the farmer had caught a cruel and ravenous ogre in his fields, and had chained him up in his barn. Some said it was not an ogre but a monster that trumpeted like an elephant and had claws like a bird.

Though the great doors of the barn were usually kept shut on the giant all day until dusk, and the farmer had stuffed up every hole he could find in its roof and timbers—and Grackel was as sensitive as any female to draughts—the roar of his snoring could be heard a full mile away, and when he laughed—which luckily was seldom—it was like a house falling down. At least so it seemed, though perhaps Dick made worse of it than was the truth. He had not yet seen Grackel's uncles.

There was at any rate no hope of keeping the giant a secret. For some reason too there was always a host of birds—rooks, daws, starlings and the like, hovering about the barn. The horses and cattle, and even the pigs, were never at peace while the giant was near; but pawing and lowing and neighing and wuffing the whole day long. And well any pig *might* wuff, since Grackel could devour him at a meal.

The result of all this was that the farmer would now often find strangers lurking in his fields. They had come in hope to get a glimpse of the giant. And whether they succeeded or not, talk of his size, his appetite, his strength and his fury spread far and wide. Worse even than this: two small urchins from a neighbouring village had managed by hiding themselves in a ditch until it was evening to creep up close to the barn and, peeping through a hole in the wood where a knot had fallen out, found themselves peering into the great staring still watery eye of the giant fixed on them as he lay in the hay on the other side. Cold as stone with terror, they had rushed away home to their mothers, been seized with fits, and one of them had nearly died.

Dick could hardly get a wink of sleep for thinking of the giant and how to be rid of him. To see the trouble and care in his father's kindly face filled him with remorse. He searched his story-books again and again but could find no help in them. Nor could he discover any advice, not a single word, about giants in *The Farmer's Friend* or *The Countryman's Companion*—books which belonged to his father.

On the next Sunday afternoon his father walked off to the vicarage, six miles away by the field paths, to ask the advice of the old parson. He was the most learned man the farmer knew. But though the old gentleman listened to him very attentively, and was sorry for the trouble he was in, his chief fear was that the giant might find his way to the church. Once in, how without damage could he be coaxed out again?

There were giants in days of old, he told the farmer, who lived for centuries; and at a hundred or more were as hale and lusty as an ordinary man of less than forty. One such in Carmarthenshire had stolen all the millstones for thirty miles around and amused himself by flinging them into the sea. There had been a dearth of meal for months. Giants can be as cunning as a fox, the parson told the farmer, and as surly as a bear, and are great gluttons. But this the farmer knew already.

At last, one night, a little less than a fortnight after

he had climbed the Beanstalk, having fallen asleep after hours of vain thinking, Dick suddenly woke up with so bright a notion in his head that it might have been whispered to him straight out of a dream.

There could be no waiting for the morning. He went off at once to his father's bedroom, woke him up, and, having made sure the giant was not listening at the window, shared it with him then and there. And the farmer thought almost as well of the notion as Dick did himself. They sat together there, Dick hooded up in a blanket at the foot of his father's bed, and for a full hour talked Dick's plan over. To and fro and up and down they discussed it, and could think of nothing better.

So as soon as light had begun to show next morning, Dick mounted his pony, and keeping him awhile on thick grass to muffle his hoofs, he galloped off by the way he had gone before.

This time he had brought with him an old pair of leathern pruning gloves and climbing irons, and he reached the top of the Beanstalk before noon. He arrived at the Castle gates while it was still full daylight. Till this moment all had gone well with him, though he had hated leaving his father alone to all the troubles of the day.

But now, as Dick was on the point of leaping up to clutch the rusty bell-chain, a distant bombilation fell on his ear—such a rumbling and bumbling as is made by huge puncheons of rum being rolled about over the hollow stones of a cellar. He had not listened long before he guessed this must be the voices of Grackel's uncles colloguing together. At sound of them he shook in his shoes. What was worse, they seemed to be in an ill humour. But whether it was anger or mere argument in their voices, there was nothing in the music of them that boded much good for Dick!

At last they ceased, and Dick (who was by now bitterly cold, for an icy wind was whiffling round the Castle walls) decided to give a tug at the bell only just strong enough for a single ding. He then hid himself behind a buttress of the wall. The woman presently looked out of the wicket in the great gates. And Dick, peeping, and seeing that she was alone, showed himself and came nearer.

'Aha,' she called at sight of him, 'so you have come back! Aye, and a fortnight late! And where, my fine young man, is my husband? Answer me that! *Grackel!*' she wailed aloud, as if beside herself, 'Where are you? Where *are* you, Grackel?'

'Not here, eh!' she went on, watching Dick out of her black eyes as closely as a cat a bird. 'So you have come back to . . .'—and with that she pounced on him. She gripped him by the slack of his coat, and stooped low over his face. 'Eh, eh, eh! So now I have you, my fine young man!' Her teeth chattered as she spoke. 'Step you in, and you shall see what you *shall* see!'

Dick had scarcely breath left to speak with. He thought his end was come at last. And then, suddenly, the woman drew back, let go of him, turned her head away and began to cry.

Then Dick knew that what had seemed only anger was chiefly grief, that she supposed her husband must be dead and would never come back to her. And he rejoiced. His plan was turning out even better than he had hoped for. As best he could he tried to comfort the poor woman. He took the long hand that hung down beside her, and assured her that her husband was in the best of health, better far then when he had started, and in such ease and comfort at his father's farm that nothing would persuade him to go on his travels in search of the Little Hen and the Harp, or induce him to come home again. 'It's no use your crying,' he said. 'That won't bring him back!'

At last the woman dried her eyes and began to listen to him. She took him into a little room this side of the kitchen, hung with smoked carcasses of beasts for the table, a room, which though cold, was secret.

'I kept on telling your husband,' Dick said, 'that he need but send you word that he is well, that he is comfortable. I thought of you, ma'am, and kept on. For though I haven't a wife myself, I know they want news of their husbands. So would my mother of my father, if she had not died when I was four. And perhaps she does even now. But your husband has grown fatter and won't stir out of the house even to take a little exercise. He eats and eats, and at mention of *home* only flies into a rage.

' "But," I said to him, "your wife will be weeping for you to come!" And all he answered was to bawl for another bucket of cider. So I came along by myself and am nearly dead-beat and starved with the cold.'

All this Dick said, and, it being chiefly lies, he said it much too boldly. But the woman was overjoyed at his news and believed him. Her one thought now was to get her husband home again, and to keep her wrath against him till then.

She told Dick she would go at once and wake her husband's uncles. 'They are taking a nap,' she said. Then he himself could go along with them, and they would soon persuade her husband to come home. 'And if he won't, they'll make him,' she said.

But this plan was by no means to Dick's liking. He asked the woman how long the giants would be sleeping and in what room they lay. 'I am too tired to talk to them just now,' he said, 'frozen. I couldn't bear the din they make. Leave them at peace awhile and take me into the kitchen, ma'am, else I shall soon perish of cold. Give me some food and a mug of milk, and I'll tell you a better plan—a far better plan—than that. But quietly!'

Now by good fortune the giants were napping in a room at the other end of the Castle where they were accustomed to play cards—*Dumps, Frogbite,* and other old games. And Dick sat up once more on his stool by the kitchen fire, and after refreshing himself, he explained to the woman his plan.

'What I want to say, ma'am, is this,' he said. And he told her that the people of his country were utterly weary of having her idle husband loafing about in their villages and doing nothing for his keep. 'Down there, we are all little like me,' he said, 'and though my father —who wouldn't hurt a fly—has done his utmost to put your husband at his ease, to feed him and keep him happy, it is all wasted. He has no more thanks in him than a flea.

'He wanders about, scares the women, frightens the children, steals from the shops, and shouts and sings at dead of night when all honest folk are asleep in their beds. And now the King's soldiers are coming, and as soon as they catch him, ma'am, they will drag him off to some great dismal underground dungeon, and he will never see daylight again. For little though we may be, there's a cage in my country that would hold nine or more giants together, and every one of them twice as big as your husband, and every one of them loaded groaning up with chains. You see, ma'am, we don't mean them any harm, but can't keep them safe else. So I came to tell you.' He took another slow sip of his greasy buttermilk, and glanced back into the fire.

'Then again,' he went on, 'if these two uncles of your husband's, who you say are big heavy men, ventured to go my way home, and that must be ten thousand feet from top to bottom, they would break every bone in their bodies. And even if they did climb safely down and came into my country, what good would that be to them? I agree, ma'am, that in mere size and shape they are much larger than we are where I come from. But for wits and quickness and cunning—why, they are no better than rabbits!

'Just think, ma'am, though I have no wish to hurt your feelings, with your husband gone and all, how a mere boy of my size and not much older, came sneaking again and again into this huge Castle of yours, and ran off with your great-grandad's treasures three times over without losing a hair of his head. I agree it was not fair dealings, between equals, as you might say. I agree that Jack borrowed the Harp without leave. But boy to giant, ma'am, *you* can't but agree he had his wits about him and was no coward.

'Besides, down there we have great cannon and what is called gunpowder, which would blow fifty giants to pieces before they could sneeze. I mean,' cried Dick, 'there would be a noise like that,' and he clapped his hands togather, 'and the next minute there wouldn't be a scrap of your husband's uncles to be seen. Except perhaps for a button here and there for a keepsake ten miles off. You must give me something to prove I have seen you.'

Dick spoke with such zest and earnestness that this poor woman began once more to be afraid that she would never see her husband again, alive or dead, for she dearly loved him even though he had given her his word of honour and not kept it. She would talk to him about that, all in good time.

'Now see here,' said Dick at last, 'your husband has been gobbling and guzzling so much that he is almost too stupid now to understand good sense when he hears it. It's true I could make a fortune out of him by leading him round from town to town and charging a piece of silver for every peep at him. But I haven't a heart as hard as that, ma'am; and if you want your husband back, there is only one thing to do.'

So after they had talked the matter over a little longer the woman fetched out from her bosom on a ribbon a locket in which was a twine of her husband's hair when he was a little boy. The hair though very coarse was almost as pale as gold. And in the back of the locket was a glass in which, said the woman, you could see your dearest friend. But she herself did not much believe in it, because when *she* looked into it she could see only herself.

So Dick peeped in, and there he saw what looked very much like his father. His cheeks grew red and he smiled into the locket; and his father seemed to give him a look back. 'And what,' Dick said to the woman, turning the locket over, 'what is this *milky* side for?'

'Oh, in that,' said the woman, 'you can see what you are dreaming about. But it's nothing but black dreams come to me.'

Dick looked; and sure enough, the milkiness cleared away in a moment, and he saw a tiny image there of Jack's Beanstalk, but fresh and green. He slipped the bauble into his jacket pocket and told the woman that it would do very well for a proof to her husband that he himself had seen and talked with her. 'For you see,' he said, 'if I had nothing to show him, he might not believe me.'

And the message the woman sent Grackel was that she had heard with joy he was happy in the place he had come to, that he must remember to behave himself, and that his uncles would not come out in search of him so long as she knew he was safe. All she desired was to have but one more glimpse of him, and that he should come back if but for one night, because a feast was preparing, the feast they had every year on his long-lost great-grandfather's birthday.

'He'll remember that,' the woman said to Dick. 'And tell him that his uncles and his nephew and his cousins and his neighbours and his friends from afar off will all be at the feast, and will never forgive him if he is absent. Tell him I haven't missed him so much as I thought I should. Tell him I cried a little when I thought he was dead, and laughed when I knew he was safe. If he thinks I don't much want him back, back he will come. If he settles for good in your country, I am a lost woman.'

'Ah,' said Dick, 'leave that to me. But what am I to have for my trouble?'

The woman offered him a bag of money. There it was in the cupboard.

'Too heavy,' said Dick.

She brought out her family's Seven-League boots.

Dick laughed. He could almost have gone to bed in one of them. She showed him her husband's drinking cup.

Dick laughed again. He said it was too big for a wash-basin and not big enough for a bath. 'Besides,' he said, 'it's only silver.'

At last the woman, as Dick hoped she would, remembered her husband's watch—the watch that had belonged to one of his aunts. This of course was but a little watch compared with the giant's father's watch, which was safe upstairs. Dick's mouth watered as he took hold of the chain and lifted the watch out of the woman's hand. What he had supposed were sapphires and emeralds were not common stones like these at all. There was a toadstone, a thunderstone, an Arabian crystal and a blagroon—though Dick didn't then know the names of them.

'But I had hoped,' he said, eyeing it and pretending to be disappointed, 'that it was not a mere pocket watch, but a watch with a little magic in it. I think perhaps, after all, I should get more money by taking your husband round to show him off at some of our country fairs. You see, as I keep on saying, he doesn't *want* to come back.'

But the woman showed him with her finger that if he pressed a secret spring at the edge of the watch near the guard-ring he could make time seem to go much slower—whenever, that is, he was truly happy; and that if he pressed the secret spring on the left he could make time seem to go much quicker—say, when he was feeling miserable, or was tired or waiting for anything or anybody. And not only this; there was a third spring. 'If you press that,' the woman said, 'you can't tell what will happen next.'

Dick was mightily pleased with the watch, and just to test it, pressed the left-hand spring. And it seemed not a moment had passed by when there came a prodigious stamping and thumping and clattering from out of the back parts of the Castle, and he knew that Grackel's two uncles had woken up. So loud was the din they were making that it sounded as if a volcano had broken out, and it scared Dick more than he liked to show. So—though he pretended to be in no hurry—he let the left-hand spring go, fixed the chain round his waist, and slipped the watch in under the front of his breeches.

'If your husband isn't with you again by sundown tomorrow evening,' he told the woman, 'then send his uncles after me. The Beanstalk, of course, *might* bear them; and even though they might never come back again, they would at least have a chance to make an end of *me*.'

'If you come along with me now,' said the woman,

'you shall have a peep at them, and they won't see you. But quietly! They have ears like the east wind!"

So, treading mimsey as a cat, Dick followed after the woman, and she led him up a flight of stairs so steep he might have been climbing a pyramid, and took him into a gallery overlooking the room in which the giants sat. Dick crept forward, and, leaning out a little between the bases of the balusters of the gallery, peeped down. They were intent on a game that looked like common dominoes, though the pieces or men they played with were almost as big as tombstones. In no story-book he had ever read had Dick chanced on the like of these giants. They sat like human mountains at their game, and the noise of the dominoes was like Pharaoh's chariots. And when one of them, laying down a domino on the table, mumbled, *Double!*, it was like the coughing of a lion. Dick didn't need to watch them long. But as soon as he was out of earshot of them again, he burst out laughing, though it was only feigned.

'It's a good thing,' he said to the woman, 'I thought of what I told you. They are fine men, your husband's uncles, and no beanstalk I have ever seen would bear even half the weight of either. I'll keep the locket safe, you can trust me, ma'am, and if my father will let me, perhaps I might come back with your husband to the feast.'

The woman was by nature mean and close, but seeing how little by comparison Dick would be likely to eat and drink, she said he would be welcome. So he bade her goodbye and off he went.

. . .

It was pitch-black night when he got home again, but his father was waiting up for him. They were so anxious for the giant to be gone that they couldn't stay till morning. They went off together with a lantern to the barn, and having gone in, shouted at the top of their voices in Grackel's ear. They managed to wake him at last, and gave him his wife's message. He was so stupid after his first sleep, and he had eaten so vast a supper, that they might as well have been conversing with a mule. Even when he understood what they were saying, he sat blinking, morose and sullen at being disturbed.

'And how can I tell', said he, 'that what you say is true? A fine story, a pretty story, but I don't believe a word of it.'

But when Dick told him of the feast that was being prepared, that all his wife wanted was to see him once again, that else his uncles might come to look for him; and when at last he showed the giant his wife's locket— then Grackel believed what was said to him (though Dick kept the watch to himself). And the very next morning the two of them set out together for the Beanstalk. And the farmer, eyes shining and all smiles, saw them off.

It was a morning fine and bright. A little hard snow had fallen in the small hours and lay on the grass like lumps of sago. The ponds were frozen hard as crystal. And as he cantered along on his pony—the giant's lank legs keeping pace with him on his right side like the arms of a windmill—Dick was so happy at the thought of at last getting rid of his guest that he whistled away like a starling as he rode.

And Grackel said, 'Why are you whistling?'

' "Why?" ' said Dick. 'Why, to think what a happy evening you are going to have, and how pleased your wife will be to see you, and what a feast they are making for you up there. I could almost smell the oxen roasting for the cold meats on the side table; and there must have been seven score of fat pigs being driven in for the black puddings.'

This only made Grackel the more eager to press on.

'And now,' said Dick, when in the height of the morning they came to the foot of the Beanstalk, which was masked thick with hoarfrost smouldering in the sun, 'here we part for a while. When you are come up to the top, give a loud *hullabaloo,* and I shall know you are safe. Then I shall ride off home again, and I will come to meet you here the day after to-morrow, about two.'

Now, though it was a great folly, Dick had not been able to resist bringing Grackel's watch with him. He had hooked the chain round his waist under his breeches, and the watch bulged out like a hump in the wrong place. By good luck the giant was on the further side away from the watch, so that he had not noticed this hump. But now that they were at a standstill, and all was quiet, he detected the ticking.

And he said, 'What is that sound I hear?'

And Dick said, 'That is my heart beating.'

'Why is it beating so loud?' said Grackel.

'Ah,' said Dick, in a doleful tone, 'it must be for sadness that you are going away, even if only for a little while! We have had our little disagreements together, you and me, about the sheep and the snoring and the cider. But now we are friends, and that is all over. Isn't there any little keepsake you could give me by which to remember you till you come back?'

At this the giant drew in his lips, and none too eagerly felt in his pockets. He brought out at last from beneath the leather flap of his side pocket a discoloured stub of candle in a box.

'It's not much to look at,' he grumbled, 'but once it's lit it will never go out till you say, *Out, candle, out!* even if it's left burning in a hurricane for a hundred years.' Dick kept this candle until the day he met his sweetheart and lit it then. It may be lighting his great-grandchildren to sleep this very evening. But that came afterwards.

'There,' said Grackel, 'take great care of it, and you shall give it me back when we meet again. Aye, and then I am sure to be hungry. So have plenty of hot supper waiting for me in my house—legs of pork soused in apples, and kids in batter, and drink to wash it down! And get in for me too some more hay and blankets and horse-cloths. I could scarcely sleep a wink last night for the cold.'

Dick nodded and laughed, and the giant began to climb the Beanstalk. Dick watched him till first he was as small to look up at as an ordinary man, and next no bigger than a dwarf, and not long after that he was out of sight. About an hour or so afterwards, for Grackel being lean and sinewy was a nimble climber, Dick heard a rumbling in the higher skies. He knew that it was the giant's hullabalooing, and that he was safe. Then as quick as lightning he set about gathering together a great heap of last year's bracken and dead

wood and dry grass, and piled it round the parched-up roots of the Beanstalk. Then he felt in his pocket for his flint and tinder-box that his father had laid out for him overnight. He felt—and felt again; and his beating heart gave one dull thump and almost stood still. In the heat and haste of getting away he had left them both on the kitchen table!

Dick hauled out Grackel's watch to see the time. It was seven minutes to twelve. It would now be impossible for him to get home before nightfall and back again much before morning. It was a long journey, and the way would be difficult to follow in the dark. And how was he to be certain that the giant, having come to the Castle and found that his watch was gone, would not climb down the Beanstalk again to fetch it? Dick pressed the right-hand spring of the watch, for though he was in great trouble of mind, he wanted to think hard and to make the time go slowly. And as, brooding on there under the Beanstalk, he stared at the second hand, though it was not much bigger than a darning needle, it was jerking so sluggishly that he could have counted twenty between every beat. The sun, that was now come to the top of his winter arch in the sky, and was glistening like a tiny furnace on the crystal of the watch, danced in his eyes so fiercely that at last he could scarcely see.

'Why,' thought Dick suddenly, 'the glass magnifies. It's a *burning*-glass!'

Instantly, after but one sharp upward glance towards the top of the Beanstalk, he took out his pocket-knife and heaved up the watch lid. The glass was as thick as half the nail-width of his little finger. He held it

close down over the dried-up leaves and bracken in
the full beams of the noonday sun. And in a few moments, to his great joy, a faint twirling wreath of grey
smoke appeared on the buff of the bracken frond.
Then there came a black pin-prick circle that rapidly
began to ring out larger. Then a little red appeared at
the edge of the circle. And at this Dick began to puff
very very softly, still tilting the glass into the direct rays
of the sun. The frond began to smoulder, and the
smoulder began to spread, and now Dick blew with all
his might.

Presently a thin reek of vapour appeared, and the
bracken broke into flames. And when once these
parched-up leaves and grasses had fairly taken fire, the
Beanstalk itself was soon ablaze. The flames—and
theirs was a strange music—roared loud in the wintry air—red, greenish, copper and gold—licking and
leaping their way from strand to strand up and up,
while a huge pale-umber tower of smoke rose billowing
into the blue air of the morning.

Dick gazed at the flames in delight and terror. Never
in all his born days had he seen such a bonfire. Even
Jock, who had been quietly browsing by the ruinous
cottage walls, turned his dark eyes at sight of this fiery
spectacle, lifted his head and whinnied. Indeed, the
flaming Beanstalk must have been visible to all
Gloucestershire's seven neighbour counties round. And
the fire burned up and up, and the pods and red-hot
bean-seeds came hailing down, with wisps of fire and
smoke. And the roaring gradually grew more and more
distant, until at last the blaze up above was dwindled to
little more than a red spark, like a tiny second sun, far

far up in the vacancy of the heavens. And then it vanished and was gone.

And Dick with a deep sigh, partly of regret and partly of relief, knew that Jack's old Beanstalk was gone for ever. At least this might be so, though he had been wise enough before he had begun gathering together the fuel for his fire to put two or three of the dry bean-seeds into his pocket. Some day he meant to plant them; just to see.

He broke the ice over a little spring that was frozen near the cottage, took a sip or two of the biting cold water underneath, and dabbled his hot cheeks and eyelids. Then he whistled for Jock, and jumped into the saddle. Yet again he dragged out Grackel's watch, pressed down the left spring, and with one last glance up over his shoulder, set off for home. And pleased beyond all words was his father the farmer to see him.

THE LORD FISH

Once upon a time there lived
in the village of Tussock in Wiltshire a young man
called John Cobbler. Cobbler being his name, there
must have been shoe-making in his family. But there
had been none in John's lifetime; nor within living
memory either. And John cobbled nothing but his own
old shoes and his mother's. Still, he was a handy young
man. He could have kept them both with ease, and with
plenty of butter to their bread, if only he had been a little different from what he was. He was lazy.

Lazy or not, his mother loved him dearly. She had
loved him ever since he was a baby, when his chief joy
was to suck his thumb and stare out of his saucer-blue
eyes at nothing in particular except what he had no
words to tell about. Nor had John lost this habit, even
when he was being a handy young man. He could make
baskets—of sorts; he was a wonder with bees; he could
mend pots and pans, if he were given the solder and
could find his iron; he could grow cabbages, hoe potatoes, patch up a hen-house or lime-wash a sty. But he
was only a jack of such trades, and master of none. He
could seldom finish off anything; not at any rate as his

namesake the Giant Killer could finish off his giants. He began well; he went on worse; and he ended, yawning. And unless his mother had managed to get a little washing and ironing and mending and sweeping and cooking and stitching from the gentry in the village, there would often have been less in the pot for them both than would keep their bodies and souls—and the two of them—together.

Yet even though John was by nature idle and a day-dreamer, he might have made his mother far easier about his future if only he could have given up but one small pleasure and pastime; he might have made not only good wages, but also his fortune—even though he would have had to leave Tussock to do it quick. It was his love of water that might some day be his ruin. Or rather, not so much his love of water as his passion for fishing in it. Let him but catch sight of a puddle, or of rain gushing from a waterspout, or hear in the middle of the night a leaky tap singing its queer *ding-dong-bell* as drop followed drop into a basin in the sink, let the wind but creep an inch or two out of the east and into the south; and every other thought would instantly vanish out of his head. All he wanted then was a rod and a line and a hook and a worm and a cork; a pond or a stream or a river—or the deep blue sea. And it wasn't even fish he pined for, merely fishing.

There would have been little harm in this craving of his if only he had been able to keep it within bounds. But he couldn't. He fished morning, noon, and even night. Through continually staring at a float, his eyes had come to be almost as round as one, and his elbows stood out like fins when he walked. The wonder was his

blood had not turned to water. And though there are
many kinds of tasty English fish, his mother at last grew
very tired of having *any* kind at every meal. As the old
rhyme goes:

> *A Friday of fish*
> *Is all man could wish.*
> *Of vittles the chief*
> *Is mustard and beef.*
> *It's only a glutton*
> *Could live on cold mutton;*
> *And bacon when green*
> *Is too fat or too lean.*
> *But all three are sweeter*
> *To see in a dish*
> *By any wise eater*
> *Than nothing but* FISH!

Quite a little fish, too, even a roach, may take as many
hours to catch and almost as many minutes to cook as a
full-sized one; and they both have the same number of
bones. Still in spite of his fish *and* his fishing, his mother
went on loving her son John. She hoped in time he
might weary of them himself. Or was there some secret
in his passion for water of which she knew nothing?
Might he some day fish up something really worth having—something to keep? A keg perhaps of rubies and
diamonds, or a coffer full of amber and gold? Then all
their troubles would be over.

Meanwhile John showed no sign at all of becoming
less lazy or of growing tired of fishing, though he was
no longer content to fish in the same places. He would

walk miles and miles in hope to find pond, pool or lake that he had never seen before, or a stream strange to him. Wherever he heard there was water within reach between dawn and dark, off he would go to look for it. Sometimes in his journeyings he would do a job of work, and bring home to his mother not only a few pence but a little present for herself—a ribbon, or a needle-case, a bag of jumbles or bull's-eyes, or a duck's egg for her tea; any little thing that might take her fancy. Sometimes the fish he caught in far-off waters tasted fresher, sweeter, richer, juicier than those from nearer home; sometimes they tasted worse—dry, poor, rank and muddy. It depended partly on the sort of fish, partly on how long he had taken to carry them home, and partly on how his mother felt at the moment.

Now there was a stream John Cobbler came to hear about which for a long time he could never find. For whenever he went to look for it—and he knew that it lay a good fourteen miles and more from Tussock—he was always baulked by a high flintstone wall. It was the highest wall he had ever seen. And, like the Great Wall of China, it went on for miles. What was more curious, although he had followed the wall on and on for hours at a stretch, he had never yet been able to find a gate or door to it, or any way in.

When he asked any stranger whom he happened to meet at such times if he knew what lay on the other side of this mysterious wall, and whether there were any good fish in the stream which he had been told ran there, and if so, of what kind, shape, size and flavour they might be—every single one of them told him a different tale. Some said there was a castle inside the wall, a good league or so away from it, and that a sorcerer lived in it who had mirrors on a tower in which he could detect any stranger that neared his walls. Others said an old, old Man of the Sea had built himself a great land mansion there in the middle of a Maze—of water and yew trees; an old Man of the Sea who had turned cannibal, and always drowned anybody who trespassed over his wall before devouring him. Others said water-witches dwelt there, in a wide lake made by the stream beside the ruinous walls of a palace which had been the abode of princes in old times. All agreed that it was a dangerous place, and that they would not venture over the wall, dark or daylight, for a pocketful of guineas. On summer nights, they said, you could hear voices coming from away over it, very strange voices, too; and would see lights in the sky. And some avowed they had heard hunting-horns at the rise of the moon. As for the fish, all agreed they must be monsters.

There was no end to the tales told John of what lay beyond the wall. And he, being a simple young man, believed each one of them in turn. But none made any difference to the longing that had come over him to get to the other side of this wall and to fish in the stream there. Walls that kept out so much, he thought, must keep something well worth having *in*. All other fishing now seemed tame and dull. His only hope was to find out the secret of what lay beyond this high, grey, massive, mossy, weed-tufted, endless wall. And he stopped setting out in its direction only for the sake of his mother.

But though for this reason he might stay at home two or three days together, the next would see him off again, hungering for the unknown waters.

John not only thought of the wall all day, he dreamed of it and of what might be beyond it by night. If the wind sighed at his window he saw moonlit lakes and water in his sleep; if a wild duck cried overhead under the stars, there would be thousands of wild duck and wild swans too and many another water-bird haunting his mind, his head on his pillow. Sometimes great whales would come swimming into his dreams. And he would hear mermaids blowing in their hollow shells and singing as they combed their hair.

With all this longing he began to pine away a little. His eye grew less clear and lively. His rib-bones began to show. And though his mother saw a good deal more of her son John since he had given up his fishing, at last she began to miss more and more and more what she had become accustomed to. Fish, that is—boiled, broiled, baked, fried or Dutch-ovened. And her longing came to such a pass at last that she laid down her knife and fork one supper-time beside a half-eaten slice of salt pork and said, 'My! John, how I would enjoy a morsel of tench again! Do you remember those tench you used to catch up at Abbot's Pool? Or a small juicy trout, John! Or some stewed eels! Or even a few roach out of the moat of the old Grange, even though they *are* mostly mud! It's funny, John, but sea-fish never did satisfy me even when we could get it; and I haven't scarcely any fancy left for meat. What's more, I notice cheese now gives you nightmares. But fish?—never!'

This was enough for John. For weeks past he had

been sitting on the see-saw of his mind, so that just the
least little tilt like that bumped him clean into a decision. It was not fear or dread indeed, all this talk of
giants and wizardry and old bygone princes that had
kept him from scaling the great wall long ago, and daring the dangers beyond it. It was not this at all. But only
a half-hidden feeling in his mind that if once he found
himself on the other side of it he might never be quite
the same creature again. You may get out of your bed
in the morning, the day's usual sunshine at the window
and the birds singing as they always sing, and yet know
for certain that in the hours to come something is going
to happen—something that hasn't happened before. So
it was with John Cobbler. At the very moment his
mother put down her knife and fork on either side of
her half-eaten slice of salt pork and said, 'My! John,
how I would enjoy a morsel of tench again! . . . Or a
small juicy trout, John!' his mind was made up.

'Why, of course, Mother dear,' he said to her, in a
voice that he tried in vain to keep from trembling. 'I'll
see what I can do for you to-morrow.' He lit his candle
there and then, and scarcely able to breathe for joy at
thought of it, clumped up the wooden stairs to his attic
to look out his best rod and get ready his tackle.

While yet next morning the eastern sky was pale blue
with the early light of dawn, wherein tiny clouds like a
shoal of silver fishes were quietly drifting on—before,
that is, the flaming sun had risen, John was posting
along out of Tussock with his rod and tackle and battered old creel, and a hunk of bread and cheese tied up
in a red spotted handkerchief. There was not a soul to
be seen. Every blind was down; the chimneys were

empty of smoke; the whole village was still snoring. He whistled as he walked, and every now and again took a look at the sky. That vanishing fleecy drift of silver fishes might mean wind, and from the south, he thought. He plodded along to such good purpose, and without meeting a soul except a shepherd with his sheep and dog and an urchin driving a handful of cows —for these were solitary parts—that he came to the wall while it was still morning, and a morning as fresh and green as even England can show.

Now John wasn't making merely for the wall, but for a certain place in it. It was where, one darkening evening some little time before, he had noticed the still-sprouting upper branches of a tree that had been blown down in a great wind over the edge of the wall and into the narrow grassy lane that skirted it. Few humans seemed ever to come this way, but there were hosts of rabbits, whose burrows were in the sandy hedgerow, and, at evening, nightjars, croodling in the dusk. It was too, John had noticed, a favourite resort of bats.

After a quick look up and down the lane to see that the coast was clear, John stood himself under the dangling branches—like the fox in the fable that was after the grapes—and he jumped, and jumped. But no matter how high he jumped, the lowermost twigs remained out of his reach. He rested awhile looking about him, and spied a large stone half-buried in the sandy hedgerow. He trundled it over until it was under the tree, and after a third attempt succeeded in swinging himself up into its branches, and had scrambled along and dropped quietly in on the other side almost before news of his coming had spread among the wild things that

lived on the other side of it. Then blackbird to blackbird sounded the alarm. There was a scurry and scamper among the leaves and bracken. A host of rooks rose
cawing into the sky. Then all was still. John peered
about him; he had never felt so lonely in his life. Never
even in his dreams had he been in a place so strange to
him as this. The foxgloves and bracken of its low hills
and hollows showed bright green where the sunshine
struck through the great forest trees. Else, so dense with
leaves were their branches that for the most part there
was only an emerald twilight beneath their boughs.
And a deep silence dwelt there.

For some little time John walked steadily on, keeping his eyes open as he went. Near and far he heard jays
screaming one to the other, and wood-pigeons went
clattering up out of the leaves into the sun. Ever and
again, too, the hollow tapping of a wood-pecker
sounded out in the silence, or its wild echoing laughter,
and once he edged along a glade just in time to see a
herd of deer fleeting in a multitude before him at sight
and scent of man. They sped soundlessly out of view
across the open glade into covert. And still John kept
steadily on, lifting his nose every now and again to snuff
the air; for his fisherman's wits had hinted that water
was near.

And he came at length to a gentle slope waist-high
with spicy bracken, and at its crest found himself looking down on the waters of a deep and gentle stream
flowing between its hollow mossy banks in the dingle
below him. 'Aha!' cried John out loud to himself; and
the sound of his voice rang so oddly in the air that he
whipped round and stared about him as if someone else

had spoken. But there was sign neither of man nor bird nor beast. All was still again. So he cautiously made his way down to the bank of the stream and began to fish.

For an hour or more he fished in vain. The trees grew thicker on the further bank, and the water was deep and dark and slow. None the less, though he could see none, he knew in his bones that it was fairly alive with fish. Yet not a single one of them had as yet cheated him even with a nibble. Still, John had often fished half a day through without getting so much as a bite, and so long as the water stole soundlessly on beneath him and he could watch the reflection of the tree boughs and of the drifts of blue sky between them in this dark looking-glass, he was happy and at ease. And then suddenly, as if to mock him, a fish with a dappled green back and silver belly and of a kind he never remembered to have seen before, leapt clean out of the water about three yards from his green and white float, seemed to stare at him a moment with fishy lidless eyes, and at once plunged back into the water again. Whether it was the mere noise of its water-splash, or whether the words had actually sounded from out of its gaping jaws he could not say, but it certainly seemed as if before it vanished he had heard a strange voice cry, 'Ho, there! John! . . . Try lower down!'

He laughed to himself; then listened. Biding a bit, he clutched his rod a little tighter, and keeping a more cautious look-out than ever on all sides of him, he followed the flow of the water, pausing every now and again to make a cast. And still not a single fish seemed so much as to have sniffed (or even sneered) at his bait, while yet the gaping mouths of those leaping up out of

the water beyond his reach seemed to utter the same hollow and watery-sounding summons he had heard before: 'Ho, John! Ho! Ho, you, John Cobbler, there! Try lower down!' So much indeed were these fish like fish enchanted that John began to wish he had kept to his old haunts and had not ventured over the wall; or that he had at least told his mother where he meant to go. Supposing he never came back? Where would she be looking for him? Where? Where? And all she had asked for, and perhaps for his own sake only, was a fish supper!

The water was now flowing more rapidly in a glass-green heavy flood, and before he was ready for it John suddenly found himself staring up at the walls of a high dark house with but two narrow windows in the stone surface that steeped up into the sky above. And the very sight of the house set his heart beating faster. He was afraid. Beyond this wall to the right showed the stony roofs of lesser buildings, and moss-clotted fruit trees gone to leaf. Busying to and fro above the roof were scores of rooks and jackdaws, their jangled cries sounding out even above the roaring of the water, for now close beneath him the stream narrowed to gush in beneath a low-rounded arch in the wall, and so into the silence and darkness beyond it.

Two thoughts had instantly sprung up in John's mind as he stared up at this strange solitary house. One that it must be bewitched, and the other that except for its birds and the fish in its stream it was forsaken and empty. He laid his rod down on the green bank and stole from one tree-trunk to another to get a better view, making up his mind that if he had time he would skirt his way round the walled garden he could see, but would not yet venture to walk out into the open on the other side of the house.

It was marvellously quiet in this dappled sunshine, and John decided to rest awhile before venturing further. Seating himself under a tree he opened his handkerchief, and found not only the hunk of bread and cheese he had packed in it, but a fat sausage and some cockled apples which his mother must have put in afterwards. He was uncommonly hungry, and keeping a wary eye on the two dark windows from under the leaves over his head, he continued to munch. And as he munched, the jackdaws, their black wings silvered by the sun, continued to jangle, and the fish silently to leap up out of their watery haunts and back again, their eyes glassily fixed on him as they did so, and the gathering water continued to gush steadily in under the dark rounded tunnel beneath the walls of the house.

But now as John listened and watched he fancied that above all these sounds interweaving themselves into a gentle chorus of the morning, he caught the faint strains as of a voice singing in the distance—and a sweet voice too. But water, as he knew of old, is a curious deceiver of the ear. At times, as one listens to it, it will sound as if drums and dulcimers are ringing in its depths; at times as if fingers are plucking on the strings of a harp, or invisible mouths calling. John stopped eating to listen more intently.

And soon there was no doubt left in his mind that this was no mere water-noise, but the singing of a human voice, and that not far away. It came as if from within the walls of the house itself, but he could not detect any words to the song. It glided on from note to note as though it were an unknown bird piping in the first cold winds of April after its sea-journey from Africa to English shores; and though he did not know it, his face as he listened puckered up almost as if he were a child again and was going to cry.

He had heard tell of the pitiless sirens, and of sea-wandering nereids, and of how they sing among their island rocks, or couched on the oceanic strands of their sunny islands, where huge sea-fish disport themselves in the salt water: porpoise and dolphin, through billows clear as glass, and green and blue as precious stones. His mother too had told him as a child—and like Simple Simon himself he had started fishing in her pail!—what dangers there may be in listening to such voices; how even sailors have stopped up their ears with wax lest they should be enticed by this music to the isles of the sirens and never sail home again. But though John remembered this warning, he continued to listen, and an intense desire came over him to discover who this secret singer was, and where she lay hid. He might peep perhaps, he thought to himself, through some lattice or cranny in the dark walls and not be seen.

But though he stole on, now in shadow, now in sun, pushing his way through the tangled brambles and briars, the bracken and bryony that grew close in even under the walls of the house, he found—at least on this side of it—no doorway or window or even slit in the masonry through which to look in. And he came back at last, hot, tired and thirsty, to the bank of the stream where he had left his rod.

And even as he knelt down to drink by the waterside,

the voice which had been silent awhile began to sing
again, as sad as it was sweet; and not more than an
arm's length from his stooping face a great fish leapt
out of the water, its tail bent almost double, its goggling
eyes fixed on him, and out of its hook-toothed mouth it
cried, '*A-whoof! Oo-ougoolkawott!*' That at least to
John was what it seemed to say. And having delivered
its message, it fell back again into the dark water and in
a wild eddy was gone. Startled by this sudden noise
John drew quickly back, and in so doing dislodged a
large moss-greened stone on the bank, which rolled
clattering down to its plunge into the stream; and the
singing again instantly ceased. He glanced back over
his shoulder at the high wall and vacant windows, and
out of the silence that had again descended he heard in
mid-day the mournful hooting as of an owl, and a cold
terror swept over him. He leapt to his feet, seized his rod
and creel, hastily tied up what was left of his lunch in
his red-spotted handkerchief, and instantly set out for
home. Nor did he once look back until the house was
hidden from view. Then his fear vanished, and he began to be heartily ashamed of himself.

And since he had by now come into sight of another
loop of the stream, he decided, however long it took
him, to fish there until he had at least caught *something*
—if only a stickleback—so that he should not disap-
point his mother of the supper she longed for. The min-
now smeared with pork marrow which he had been
using for bait on his hook was already dry. None the
less he flung it into the stream, and almost before the
float touched the water a swirl of ripples came sweeping
from the further bank, and a greedy pike, grey and

silver, at least two feet long if he was an inch, had instantly gobbled down bait and hook. John could hardly believe his own eyes. It was as if it had been actually lying in wait to be caught. He stooped to look into its strange motionless eye as it lay on the grass at his feet. Sullenly it stared back at him as though, even if it had only a minute or two left to live in, it were trying heroically to give him a message, yet one that he could not understand.

Happy at heart, he stayed no longer. Yet with every mile of his journey home the desire grew in him to return to the house, if only to hear again that dolorous voice singing from out of the darkness within its walls. But he told his mother nothing about his adventures, and the two of them sat down to as handsome a dish of fish for supper as they had ever tasted.

'What's strange to me, John,' said his mother at last, for they had talked very little, being so hungry, 'is that though this fish here is a pike, and cooked as usual, with a picking of thyme and marjoram, a bit of butter, a squeeze of lemon and some chopped shallots, there's a good deal more to him than just that. There's a sort of savour and sweetness to him, as if he had been daintily fed. Where did you catch him, John?'

But at this question John was seized by such a fit of coughing—as if a bone had stuck in his throat—that it seemed at any moment he might choke. And when his mother had stopped thumping him on his back she had forgotten what she had asked him. With her next mouthful, too, she had something else to think about; and it was fortunate that she had such a neat strong row of teeth, else the crunch she gave to it would certainly have broken two or three of them in half.

'Excuse me, John,' she said, and drew out of her mouth not a bone, but something tiny, hard and shiny, which after being washed under the kitchen tap proved to be a key. It was etched over with figures of birds and beasts and fishes, that might be all ornament or might, thought John, his cheeks red as beetroot, be a secret writing.

'Well I never! Brass!' said his mother, staring at the key in the palm of her hand.

'Nor didn't I,' said John. 'I'll take it off to the blacksmith's at once, Mother, and see what he makes of it.'

Before she could say Yes or No to this, John was gone. In half an hour he was back again.

'He says, Mother,' said he, 'it's a key, Mother; and not brass but solid gold. A gold key! Whoever? And in a fish!'

'Well, John,' said his mother, who was a little sleepy after so hearty a supper, 'I never—mind you—did see much good in fishing except the fish, but if there are any more gold keys from where that pike came from, let's both get up early, and we'll soon be as rich as Old Creatures.'

John needed no telling. He was off next morning long before the sun had begun to gild the dewdrops in the meadows, and he found himself, rod, creel and bait, under the magician's wall a good three hours before noon. There was not a cloud in the sky. The stream flowed quiet as molten glass, reflecting the towering forest trees, the dark stone walls, and the motionless flowers and grass-blades at its brim. John stood there gazing awhile into the water, just as if to-day were yesterday over again, then sat himself down on the bank and fell into a kind of daydream, his rod idle at his side. Neither fish nor key nor the freshness of the morning nor any wish or thought was in his mind but only a longing to hear again the voice of the secret one. And the shadows around him had crept less even than an inch on their daily round, and a cuckoo under the hollow sky had but thrice cuckoo'd in some green dell of the forest, when there slid up into the air the very notes that had haunted him, waking and sleeping, ever since they had first fallen on his ear. They rang gently on and on, in the hush, clear as a cherub in some quiet gallery of paradise, and John knew in his heart that she who sang was no longer timid in his company, but out of her solitude was beseeching his aid.

He rose to his feet, and once more searched the vast frowning walls above his head. Nothing there but the croaking choughs and jackdaws among the chimneys, and a sulphur-coloured butterfly wavering in flight along the darkness of their stones. They filled him with dread, these echoing walls; and still the voice pined on. And at last he fixed his eyes on the dark arch beneath which coursed in heavy leaden flow the heaped-up volume of the stream. No way in, indeed! Surely, where water could go, mightn't *he?*

Without waiting a moment to consider the dangers that might lie in wait for him in the dark water beneath the walls, he had slipped out of his coat and shoes and had plunged in. He swam on with the stream until he was within a little way of the yawning arch; then took a deep breath and dived down and down. When he could hold it no longer he slipped up out of the water—and in the nick of time. He had clutched something as he came to the surface, and found himself in a dusky twilight looking up from the foot of a narrow flight of stone steps—with a rusty chain dangling down the middle of it. He hauled himself up out of the water and sat down a moment to recover his breath, then made his way up the steps. At the top he came to a low stone corridor. There he stayed again.

But here the voice was more clearly to be heard. He hastened down the corridor and came at last to a high narrow room full of sunlight from the window in its walls looking out over the forest. And, reclining there by the window, the wan green light shining in on her pale face and plaited copper-coloured hair, was what John took at first to be a mermaid; and for the very good reason that she had a human head and body, but a fish's tail. He stayed quite still, gazing at her, and she at him, but he could think of nothing to say. He merely kept his mouth open in case any words should come, while the water-drops dripped from his clothes and hair on to the stone flags around him. And when the lips in the odd small face of this strange creature began to speak to him, he could hardly make head or tail of the words. Indeed she had been long shut up alone in this old mansion from which the magician who had given her her fish's tail, so that she should not be able to stray from the house, had some years gone his way, never to come back. She had now almost forgotten her natural language. But there is a music in the voice that tells more to those who understand it than can any words in a dictionary. And it didn't take John very long to discover that this poor fish-tailed creature, with nothing but the sound of her own sad voice to comfort her, was mortally unhappy; that all she longed for was to rid herself of her cold fish's tail, and so win out into the light and sunshine again, freed from the spell of the wizard who had shut her up in these stone walls.

John sat down on an old wooden stool that stood beside the table, and listened. And now and then he himself sighed deep or nodded. He learned—though he learned it very slowly—that the only company she had was a deaf old steward who twice every day, morning and evening, brought her food and water, and for the rest of the time shut himself up in a tower on the further side of the house looking out over the deserted gardens and orchards that once had flourished with peach and quince and apricot, and all the roses of Damascus. Else, she said, sighing, she was always alone. And John, as best he could, told her in turn about himself and about his mother. 'She'd help you all she could to escape away from here—I know *that,* if so be she *could.* The only question is, How? Since, you see, first it's a good long step for Mother to come and there's no proper way over the wall, and next if she managed it, it wouldn't be easy with nothing but a tail to walk on. I mean, lady, for you to walk on.' At this he left his mouth open, and looked away, afraid that he might have hurt her feelings. And in the same moment he bethought himself of the key, which, if he had not been on the verge of choking, his mother might have swallowed in mistake for a mouthful of fish. He took it out of his breeches' pocket and held it up towards the window, so that the light should shine on it. And at sight of it it seemed that something between grief and gladness had suddenly overcome the poor creature with the fish's tail, for she hid her face in her fingers and wept aloud.

This was not much help to poor John. With his idle ways and love of fishing, he had been a sad trial at times to his mother. But she, though little to look at, was as brave as a lion, and if ever she shed tears at all, it was in secret. This perhaps was a pity, for if John had but once seen her cry he might have known what to do now. All that he actually did do was to look very glum himself and turn his eyes away. And as they roved slowly round the bare walls he perceived what looked like the crack of a little door in the stones and beside it a tiny keyhole. The one thing in the world he craved was to comfort this poor damsel with the fish's tail, to persuade her to dry her eyes and smile at him. But as nothing he could think to say could be of any help, he tiptoed across and examined the wall more closely. And cut into the stone above the keyhole he read the four letters—*C.A.V.E.!* What they meant John had no notion, except that a cave is something hollow—and usually empty. Still, since here was a lock and John had a key, he naturally put the key into the lock with his clumsy fingers to see if it would fit. He gave the key a gentle twist. And lo and behold, there came a faint click. He tugged, drew the stone out upon its iron hinges, and looked inside.

What he had expected to see he did not know. All that was actually within this narrow stone cupboard was a little green pot, and beside it a scrap of what looked like parchment, but was actually monkey skin. John had never been much of a scholar at his books. He was a dunce. When he was small he had liked watching the clouds and butterflies and birds flitting to and fro and the green leaves twinkling in the sun, and found drogs and newts and sticklebacks and minnows better company than anything he could read in print on paper. Still he had managed at last to learn all his letters and even to read, though he read so slowly that he sometimes forgot the first letters of a long word before he had spelled out the last. He took the piece of parchment into the light, held it tight between his fingers, and, syllable by syllable, muttered over to himself what it said—leaving the longer words until he had more time.

And now the pale-cheeked creature reclining by the window had stopped weeping, and between the long strands of her copper hair was watching him through her tears. And this is what John read:

> *Thou who wouldst dare*
> *To free this Fair*
> *From fish's shape,*
> *And yet escape*
> *O'er sea and land*
> *My vengeful hand:—*
> *Smear this fish-fat on thy heart,*
> *And prove thyself the jack thou art!*
>
> *With tail and fin*
> *Then plunge thou in!*
> *And thou shalt surely have thy wish*
> *To see the great, the good Lord Fish!*

Swallow his bait in haste, for he
Is master of all wizardry.
And if he gentle be inclined,
He'll show thee where to seek and find
The Magic Unguent that did make
This human maid a fish-tail take.

> *But have a care*
> *To make short stay*
> *Where wields his sway,*
> *The Great Lord Fish;*
> *'Twill be too late*
> *To moan your fate*
> *When served with sauce*
> *Upon his dish!*

John read this doggerel once, he read it twice, and though he couldn't understand it all even when he read it a third time, he understood a good deal of it. The one thing he could not discover, though it seemed the most important, was what would happen to him if he did as the rhyme itself bade him do—smeared the fish-fat over his heart. But this he meant to find out.

And why not at once, thought John, though except when he hooked a fish, he was seldom as prompt as that. He folded up the parchment very small, and slipped it into his breeches' pocket. Then imitating as best he could the motion of descending the steps and diving into the water, he promised the maid he would return to her the first moment he could, and entreated her not to sing again until he came back. 'Because . . .' he began, but could get no further. At which, poor mortal, she began to weep again, making John, for very sadness to see her, only the more anxious to be gone. So he took the little pot out of the stone cupboard, and giving her for farewell as smiling and consoling a bob of his head as he knew how, hurried off along the long narrow corridor, and so down the steep stone steps to the water.

There, having first very carefully felt with his fingertips exactly where his heart lay beating, he dipped his finger into the green ointment and rubbed it over his ribs. And with that, at once, a dreadful darkness and giddiness swept over him. He felt his body narrowing and shortening and shrinking and dwindling. His bones were drawing themselves together inside his skin; his arms and legs ceased at last to wave and scuffle, his eyes seemed to be settling into his head. The next moment, with one convulsive twist of his whole body, he had fallen plump into the water. There he lay a while in a motionless horror. Then he began to stir again, and after a few black dreadful moments found himself coursing along so swiftly that in a trice he was out from under the arch and into the green gloaming of the stream beyond it. Never before had he slipped through the water with such ease. And no wonder!

For when he twisted himself about to see what had happened to him, a sight indeed met his eye. Where once had been arms were now small blunt fins. A gristly little beard or barbel hung on either side of his mouth. His short dumpy body was of a greeny brown, and for human legs he could boast of nothing now but a fluted wavering tail. If he had been less idle in his young days he might have found himself a fine mottled trout, a barbel, a mullet, or a lively eel, or being a John he might well have become a jack. But no, he was fisherman enough to recognize himself at sight—a common tench, and not a very handsome one either! A mere middling fish, John judged. At this horrifying discovery, though the rhyme should have warned him of it, shudder after shudder ran along his backbone and he dashed blindly through the water as if he were out of his senses. Where could he hide himself? How flee away? What would his mother say to him? And alackaday, what had become of the pot of ointment? 'Oh mercy me, oh misery me!' he moaned within himself, though not the faintest whisper sounded from his bony jaws. A pretty bargain this!

He plunged on deeper and deeper, and at length, nuzzling softly the sandy bed of the stream with his blunt fish's snout, he hid his head between two boulders at the bottom. There, under a net of bright green waterweed, he lay for a while utterly still, brooding again on his mother and on what her feelings would be if she should see him no more—or in the shape he was! Would that he had listened to her counsel, and had never so much as set eyes on rod or hook or line or float or water. He had wasted his young days in fishing, and now was fish for evermore.

But as the watery moments sped by, this grief and despondency began to thin away and remembrance of the crafty and cruel magician came back to mind. Whatever he might look like from outside, John began to be himself again within. Courage, even a faint gleam of hope, welled back into his dull fish's brains. With a flick of his tail he had drawn back out of the gloomy cranny between the boulders, and was soon disporting himself but a few inches below the surface of the stream, the sunlight gleaming golden on his scales, the cold blood coursing through his body, and but one desire in his heart.

These high spirits indeed almost proved the end of him. For at this moment a prowling and hungry pike having from its hiding-place spied this plump young tench, came flashing through the water like an arrow from a bow, and John escaped the snap of its sharp-toothed jaws by less than half an inch. And when on land he had always supposed that the tench who is the fishes' doctor was safe from any glutton! After this dizzying experience he swam on more heedfully, playing a kind of hide-and-seek among the stones and weeds, and nibbling every now and again at anything he found to his taste. And the world of trees and sky in which but a few hours before he had walked about on his two human legs was a very strange thing to see from out of the rippling and distorting wavelets of the water.

When evening began to darken overhead he sought out what seemed to be a safe lair for the night, and must soon have fallen into a long and peaceful fish's sleep— a queer sleep too, for having no lids to his eyes they both remained open, whereas even a hare when he is asleep shuts only one!

Next morning very early John was about again. A south wind must be blowing, he fancied, for there was a peculiar mildness and liveliness in the water, and he snapped at every passing tit-bit carried along by the stream with a zest and hunger that nothing could satisfy. Poor John, he had never dreamed a drowned fly or bee or a grub or caterpillar, or even water-weed, could taste so sweet. But then he had never tried to find out. And presently, dangling only a foot or two above his head, he espied a particularly juicy-looking and wriggling red worm.

Now though, as has been said already, John as a child or even as a small boy, had refrained from tasting caterpillars or beetles or snails or woodlice, he had once —when making mud pies in his mother's garden—nib- bled at a little earth-worm. But he had not nibbled much. For this reason only perhaps, he stayed eyeing this wriggling coral-coloured morsel above his head. Memory too had told him that it is not a habit of worms to float wriggling in the water like this. And though at sight of it he grew hungrier and hungrier as he finned softly on, he had the good sense to cast a glance up out of the water. And there—lank and lean upon the bank above—he perceived the strangest shape in hu- man kind he had ever set eyes on. This bony old being had scarcely any shoulders. His grey glassy eyes bulged out of his head above his flat nose. A tuft of beard hung from his cod-like chin, and the hand that clutched his fishing-rod was little else but skin and bone.

'Now,' thought John to himself, as he watched him steadily from out of the water, 'if that old rascal there ain't the Lord Fish in the rhyme, I'll eat my buttons.' Which was an easy thing to promise, since at this mo- ment John hadn't any buttons to eat. It was by no means so easy to make up his hungry fishy mind to snap at the worm and chance what might come after. He longed beyond words to be home again; he longed be-

yond words to get back into his own body again—but
only (and John seemed to be even stubborner as a fish
than he had been as a human), *only* if the beautiful
lady could be relieved of her tail. And how could there
be hope of any of these things if he gave up this chance
of meeting the Lord Fish and of finding the pot of
'unguent' he had read of in the rhyme? The other had
done its work with him quick enough!

If nothing had come to interrupt these cogitations,
John might have cogitated too long. But a quick-eyed
perch had at this moment finned into John's pool and
had caught sight of the savoury morsel wriggling and
waggling in the glass-clear water. At very first glimpse
of him John paused no longer. With gaping jaws and
one mad swirl of his fish-tail he sprang at the worm. A
dart of pain flashed through his body. He was whirled
out of the water and into the air. He seemed on the point
of suffocation. And the next instant found him gasping
and floundering in the lush green grass that grew beside
the water's brink. But the old angler who had caught
him was even more skilful in the craft of fishing than
John Cobbler was himself. Almost before John could
sob twice, the hook had been extracted from his mouth,
he had been swathed up from head to tail in cool green
moss, a noose had been slipped around that tail, and
poor John, dangling head downwards from the fisherman's long skinny fingers, was being lugged away he
knew not where. Few, fogged and solemn were the
thoughts that passed through his gaping, gasping head
on this dismal journey.

Now the Lord Fish who had caught him lived in a
low stone house which was surrounded on three sides

by a lake of water, and was not far distant from his master's—the Sorcerer. Fountains jetted in its hollow echoing chambers, and water lapped its walls on every side. Not even the barking of a fox or the scream of a peacock or any sound of birds could be heard in it; it was so full of the suffling and sighing, the music and murmuration of water, all day, all night long. But poor John being upside down had little opportunity to view or heed its marvels. And still muffled up in his thick green overcoat of moss he presently found himself suspended by his tail from a hook in the Lord Fish's larder, a long cool dusky room or vault with but one window to it, and that only a hole in the upper part of the wall. This larder too was of stone, and apart from other fish as luckless as John who hung there gaping from their hooks, many more, plumper and heavier than he, lay still and cold on the slate slab shelves around him. Indeed, if he could have done so, he might have hung his head a little lower at being so poor a fish by comparison.

Now there was a little maid who was in the service of this Lord Fish. She was the guardian of his larder. And early next morning she came in and set about her day's work. John watched her without ceasing. So fish-like was the narrow face that looked out from between the grey-green plaits of her hair that he could not even guess how old she was. She might, he thought, be twelve; she *might,* if age had not changed her much, be sixty. But he guessed she must be about seventeen. She was not of much beauty to human eyes—so abrupt was the slope of her narrow shoulders, so skinny were her hands and feet.

First she swept out the larder with a besom and flushed it out with buckets of water. Then, with an earthenware watering pot, and each in turn, she sprinkled the moss and weed and grasses in which John and his fellows were enwrapped. For the Lord Fish, John soon discovered, devoured his fish raw, and liked them fresh. When one of them, especially of those on the shelves, looked more solemn and motionless than was good for him, she dipped him into a shallow trough of running water that lay outside the door of the larder. John indeed heard running water all day long—while he himself could scarcely flick a fin. And when all this was done, and it was done twice a day, the larder-maid each morning chose out one or two or even three of her handsomest fish and carried them off with her. John knew—to his horror—to what end.

But there were two things that gave him heart and courage in this gruesome abode. The first was that after her second visit the larder-maid treated him with uncommon kindness. Perhaps there was a look on his face not quite like that of her other charges. For John with his goggling ogling eyes would try to twist up his poor fish face into something of a smile when she came near him, and—though very faintly—to waggle his tail tips, as if in greeting. However that might be, there was no doubt she had taken a liking to him. She not only gave him more of her fish-pap than she gave the rest, to fatten him up, but picked him out special dainties. She sprinkled him more slowly than the others with her water-pot so that he could enjoy the refreshment the more. And, after a quick, sly glance over her shoulder one morning she changed his place in the larder, and

hung him up in a darker corner all to himself. Surely, surely, this must mean, John thought, that she wished to keep him as long as she could from sharing her master's table. John did his best to croak his thanks, but was uncertain if the larder-maid had heard.

This was one happy thing. His other joy was this. Almost as soon as he found himself safe in his corner, he had discovered that on a level with his head there stood on a shelf a number of jars and gallipots and jorams of glass and earthenware. In some were dried roots, in some what seemed to be hanks of grass, in others black-veined lily bulbs, or scraps of twig, or dried-up buds and leaves, like tea. John guessed they must be savourings his cook-maid kept for the Fish Lord to soak his fish in, and wondered sadly which, when his own turn came, would be his. But a little apart from the rest and not above eighteen inches from his nose, there stood yet another small glass jar, with greenish stuff inside it. And after many attempts and often with eyes too dry to read, John spelled out at last from the label of this jar these outlandish words: UNGUENTUM AD PISCES HOMINIBUS TRANSMOGRIFICANDOS. And he went over them again and again until he knew them by heart.

Now John had left school very early. He had taken up crow-scaring at seven, pig-keeping at nine, turnip-hoeing at twelve—though he had kept up none of them for very long. But even if John had stayed at school until he was grown-up, he would never have learned any Latin—none at all, not even dog Latin—since the old dame who kept the village school at Tussock didn't know any herself. She could cut and come again as easily as you please with the cane she kept in her cupboard, but this had never done John much good, and she didn't know any Latin.

John's only certainty then, even when he had learned these words by heart, was that they were not good honest English words. Still, he had his wits about him. He remembered that there had been words like these written in red on the parchment over the top of the rhyme that now must be where his breeches were, since he had tucked it into his pocket—though where *that* was he hadn't the least notion. But *unguent* was a word he now knew as well as his own name; and it meant ointment. Not many months before this, too, he had mended a chair for a great lady that lived in a high house on the village green—a queer lady too though she was the youngest daughter of a marquis of those parts. It was a job that had not taken John very long, and she was mightily pleased with it. 'Sakes, John,' she had said, when he had taken the chair back and put it down in the light of a window, 'sakes, John, what a *transmogrification!*' And John had blushed all over as he grinned back at the ladȳ, guessing that she meant that the chair showed a change for the better.

Then, too, when he was a little boy, his mother had often told him tales of the *piskies*. 'Piskies, PISCES,' muttered John to himself on his hook. It sounded even to *his* ear poor spelling, but it would do. Then too, HOMINIBUS. If you make a full round O of the first syllable it sounds uncommonly like *home*. So what the Lord Fish, John thought at last, had meant by this lingo on his glass pot must be that it contained an UNGENT to which some secret PISKY stuff or what is known as wizardry had been added, and that it was useful for 'changing' for the better anything or anybody on which it was rubbed when away from HOME. Nobody could call the stony cell in which the enchanted maid with the fish-tail was kept shut up a *home;* and John himself at this moment was a good many miles from his mother!

Besides, the stuff in the glass pot was uncommonly like the ointment which he had taken from the other pot and had smeared on his ribs. After all this thinking John was just clever enough to come to the conclusion that the one unguent had been meant for turning humans into fish, and that this in the pot beside him was for turning fish into humans again. At this his flat eyes bulged indeed in his head, and in spite of the moss around them his fins stood out stiff as knitting needles. He gasped to himself—like a tench out of water. And while he was still brooding on his discovery, the larder-maid opened the door of the larder with her iron key to set about her morning duties.

'*Ackh*,' she called softly, hastening towards him, for now she never failed to visit him first of all her charges, '*ackh*, what's wrong with 'ee? What's amiss with 'ee?' and with her lean finger she gently stroked the top of his head, her narrow bony face crooked up with care at seeing this sudden change in his looks. She did not realise that it was not merely a change but a transmogrification! She sprinkled him twice, and yet a third time, with her ice-cold water, and with the tips of her small fingers pushed tiny gobbet after gobbet of milk-pap out of her basin into his mouth until John could swallow no more. Then with gaspings and gapings he fixed his nearer eye on the jar of unguent or ointment,

THE LORD FISH • 199 •

gazed back rapidly at the little larder-maid, then once again upon the jar.

Now this larder-maid was a great-grandniece of the Lord Fish, and had learned a little magic. 'Aha,' she whispered, smiling softly and wagging her finger at him. 'So that's what you are after, Master Tench? That's what you are after, you crafty Master Sobersides. Oh, what a scare you gave me!'

Her words rang out shrill as a whistle, and John's fellow fish, trussed up around him in their moss and grass and rushes on their dishes, or dangling from their hooks, trembled at sound of it. A faint chuffling, a lisping and quiet gaggling, tiny squeaks and groans filled the larder. John had heard these small noises before, and had supposed them to be fish talk, but though he had tried to imitate them he had never been sure of an answer. All he could do, then, was what he had done before—he fixed again his round glassy eye first on the jar and then on the little larder-maid, and this with as much gentle flattery and affection as he could manage. Just as when he was a child at his mother's knee he would coax her to give him a slice of bread pudding or a spoonful of jam.

'Now I wonder,' muttered the larder-maid as if to herself, 'if you, my dear, are the one kind or the other. And if you are the *other, shall* I, my gold-green Tinker, take the top off the jar?'

At this John wriggled might and main, chapping with his jaws as wide and loud as he could, looking indeed as if at any moment he might burst into song.

'Ah,' cried the maid, watching him with delight, 'he

understands! That he does! But if I did, precious, what would my lord the Lord Fish say to me? What would happen to *me,* eh? You Master Tench, I am afraid, are thinking only of your own comfort.'

At this John sighed and hung limp as if in sadness and dudgeon and remorse. The larder-maid eyed him a few moments longer, then set about her morning work so quickly and with so intense a look on her lean narrow face, with its lank dangling tresses of green-grey hair, that between hope and fear John hardly knew how to contain himself. And while she worked on, sprinkling, feeding, scouring, dipping, she spoke to her charges in much the same way that a groom talks to his horses, a nurse to a baby, or a man to his dogs. At last, her work over, she hastened out of the larder and shut the door.

Now it was the habit of the Lord Fish on the Tuesdays, Thursdays and Saturdays of every week, to make the round of his larder, eyeing all it held, plump fish or puny, old or new, ailing or active; sometimes gently pushing his finger in under the moss to see how they were prospering for his table. This was a Thursday. And sure enough the larder-maid presently hastened back, and coming close whispered up at John, 'Hst, he comes! The Lord Fish! Angry and hungry. Beware! Stay mum as mum can be, you precious thing. Flat and limp and sulky, look 'ee, for if the Lord Fish makes his choice of 'ee now, it is too late and all is over. And above all things, don't so much as goggle for a moment at that jar!"

She was out again like a swallow at nesting-time, and presently there came the sound of slow scraping footsteps on the flagstones and there entered the Lord Fish into the larder, the maid at his heels. He was no lord to look at, thought John; no marquis, anyhow. He looked as glum and sullen as some old Lenten cod in a fish-monger's, in his stiff drab-coloured overclothes. And John hardly dared to breathe, but hung—mouth open and eyes fixed—as limp and lifeless from his hook in the ceiling as he knew how.

'*Hoy, hoy, hoy,*' grumbled the Lord Fish, when at last he came into John's corner. 'Here's a dullard. Here's a rack of bones. Here's a sandy gristle-trap. Here's a good-as-dead-and-gone-and-useless! Ay, now my dear, you can't have seen him. Not this one. You must have let him go by, up there in the shadows. A quick eye, my dear, a quick watchful eye! He's naught but muddy sluggard tench 'tis true. But, oh yes, we can better him! He wants life, he wants exercise, he wants cosseting and feeding and *fattening*. And then—why then, there's the makings in him of as comely a platter of fish as would satisfy my Lord Bishop of the Seven Sturgeons himself.' And the little larder-maid, her one hand clutching a swab of moss and the other demurely knuckled over her mouth, sedately nodded.

'Ay, master,' said she, 'he's hung up there in the shadows, he is. In the dark. He's a mumper, that one, he's a moper. He takes his pap but poorly. He shall have a washabout and a dose of sunshine in the trough. Trust me, master, I'll soon put a little life into him. Come next Saturday, now!'

'So, so, so,' said the Lord Fish. And having made the round of John's companions he retired at last from out of his larder, well content with his morning's visit. And with but one quick reassuring nod at John over her narrow shoulder, his nimble larder-maid followed after him. John was safe until Saturday.

Hardly had the Lord Fish's scuffling footsteps died away when back came the little maid, wringing her hands in glee, and scarcely able to speak for laughing. 'Ay, Master Tench, did you hear that? "Up there in the shadows. Here's a dullard; here's a rack of bones; here's a gristle-trap. He wants cosseting and feeding and fattening."—Did he not now? Was I sly? Was I cunning? Did the old Lord nibble my bait, Master Tench? Did he *not* now? Oho, my poor beautiful; "fatten," indeed!' And she lightly stroked John's snout again. 'What's wrong with the old Lord Fish is that he eats too much and sleeps too long. Come 'ee now, let's make no more ado about it.'

She dragged up a wooden stool that stood close by, and, holding her breath, with both hands she carefully lifted down the jar of green fat or grease or unguent. Then she unlatched John from his hook, and laid him gently on the stone slab beside her, bidding him meanwhile have no fear at all of what might happen. She stripped off his verdant coat of moss, and, dipping her finger in the ointment, smeared it on him, from the nape of his neck clean down his spine to the very tip of his tail.

For a few moments John felt like a cork that, after bobbing softly along down a softly-flowing river, is suddenly drawn into a roaring whirlpool. He felt like a firework squib when the gushing sparks are nearly all out of it and it is about to burst. Then gradually the fog in his eyes and the clamour in his ears faded and waned away, and lo and behold, he found himself returned safe and sound into his own skin, shape and appearance again. There he stood in the Lord Fish's fish larder, grinning down out of his cheerful face at the maid who in stature reached not much above his elbow.

'Ah,' she cried, peering up at him out of her small water-clear eyes, and a little dazed and dazzled herself at this transmogrification. 'So you *were* the other kind, Master Tench!' And the larder-maid looked at him so sorrowfully and fondly that poor John could only blush and turn away. 'And now,' she continued, 'all you will be wanting, I suppose, is to be gone. I beseech you then make haste and be off, or my own skin will pay for it.'

John had always been a dullard with words. But he thanked the larder-maid for all she had done for him as best he could. And he slipped from off his little finger a silver ring which had belonged to his father, and put it into the palm of the larder-maid's hand; for just as when he had been changed into a fish, all his clothes and everything about him had become fish itself, so now when he was transformed into human shape again, all that had then been his returned into its own place, even to the parchment in his breeches' pocket. Such it seems is the law of enchantment. And he entreated the maid, if ever she should find herself on the other side of the great wall, to ask for the village of Tussock, and when she came to Tussock to ask for Mrs. Cobbler.

'That's my mother,' said John, 'is Mrs. Cobbler. And she'll be mighty pleased to see you, I promise you. And so will I.'

The larder-maid looked at John. Then she took the

ring between finger and thumb, and with a sigh pushed it into a cranny between the slabs of stone for a hiding-place. 'Stay there,' she whispered to the ring, 'and I'll come back to 'ee anon.'

Then John, having nothing else handy, and knowing that for the larder-maid's sake he must leave the pot behind him, took out of the fob in his breeches' pocket a great silver watch that had belonged to his grandfather. It was nothing now but a watch *case,* since he had one day taken out the works in hopes to make it go better, and had been too lazy to put them back again. Into this case he smeared as much of the grease out of the pot as it would hold.

'And now, Master Tench, this way,' said the larder-maid, twisting round on him. 'You must be going, and you must be going for good. Follow that wall as far as it leads you, and then cross the garden where the Lord Fish grows his herbs. You will know it by the scent of them in the air. Climb the wall and go on until you come to the river. Swim across that, and turn sunwards while it is morning. The Lord Fish has the nose of a she-wolf. He'd smell 'ee out across a bean field. Get you gone at once then, and meddle with him no more. Ay, and I know it is not on *me* your thoughts will be thinking when you get to safety again.'

John, knowing no other, stooped down and kissed this little wiseacre's lean cold fingers, and casting one helpless and doleful look all about the larder at the fish on hook and slab, and seeing none, he fancied, that could possibly be in the same state as his had been, he hastened out.

There was no missing his way. The Lord Fish's walls

and water conduits were all of stone so solid that they might have been built by the Romans, though, truly, they were chiefly of magic, which has nothing to do with time. John hurried along in the morning sunshine, and came at length to the stream. With his silver watch between his teeth for safety he swam to the other side. Here grew very tall rough spiny reeds and grasses, some seven to nine feet high. He pushed his way through them, heedless of their clawing and rasping, and only just in time. For as soon as he was safely hidden in the low bushes beyond them, whom did he now see approaching on the other side of the stream, rod in hand, and creel at his elbow, but the Lord Fish himself—his lank face erected up into the air and his nose sniffing the morning as if it were laden with the spices of Arabia. The larder-maid had told the truth indeed. For at least an hour the Lord Fish stood there motionless on the other side of the stream immediately opposite John's hiding-place. For at least an hour he pried and peeped about him, gently sniffing on. And, though teased by flies and stung with nettles, John dared not stir a finger. At last even the Lord Fish grew weary of watching and waiting, and John, having seen him well out of sight, continued on his way. . . .

What more is there to tell? Sad and sorrowful had been the maid's waiting for him, sad beyond anything else in the fish-tailed damsel's memory. For, ever since she had so promised him, she had not even been able to sing to keep herself company. But when seventeen days after he had vanished, John plunged in again under the stone arch and climbed the steep stone steps to her chamber, he spent no time in trying to find words and speeches that would not come. Having opened the glass of his watch, he just knelt down beside her, and said, *'Now,* if you please, lady. If you can keep quite still, I will be quick. If only *I* could bear the pain I'd do it three times over, but I promise 'ee it's soon gone.' And with his finger he gently smeared the magic unguent on the maid's tail down at last to the very tip.

Life is full of curiosities, and curious indeed it was that though at one moment John's talk to the enchanted creature had seemed to her little better than Double Dutch, and she could do his bidding only by the signs he had made to her, at the next they were chattering together as merrily as if they had done nothing else all their lives. But they did not talk for long, since of a sudden there came the clatter of oars, and presently a skinny hand was thrust over the window-sill, and her daily portion of bread and fruit and water was laid out on the sill. The sound of the Lord Fish's 'Halloo!' when he had lowered his basket into the boat made the blood run cold again in John's body. He waited only until the rap and grinding of the oars had died away. Then he took the maid by the hand, and they went down the stone steps together. There they plunged into the dark water, and presently found themselves breathless but happy beyond words seated together on the green grass bank in the afternoon sunshine. And there came such a chattering and cawing from the rooks and jackdaws over their heads that it seemed as if they were giving thanks to see them there. And when John had shaken out the coat he had left under the tree seventeen days before, brushed off the mildew, and dried it in the sun, he put it over the maid's shoulders.

It was long after dark when they came to Tussock, and not a soul was to be seen in the village street or on the green. John looked in through the window at his mother. She sat alone by the hearthside, staring into the fire, and it seemed to her that she would never get warm again. When John came in and she was clasped in his arms, first she thought she was going to faint, then she began to cry a little, and then to scold him as she had never scolded him before. John dried her tears and hushed her scoldings. And when he had told her a little of his story, he brought the maid in. And John's mother first bobbed her a curtsey, then kissed her and made her welcome. And she listened to John's story all over again from the beginning to the end before they went to bed—though John's bed that night was an old armchair.

Now before the bells of Tussock church—which was a small one and old—rang out a peal for John's and the fish-maid's wedding, he set off as early as ever one morning to climb the wall again. In their haste to be gone from the Sorcerer's mansion she had left her belongings behind her, and particularly, she told John, a leaden box or casket, stamped with a great A—for Almanara; that being her name.

Very warily John stripped again, and, diving quietly, swam in under the stone arch. And lo, safe and sound, in the far corner of the room of all her grief and captivity, stood the leaden casket. But when he stooped to lift it, his troubles began. It was exceedingly heavy, and to swim with it even on his shoulders would be to swim to the bottom! He sat awhile and pondered, and at last climbed up to the stone window, carved curiously with flowers and birds and fish, and looked out. Water lay beneath him in a moat afloat with lilies, though he couldn't tell how deep. But by good fortune a knotted rope hung from a hook in the window-sill—for use, no doubt, of the Lord Fish in his boat, John hauled the rope in, tied one end of it to the ring in the leaden casket and one to a small wooden stool. At last after long heaving and hoisting he managed to haul the casket on to the sill. He pushed it over, and—as lively as a small pig—away went the stool after it. John clambered up to the window again and again looked out. The stool, still bobbing, floated on the water beneath him. Only a deeper quiet had followed the splash of the casket. So, after he had dragged it out of the moat and on to the bank, John ventured on beyond the walls of the great house in search of the Lord Fish's larder. He dearly wanted to thank the larder-maid again. When at last he found it, it was all shut up and deserted. He climbed up to the window and looked in, but quickly jumped down again, for every fish that hung inside it hung dead as mutton. The little larder-maid was gone. But whether she had first used the magic unguent on the Lord Fish himself and then in dismay of what followed had run away, or whether she had tried it on them both and now was what John couldn't guess, he never knew and could never discover. He grieved not to see her again, and always thought of her with kindness.

Walking and resting, walking and resting, it took him three days, even though he managed to borrow a wheelbarrow for the last two miles, to get the casket home. But it was worth the trouble. When he managed at last to prise the lid open, it was as though lumps of a frozen rainbow had suddenly spilled over in the kitchen, the casket was crammed so full of precious stones. And after the wedding Almanara had a great J punched into the lead of the box immediately after her great A—since now what it held belonged to them both.

But though John was now married, and not only less idle but as happy as a king-fisher, *still* when the sweet south wind came blowing, and the leaves were green on the trees, and the birds in song, he could not keep his thoughts from hankering after water. So sometimes he made himself a little paste or dug up a few worms, and went off fishing. But he made two rules for himself. First, whenever he hooked anything—and especially a tench—he would always smear a speck or two of the unguent out of his grandfather's silver watch-case on the top of its head; and next, having made sure that his fish was fish, wholly fish, and nothing but fish, he would put it back into the water again. As for the mansion of the Sorcerer, he had made a vow to Almanara and to his mother that he would never go fishing *there*. And he never did.

A NOTE ON THE TYPE

The text of this book was set on the Linotype in a face called *TIMES ROMAN*, designed by *STANLEY MORISON* for The Times (London), and first introduced by that newspaper in 1932.

Among typographers and designers of the twentieth century, Stanley Morison has been a strong forming influence, as typographical adviser to the English Monotype Corporation, as a director of two distinguished English publishing houses, and as a writer of sensibility, erudition, and keen practical sense.

In 1930 Morison wrote: "Type design moves at the pace of the most conservative reader. The good type-designer therefore realises that, for a new fount to be successful, it has to be so good that only mate reticence and rare discipline of a new type, it is probably a good letter." It is now generally recognized that in the creation of *TIMES ROMAN* Morison successfully met the qualifications of this theoretical doctrine.

Composed, printed, and bound by H. WOLFF, *New York*
Typography by TERE LOPRETE